By LYN GALA

NOVELS
Desert World Allegiances • Desert World Rebirth
Fettered
Gathering Storm
Mountain Prey
Urban Shaman

NOVELLAS
Lines in the Sand
Long Lonely Howl

Published by DREAMSPINNER PRESS
http://www.dreamspinnerpress.com

MOUNTAIN Prey

LYN GALA

Dreamspinner Press

Published by
Dreamspinner Press
5032 Capital Circle SW
Ste 2, PMB# 279
Tallahassee, FL 32305-7886
USA
http://www.dreamspinnerpress.com/

Mountain Prey

Cover Art by AngstyG
www.angstyg.com

Cover content is being used for illustrative purposes only
and any person depicted on the cover is a model.

ISBN: 978-1-62380-583-8
Digital ISBN: 978-1-62380-584-5

Printed in the United States of America
First Edition
June 2013

A discussion of guilty pleasures led to the discovery of a shared kink—the shotgun wedding. Personally, I blame my love for this trope on *Seven Brides for Seven Brothers* (*hums a few bars of "Goin' Courtin'"). As much as I know the musical and the trope are a little silly, I found myself obsessed with the idea. Luckily I have a great group of beta readers who stuck with me through some pretty serious rewrites. I especially appreciate the ladies from the South who helped me create this world. While it is fantasy and you'll never find Stunt's beloved mountain on a map, they helped me create a fantasy based on a unique people with their own strengths and quirks.

CHAPTER
1

STUNT turned in a slow circle, trying to figure out why he had the feeling that someone was staring a hole in the back of his head. He didn't know of anyone running a still or making meth in this area, and the forestry service had finally torn down the old shacks squatters used, so he should be safe. Still, his gut screamed at him. He even checked the shadows for bamboo. The weed growers used the fast-growing plants to hide their crops, so even a few bamboo shoots could mean trouble.

Nope. No bamboo, no pot, no scent of sweet mash, and no reason in the world for his skin to crawl. However, he was a good sight west of the official trail here—near where private land started—which could be dangerous at times. He couldn't escape that cold shiver you got when there was something particularly nasty sneaking up on you.

The day was relatively cool, the trail littered with little saplings struggling up out of the hard-packed brown earth and between the gray shale rocks with their edges stained green with moss. The sugar maples shimmered in the breeze, their thick leaves leaving the younger beech and white ash to starve in their shadows. It wasn't healthy, a whole cluster of one kind of tree, and Stunt figured humans probably mucked something up in the ecology 'round here, but other than a lack of diversification in the flora, all seemed quiet.

But occasionally the mountain lied. It made you see things that weren't there. Stunt still swore he could feel Wicked John rushing by him on the breeze from time to time, his soul exiled from heaven for sinning and from hell because he'd given the devil so much grief before he died. It was a stupid kid's story, but Stunt turned a full circle as he searched for something that didn't exist.

"You're a-fixin' ta lose your mind out here," he told himself out loud, hoping the sound of his voice would scare off any spirits. The only answer was the stirring of the wind through the branches so that shadows danced on the ground.

"The work ain't going to start doing itself," he chastised himself as he pulled on a set of gloves. After he wrapped his hands around a thin beech trunk that had invaded the official path, he gave it a good yank. Once the roots ripped free, he tossed it far back into the maples.

Stunt had bent down to pull another sapling when a flash of something caught his eye. He couldn't say if it was a shape or a color or a movement, but he peered at a rough-shaped lump near the base of a tree, struggling to figure out what he was looking at.

He focused so hard and so long that when the lump turned into a man leaping at him, Stunt couldn't do more than stumble back a step. His heel caught on a bit of shale, and he windmilled his arms and staggered back, trying to not fall on his ass. By the time he'd gotten both feet directly under him, the man had a pretty impressive rifle pointed right at Stunt's midsection.

Stunt raised his hands high. "Now, no need to do anything drastic," he said. "If you have a claim on this bit of land, I am more than happy to find myself someplace else to be." This wasn't the first time Stunt had had a gun pointed at him, and it wasn't the first time he'd decided a certain bit of the federal trail system could do without maintenance. Hell, Stunt chose to let trails go back to nature on a semiregular basis because they came too close to some cranky soul with a gun. They were kind of a dime a dozen in these parts.

"Who are you?" The man was about Stunt's age—mid to late twenties. Unlike Stunt, who had a real talent at being average-looking, this guy was seriously gorgeous, especially for a gun-toting psycho.

Stunt coughed to clear the fear that'd gotten stuck at the base of his throat. "Stunt Folger," he introduced himself. "Very pleased to make your acquaintance, and if it doesn't bother you none, I will be taking myself back down the trail." Stunt eased his way back. Mr. Gun might be cute as hell, with dark-brown hair, a clean-shaven face, and blue eyes a darker shade than Stunt had seen in a while, but that gun was a very big deterrent when it came to chatting.

"Freeze!" Mr. Gun raised his rifle, and Stunt froze.

"Now, let's all calm down," he urged.

"I am calm," Mr. Gun announced as he climbed up onto the trail, leaves falling away with each step. He'd buried himself in the leaf litter, which did tend to indicate he was up to no good. No self-respecting moonshiner would bury himself in leaves just to avoid one little forestry technician. With each passing second, this was looking a little bit worse.

"You may be calm, but I'm not," Stunt said as Mr. Gun kept on coming closer. "In fact, I'm freaking out a bit, so how about we just cool things down a little… take a second to think?"

"Think with your hands behind your head, fingers interlocked," Mr. Gun ordered. Okay, this was bad. Stunt really didn't want to be helpless in front of this guy, but at least the man was issuing orders instead of shooting him, which was one small point in Stunt's favor. "Now!"

Stunt took a step back as the rifle came dangerously close. "Yes, sir. If it keeps you from shooting me, no problem." He put his hands behind his head and interlocked his fingers. "Whatever you want, I'm not in any position to give you grief, so why don't you just move on?"

"Turn around."

With his heart pounding painfully hard, Stunt studied the man and tried figuring out if his life expectancy had just dropped from years to minutes. "You don't want trouble any more than I do. You don't want to pull that trigger." Stunt kept his voice nice and quiet, like when some neighbor had his crazy-ass dog ready to bite you in the balls if you didn't run fast enough.

Mr. Gun gave Stunt a real dirty look, the kind teachers and mothers loved to inflict on others. "I don't plan to shoot you."

"That whopper of a gun there is saying something else. I'm hoping it's a liar." Knowing he didn't have a whole lot of choices, Stunt turned around, putting his back to Mr. Gun.

"On your knees."

Before this day was done, Stunt was going to have a heart attack if he didn't get shot in the head first. "If you're going to shoot me—"

"I already said I wasn't." From the tone, Stunt had managed to offend the crazy man. Great. "I may, however, gag you if you don't shut up and start following orders."

"You might want to stop with the threats before my heart gives out," Stunt countered as he went to his knees. It wasn't easy with his hands behind his head. It made the angle very awkward, even for someone who was normally talented at going to his knees. While he might be exaggerating a mite about his heart, his chest did hurt. It'd been a good long time since he'd been this afraid.

"You look healthy enough."

"And you look sane. Imagine that," Stunt shot right back. His common sense kicked in about a second too late to save him from his mouth, and there was a long silence. Insulting the man holding you at gunpoint showed a real lack of common sense. Insulting him and then not being able to see the reaction because your back was turned and he'd gone utterly silent was so very much worse.

"You'd be safer if I did gag you," Mr. Gun finally said, but he almost sounded amused. Stunt started breathing again and silently promised the Lord to take up regular churchgoing in the very near future.

"That's a possibility," Stunt admitted. "I have been known to insert two or three feet into my mouth at once. But feel free to tie me to a tree and leave me, only could you give someone a call and let them know where to find me? I'm not fond of the idea of dying of thirst out here."

Hands patted Stunt down, pulling his pockets out and running up and down Stunt's thighs. Normally, Stunt's dick would have embarrassed itself by now, but luckily it was too busy trying to climb back up and become an internal organ to care. "You're coming with me," Mr. Gun announced when he finished.

"That doesn't sound ominous, not at all."

"I'm not going to leave you behind to describe me to the state police."

"And the ominous just keeps on a'coming," Stunt muttered.

Behind him, Mr. Gun made a noise that sounded a little like a growl. "Look, I'm only going to say this one more time. I wouldn't shoot an innocent man. So relax and you'll get through this."

"Relax. I'll get right on that." Fear had loosened Stunt's tongue, and he couldn't quite stop the idiot thing from blurting out what he was thinking. Around here, people likely to take hostages generally would have had a little too much to drink the night before. If they didn't shoot you before they fell asleep, they'd cut you loose in the morning. Jack Donnally had done that Stunt's first year back from college. But this guy had him a Western accent, something from the middle of the country or the West Coast even, and Stunt didn't know those folk real well. It did seem like they were less likely to go taking people hostage, but more likely to do some killing when it came right down to it.

"Cross your ankles and do not move."

"Does shaking count?" Feeling like he was walking to his own execution, Stunt complied since he couldn't figure out what else to do.

"Look at it this way, you're going to have one hell of a story to tell your buddies." Mr. Gun stepped on the back of Stunt's top leg, pinning both his feet to the ground and making a sharp rock dig into the flesh of Stunt's shin. Damn, that hurt.

"Have you considered therapy?" Stunt flinched as metal ratcheted closed around his right wrist. Of course this man carried handcuffs. Perfect. Ropes wouldn't have been a problem, but cuffs…. Shit.

"You're insulting your captor? I'm not the only one who might want to sign up for a few sessions," Mr. Gun pointed out.

Stunt sighed as he realized that the guy was probably right. "Yeah, I'll get right on that."

"Where's your gun?" Mr. Gun pulled Stunt's hands behind his back and closed the other cuff around his left wrist. Panic nearly crawled up Stunt's throat and choked him to death before he could swallow it back down.

"Considering you just frisked me, you already know I don't have one."

Mr. Gun's warm hands left him, and Stunt stared ahead at the split trunk of a maple, his brain spinning off into trivial thoughts about how they should come out here and thin the trees and clear a few damaged ones. A cold barrel pressed against the back of his neck. "I won't ask you again," Mr. Gun warned in a cold voice.

"In my truck. It's under the front seat," Stunt offered up. He definitely wasn't winning any points here.

"Not smart, walking around without a gun."

"Have you seen our little town? This isn't exactly crime central. At least, it wasn't before you showed up."

"I don't know about that." The gun barrel withdrew, and Stunt took a couple of deep breaths to stave off a pending case of unconsciousness. "You seem to have some new neighbors. Trust me, you should keep your weapon on hand."

"I tell you what, cut me loose, and I'll go get it now." Danger always had made Stunt a little giddy and stupid… which is how he'd earned his nickname. If he had his druthers, he'd be out cliff jumping or cave diving or having the most dangerous sex he could find six days a week, but this was far beyond even his comfort level.

"Funny."

"Not really. Terror makes it hard to tell a good joke."

Mr. Gun reached up between Stunt's legs and pressed up, nearly sending Stunt falling forward on his face, only Mr. Gun grabbed his shoulder and righted him before reaching around and fumbling with Stunt's belt.

"Hey, hey, hey, if you're looking for a partner who is into serious kink, I can give you the name of a club. Or two clubs. There's more variety in the city than you might think. I mean, Southern gentlemen and genteel ladies can be just as sadistic and kinky as you want if you just find the right club. Or masochistic and kinky. It's all good, so you do not have to do this."

"I'm not going to rape you. I'm checking for knives."

Stunt's heart slowed a half notch. No killing and no rape... that sounded good. It didn't match the hand groping him, but it sounded good. "Okay, if you think I could still have a hidden knife on me, I have to ask. Where the hell do you keep your knife?"

Mr. Gun chuckled. "You'd be surprised at what a man can hide in his pants."

"After this, you pretty much know everything I have in my pants. Feel free to have your homophobia kick in, you know, the sense that maybe you shouldn't look at another man's dick in the school showers or ever touch a man's crotch. Ever. I'm okay with that sort of homophobia right now."

Mr. Gun's hand ran along the inside of Stunt's pants before pulling out the belt. "I'm gay."

Stunt closed his eyes. Of course. Shit. Under normal circumstance, he'd love to meet a gay man this good with a set of cuffs. Right now, he was figuring this couldn't get too much worse. "You do know that does not make me feel better, right?"

"I told you, your virtue's safe with me." His voice had a bit of frustration in it as he checked Stunt's right boot.

"You have a bit of a credibility issue with me," Stunt said, groaning when Mr. Gun checked his left boot and found the sweet little Mini Tac Beaver Tail skinning knife tucked down in it.

"Yep. I figure we both have trust issues at this point." Mr. Gun stepped to the side and pulled on Stunt's right arm to get him up onto his feet. "Let's head to your truck. You do not want me to get spooked, so be a good boy and I won't have to shoot you in the back."

\

CHAPTER 2

WALKING down the trail, Stunt sorted through every fact he knew about hostage situations. The realization that most of them came from television was not exactly comforting. "So, what do you want?" Stunt's words came out a little more aggressive than he intended. Mr. Gun's hand tightened, and for a second, Stunt thought he was being warned to shut up. However, Mr. Gun yanked him off to the side of the trail so they both slid down the leaf litter and into the trees. Without hands to slow his descent, Stunt ended up with his face shoved into the leaves and mold, the warm smell of rot rising up from the dirt. He sneezed and felt snot slide toward his lip. Instinct told him to wipe it away, which left him fighting the cuffs.

Mr. Gun lay on top of him, the cold barrel of the gun pressed into the spot just under Stunt's ear. "Shhh," he said. For someone who kept claiming he didn't plan to do any killing, the man spent a considerable amount of time shoving a gun barrel into Stunt's flesh.

"They come through here about once a month," a male voice said.

"I don't like it."

"They're not cops. They're more like yard boys, only paid by the feds."

"It's the paid by the feds part that's not going to make the boss happy," the second man said. He had a strong accent, something sharper than Mr. Gun's Western flavor of bland. They sure weren't local, not any of them. Up until this point, Stunt would have been quick to say that folks on the mountain were all shades and colors of crazy, but these out-of-town guys were making the locals look sane, and that wasn't an easy task.

"Around here, even feds know to mind their own business," the first guy said.

"Where is he now? If he's playing yard boy on the trail, shouldn't we see him?"

"Chances are he has to check all the trails and streams for miles around. We'll probably never see him, and he'll sure as hell never see us, since he doesn't have the right to come onto private property."

The voices were fading now, and Stunt frowned. Why the hell were two strangers worrying about him doing his job? Hell, even moonshiners knew he was pretty impotent, in the legal department anyway. Of course, that didn't prevent them from pointing guns at him, but at least they generally weren't willing to take it further than that. This new crop of crazy though…. Stunt wasn't sure about them.

"We move fast and quiet," Mr. Gun ordered in a rough whisper. "Those two will shoot you on sight."

"And you won't?" Stunt whispered back, but he struggled to cooperate and get his feet under him as Mr. Gun pulled him upright.

"I'm getting sick of telling you I don't plan to kill you."

"Imagine that. I'm annoying you," Stunt said in a flat voice. He somehow wasn't feeling too much sympathy for the man. A glance over his shoulder revealed Mr. Gun had on his unhappy face. He scowled darkly, the blue of his eyes turning into narrow bands of color. Either the man was scared out of his mind—scared enough to make his eyes dilate—or he was stoned off his gourd. Stunt wondered which would be worse, but he didn't have much time for contemplating. Mr. Gun pushed him toward the path.

He had to really give Stunt some good shoving to get him back up to the trail, since Stunt was pretty much helpless against the slippery ground without his hands. Under the dry layer of leaves, slick mold crept from leaf to leaf, turning the detritus into a layer of slime that soaked into Stunt's pants every time he went to one knee… which was too often.

After nearly silent curses from both of them, they got back up on the trail, and Mr. Gun broke into a trot, hurrying Stunt along with a hand around his arm.

Stunt tried pulling off the trail. "Wait, hey."

"Keep moving."

Stunt planted his feet and nearly got pulled to the ground before Mr. Gun stopped. "You said you wanted to go to my truck. It's this a'way." Stunt jerked his head up the gentle slope. Here most of the leaves had been whisked away by some quirk of summer rains or wind, leaving the trees' roots peeking through the dry forest floor in search of oxygen.

"If you're playing a trick…."

"I'm unarmed and handcuffed. Exactly what sort of trick do you think I'd be playing?"

Mr. Gun eyed him. "I'm not sure. I get the feeling that cute smile of yours has led more than one man straight into trouble."

Stunt cleared his throat. He couldn't exactly deny that, but he was playing this one straight. A weapon pointed at his midsection did tend to make him mind his p's and q's. "Now, I ain't saying that I wouldn't love to trick you, but right now, I'm one plan short of a plan. I just don't feel like following a loop of the trail an extra two miles when I'm dirty, sore, and scared enough to make my heart stutter like Jimmy Bolleau."

"Bolleau?"

"Jimmy Bolleau. When teachers made him do presentations in school, he did stutter up a storm, and that's what my heart's feeling like right now. So I'm not likely to be trying to play any games at all."

Mr. Gun narrowed his eyes and considered the slope before looking back at Stunt. "If we run into someone, you do not want to know what I am capable of," he warned.

"I pretty much figure I know already, seeing as how you keep threatening to shoot me right before promising to not shoot me. Trust me, I'm very fond of my skin being in one piece."

Mr. Gun's gaze skittered to the section of trail they'd come down as though looking for those two guys to come back, and then to the other end of the trail, and then up the slope before coming back to Stunt. "Your face is dirty," he observed, which seemed a mite bit like a non sequitur, but seeing as how Stunt's own brain wasn't exactly tracking real well, he couldn't blame the man for any lapses in logic.

"You shoved my face into leaf mold. I reckon it's all kinds of dirty," he agreed, but Mr. Gun looked more concerned than he rightly should over a bit of mud.

Mr. Gun pulled a cloth out of his pocket and pulled one of those green plastic canteens off his belt, and then poured some water onto the cloth before wringing it out. Stunt watched, not quite sure what to think as Mr. Gun reached up to stroke the damp cloth over Stunt's face. The word surreal was making an appearance, that was for sure.

"You're bleeding," Mr. Gun said as his fingers moved up to explore the side of Stunt's head. Stunt kept his blond hair real short, seeing as how he ended up crawling through underbrush more times than not, but still, muck had gotten caught up in it. Mr. Gun yanked on something, and Stunt flinched as several hairs came loose. "Sorry about that," the man offered before tossing a twig to one side. "Looks like you hit your head."

"Any chance you'd want to drop me off at the emergency room?"

"You didn't hit it that hard." Moving slow and easy, Mr. Gun wiped Stunt's forehead and then down over his left temple before cleaning his left cheek and then his right one. As he worked, Stunt could see the tattoo on his right forearm—a simple cross with uneven black lines that pretty much screamed "prison tattoo."

Stunt bit down on the urge to say something inappropriate. If he wanted to come out of this alive, he needed to stop poking the ex-con who had taken him captive. It was hard to keep that in mind when the ex-con in question ran the cloth down Stunt's nose, cleaning off the mud and running snot as carefully as a mother. This guy had issues with his issues, that was for sure.

Clearing his throat, Mr. Gun took a quick step back and shoved the cloth in his pocket—mud, snot, and all. "Let's go," he ordered, a gruffness in his voice as he tightened his hand around his rifle. He wasn't as comfortable carrying it as most mountain folk. So, he didn't normally take hostages, and he felt guilty about shoving Stunt's face in the muck. Mr. Gun was just a mass of contradictions, and that wasn't necessarily a point in Stunt's favor. People could make mighty big mistakes when they weren't familiar with a weapon, and given that this guy tended to point his gun at Stunt on a regular basis, that was not a comfort.

"This way," Stunt said, which was rather redundant seeing as how he was already heading up the slope. Mr. Gun stayed just to the side of him, looking around with those blue eyes like he expected Wicked John to come flying out from behind a tree.

"Who are we running from?" Stunt finally asked as they cleared the dry creek that always took out Thompson's road in spring.

"You don't want to know."

"I'd sooner know than get shot over something that isn't making a lick of sense. I mean, as far as I can tell, you're all funny turned."

"Are you talking like that for my benefit?" Mr. Gun's voice had a suspicious edge to it.

Stunt gave Mr. Gun a confused look. "Excuse me?"

"You sound smarter than most people around here, so I'm wondering if you're trying to pull some game by talking like that, like you're a hick."

Stunt stopped long enough to really and truly glare at Mr. Gun. Not only was his accent a particular sore spot with him, but he hated feeling helpless, which was a mite strange because he loved being dominated. But Stunt wasn't into introspection. He only knew that his anger was about to roar out of control. Fear and anger and about a dozen more emotions he couldn't pin down raged through him, and he worked to keep his voice even.

"Just because I have an accent does not mean I ain't intelligent. I know as well as the next person that 'ain't' ain't a word, and if you're going to get all brigedy about how I talk, we're going to have a problem."

For a second, Mr. Gun just blinked at him like he couldn't exactly understand what he was hearing. "Funny, I thought we had a problem because I pulled a gun on you," Mr. Gun commented in a perfectly droll tone.

Stunt only stared back, all that anger derailed with one smartass comment. This man was just bending Stunt's head every which way. "You have issues," Stunt finally proclaimed.

"I have an alphabetized and indexed library of issues," Mr. Gun agreed, tugging at Stunt's arm to get him moving again. "Do you think I'd be running around these mountains taking hostages if I didn't?"

"There is that."

"Yeah, there is." With that, Mr. Gun fell silent, and Stunt couldn't think of much to say. Usually, his mouth was willing to run away with the rest of him, but right now, he had so many questions his brain was spinning, and he wasn't sure he wanted any of the answers. If he knew what was going on, would he be more or less likely to end up facedown in a shallow grave? He wished he had an answer to that. Desperately wished.

"So how far is this truck of yours?" Mr. Gun asked as they approached a low ridge.

"Other side of the hill."

"So, you just parked in the middle of the forest?"

"The trail loops back. I'm parked just off Thompson Road."

"I can check the map when we get there," Mr. Gun said. "If you're trying to trick me...."

Stunt grunted, but he didn't comment. Around here, maps were nigh-on worthless. People changed roads when it suited them, and let them fall back to forest land when it didn't. Every time a good-old boy moved a still or a meth shed, it seemed like the whole network of roads shifted to accommodate. If that wasn't bad enough, most everyone Stunt knew had stolen at least one street sign, himself included. It was a sort of prank, something to challenge the local law. Challenging the law was a rite of passage, and confusing strangers was another, which was why stealing street signs was such a popular pastime, seeing as how a boy could kill two birds with one stone.

Shoulders aching, Stunt finally got to the top of the rise where they could see his pickup. He had parked with two wheels on the slope so the vehicle listed to one side, leaving enough room for another truck to pass. "Right where I promised," Stunt pointed out. See, he was playing nice. His high school English teacher would be amazed at how nice he could play when he had a gun pointed at his back. Mind, he wasn't advocating the teaching of English at gunpoint, but it might have improved his GPA.

"Gun under the seat?"

"Unless someone has stolen it, but given how my day is going, I ain't discounting that possibility."

"Your day could have been worse if the other two had caught you," Mr. Gun said. "Trust me, you're better off with me."

Stunt wasn't sure he agreed, given the other two seemed ready to live and let live, even if they didn't like him. Mr. Gun here kept promising he wasn't into killing innocent men, but the prison tattoo was a little worrisome, and Stunt wasn't sure how Mr. Gun intended to end this. It seemed as if Stunt had a mighty good description of Mr. Gun right now.

He had a long-sleeved black shirt pushed up to his elbows and camouflage pants, military surplus boots and gear, and a Remington Model 700 SPS Buckmaster hunting rifle. He had dark blue eyes, a strong, straight nose, and what people called a manly jaw line, dark brown hair, and long fingers that felt good as they wiped your face clean. Honestly, though, Stunt should probably edit that last part out of any statement to the police, at least unless he wanted to end up sounding crazy as a bedbug. And he couldn't figure out what this guy was thinking because Stunt could give the police all that… as long as he survived. That last was the rub.

Mr. Gun had already taken Stunt's keys, so when they reached the truck, Stunt got shoved stomach-first into the side of the truck. Without a word, Mr. Gun kicked his legs apart until they were obscenely spread like one of those men on a police show getting frisked or one of those guys in porn about to get seriously nailed. It was funny how the pose was so similar. "Stay," Mr. Gun ordered.

Without moving, Stunt answered with a "Woof."

"Keep it up and you'll be on a leash, Rover."

"Stunt."

"What?" Mr. Gun had already opened the driver's side door, and he started tossing aside the fast-food trash from under the seat in his search for the gun.

"Stunt Folger. Stewart Folger actually, but no one ever called me Stewart except the preacher and my momma, and no one at all calls me Rover."

Mr. Gun pulled back and gave Stunt a real good looking over. "So we're having introductions now?" Mr. Gun seemed to think about that, and Stunt swallowed as it occurred to him Mr. Gun might not have realized how much information Stunt was gathering up on him until this very moment. After all, hanging out in the leaf litter wasn't exactly a sign of great intelligence.

"Alex," Mr. Gun offered. It was such a normal name that it took a second for it to sink in. Oh, Stunt hadn't exactly expected him to be named "Killer," but "Alex" seemed pretty pedestrian for a guy who ran around taking hostages. Alex went back to searching under the seat. It took him a minute or so before he finally came up with Stunt's Jericho 941 pistol. He held it up, studying it in the light. "Well, this is fancier than I expected."

"You mean from us hicks?" Stunt said.

"Yep," Alex agreed without rancor, checking the gun and pulling the ammo out quickly. He was better with a pistol than his hunting rifle, that was for sure. "Any more weapons?"

"I have a nice booby trap in the glove compartment that will blow your hand off," Stunt said with a sweet smile. "Want to try it out?"

Alex shoved the gun into the back of his pants and pulled his shirt over to hide it, not that anyone would care around here. Most people did go armed. "Do you need a gag? I could dig one up if you can't control that mouth of yours."

"Oh no. Do not blame me if you get a wild hair and feel like getting into more bondage. This is all about you and your mighty powerful dysfunction," Stunt said. He grunted as he shifted to push one of his shoulders against the side of the truck without moving his feet.

Alex struck him as someone who wouldn't appreciate him moving too much, but his shoulders were hurting.

Stunt got tied up often enough, but usually he was on his bed and his hands were over his head, not wrenched behind him. This was more annoying than he would have thought, and sadly, he had come up with scenarios pretty close to this more than once. He did like his sexual fantasies to have a little more adrenaline than most folk.

"My dysfunction wouldn't include an unwilling partner, so how about you stop pushing that button before you ruin my favorite fantasies?" Alex asked.

"Oh yeah, because I really worry about your sex life. As long as it doesn't involve me, I don't care about your kinks." Stunt blinked. Wait. Alex's fantasies? Alex's favorite fantasies included handcuffing someone and holding them hostage? Either Stunt had a whole lot of brain cells offline or Alex had just admitted to being on the kinky side.

"Really? Because you're the one who offered me a club where this would be considered foreplay," Alex said with a chuckle, and Stunt had to do some mental scrambling to catch up with the conversation. "I think that implies I'm not the only one with kinks."

Stunt cringed. Okay, so first, Alex wasn't as dumb as Stunt had hoped, and second, Stunt needed to work on being more subtle. Usually, he was pretty good at not shoving his gayness or his kinkiness in anyone's face, since it wasn't exactly open-minded central around these parts, but Stunt had definitely outed himself in the kink department. "My kinks include the word consensual."

"And safe and sane, I bet," Alex said with a grin that quickly fell away when Stunt didn't return it. As the person tied up, helpless, and terrified, Stunt didn't want to even think about what it meant that his sex life so often included "consensual" and "safe," and how often it excluded "sane."

Alex cleared this throat. "Look, if I ran into someone with your clever mouth in a gay bar, I would offer you a drink and a long night of debauchery. I'm not denying that. However, I'm not into rape and I'm not into murder. I'm absolutely not going to hurt an innocent man unless he does something stupid, like back me into a corner. So can you please stop assuming the worst of me?" asked the man with the big gun and the keys to the cuffs. The irony wasn't lost on Stunt.

"Yeah, I'll get right on that," Stunt said wearily. "You could always drop me off in town and let me look for a good shrink with emergency office hours," he offered.

"Your mouth must get you into a lot of trouble."

"Your tendency of taking hostages must do the same."

Alex gave a quick huff of laughter. "You're my first. I'm in virgin territory here." After grabbing Stunt's arm, Alex dragged him around to the other side of the truck.

Stunt figured that meant, if he took Alex's word for things, kidnapping, murder, and rape were off the list of Alex's potential previous crimes. That still left a lot of terrifying territory. Some guy in the hoosegow for shoplifting wouldn't exactly be getting a prison tattoo. Alex had done something plenty bad.

Alex forced him up against the truck's side, pushing his legs apart like before. Sighing, Stunt cooperated, watching while Alex searched the passenger side. Unfortunately, the glove compartment wasn't booby-trapped, and all Alex got out of it was the department's credit card for a local gas station. He pulled a blanket out from behind the seat and folded it before arranging it on the floor of the passenger side.

"Okay, in you go, knees on the blanket," Alex ordered. Stunt frowned, but he didn't have much choice but to climb awkwardly into the passenger side and kneel on the floor. The space was too small for comfort, and he had to jam himself between the glove box and the seat. Between that and the cuffs, he would not be trying anything heroically stupid in the near future.

Alex got into the driver's side and started the truck before he pulled out a map and opened it on the bench seat. "Comfortable?" he asked as he studied the network of roads that totally didn't match reality.

"Bite me," Stunt answered. Alex's gaze flickered toward him, and he smiled, but he didn't comment as he searched the map for something. It looked like they were taking a road trip.

CHAPTER
3

"SO, WHY Stunt?"

Stunt had to arch his back and squirm to look up from his awkward spot on the floor. "You want to engage in small talk?" For the last ten or fifteen minutes, Alex had driven the pitted roads in silence, and Stunt had used the time to have a quiet little panic attack. Honestly, he resented Alex for interrupting that, and when a panic attack became his happy place, he was in all sorts of trouble.

Alex frowned. "I'm trying to be friendly here."

"Friendly?" Stunt raised his eyebrows and bit down on an urge to tell Alex where to shove his friendly. His emotions were churning a little more than was healthy. However, with a sigh, he answered. "Up until about an hour ago, I figured I liked adrenaline. I did some pretty crazy stunts in school, so the kids started calling me Stunt." He'd engaged in more than a few stupid and life-threatening moments, but jumping off Miller's cliff into the river or kissing Howie LaMont on a dare couldn't touch the adrenaline of being helpless in his own truck with a man who was trying to be "friendly."

"I guess it's better than Stewart."

"Excuse me?"

"No offense," Alex said in a voice that almost sounded apologetic. "It's just that when I hear the name Stewart, I think animated mice and grandfathers. But Stunt... that's a good name."

"I'm so glad you approve," Stunt said wearily. He was in hell. That was the best explanation for this. He was dead, and his grandmother was right about fornicators going to hell. 'Course, if he listened to his grandmother, folks that spit on the sidewalk were headed there too, so he wasn't sure she was a real good authority on the issue.

"Hey, I'm trying to be nice."

"Says the man who's holding me captive." Stunt let his head hang forward as he tried to take the strain off his shoulders. That gave him a good view of the dirt and broken Fritos and crumbled dry leaves ground into the tan carpet. If Stunt had known he was going to be held captive and shoved onto the floor, he would have cleaned up the truck.

"Believe it or not, you weren't the one I was hunting. Maybe if you hadn't gotten in the middle, you wouldn't be here."

"Oh yes. I apologize. I should have avoided the crazy man hiding in the leaves."

Alex gave a huge sigh, as if Stunt was being unreasonable. Then again, maybe Stunt was. It occurred to him that proper hostages probably spent less time complaining and being sarcastic. Too bad for Alex, adrenaline had always freed Stunt from his inhibitions and common sense. That was why he liked to play so hard sexually.

Let him feel a sharp edge of fear or the little animal panic at being tied down tight, and suddenly he was free to fight. He could spew out his frustration without having to wonder if he would hurt his partner, or feel guilty if he did. Maybe it was the release of control after being raised to believe that good manners trumped every other concern, but getting dominated did tend to turn a harder, more adventurous version of himself loose on the world.

Some days he suspected that made him just one step to the far side of crazy. Other days he figured he was about the sanest person he knew since he'd figured out which buttons were likely to poke his psyche. However, right now, every wire he had was getting crossed. His good buddy, adrenaline, had turned foe, and the helplessness he had always associated with cutting loose was about to get him killed if he didn't start biting his tongue and using the good manners his momma and memaw had taught him.

The truck bounced up onto blacktop. The smooth road meant Stunt wasn't shoved into the dashboard on every pothole, and he sank down, his chest resting against his thighs and his head nearly to the floor.

The hum of the road under the truck was almost soothing, and Stunt closed his eyes and thought back to his Eastern Traditions class and the professor's discussion of meditation. It was a subject he normally didn't go thinking on much. Actually, it was a subject he normally considered one big steaming pile of shit. However, he could feel himself drifting away from reality as the buzz of the tires against the blacktop soothed him, each tarred crack in the pavement sending him deeper into a sort of limbo.

The worst part was the quiet he felt was a lot like the sort of quiet he got during a really good scene where his partner tied him down so tight all he could do was drift in and out of reality as his body sang whatever tune his Dom chose. The mental gray sank into him. It spoke volumes of how fucked up his sex life was that he could almost feel himself relaxing into the helplessness. *Volumes.* Normally, Stunt embraced his sexual deviance right up there with the best of them, but he was thinking he was taking this a little too far if his brain was confusing this with fun. Luckily, his balls had the good sense his brain didn't. They were still trying to crawl back up inside.

"You okay down there?"

Stunt didn't open his eyes. It'd be a lot easier to play nice if this guy would stop verbally poking him and just let Stunt have a quiet little breakdown. "Peachy," he offered dryly.

Alex chuckled, and Stunt felt a stab of annoyance. He didn't want this asshole to appreciate his humor. "We're almost there," Alex offered.

"Good to know," Stunt answered in the same flat tone. He didn't know where "there" was, but he was pretty sure he didn't want the truck to stop. As long as they were just driving, nothing too bad was happening… nothing besides sore shoulders. It seemed like ever since they'd gone tumbling down that slope, Stunt's right shoulder had been right stove-up. With his luck, he'd pulled something.

"My truck will be more comfortable for you."

Stunt grunted. Alex seemed to be carrying on the conversation fine without any help from him.

"How long will it take for anyone to notice you haven't checked back in?"

Stunt raised himself up and considered his answer. Truth was, if he didn't check in until tomorrow, his boss would assume that he'd run his truck in a ditch or found some good old boy trying to set up a still too close to the trails and gone off to negotiate with him, or maybe Drew would just assume Stunt had taken off for the day. If he didn't check in until the day after, most likely Drew would start doing a little worrying—calling around to the café and asking the sheriff's department to keep an eye out. Stunt figured it would probably take at least three days before anyone started hitting any panic buttons. Never before in his life had he regretted being such a marginal employee.

"That long, huh?" Alex asked even though Stunt hadn't answered.

Figuring his chance to lie had already passed him by, Stunt rested back on his heels. "Probably. Two or three days, at least. I have a reputation for handling problems on my own, so a few days missing isn't exactly unknown."

"What about your friends? Your family?"

Stunt sighed. "I don't have much family left alive or I'd be threatening you with all kinds of mountain justice. You ain't seen much until you've seen a mountain feud get out of hand. And as for friends, let's just say I'm not the most popular man in town. I don't suppose you have too much to worry about on that front."

If Stunt missed the weekend down at Matthew's Place, guys would notice, but they'd move on to another partner. If he missed a few weeks in a row, they'd start wondering and maybe they'd even try to check on him, but he suspected that was more because of his unusual sexual aptitude rather than any concern for him as a person. The guys appreciated his cock, but the personality that came with it—they never had shown much interest in Stunt as an individual.

And people in town were nice enough to his face, but in their worldview, he was a sodomizer and fornicator. They definitely kept a certain distance. They'd check on him after a storm to make sure he was alive, but none of them would be borrowing a cup of sugar anytime soon.

Alex nodded. "Hopefully by then it'll all be over."

A cold chill went through Stunt. "All what?"

Alex pulled off the blacktop, the truck bouncing over rain-rutted dirt. "All this. Hopefully in two or three days, I will have killed Michael Garrido."

The cold chills kept a'coming. Stunt pressed his lips together and tried very hard to not think about what it meant that Alex had just confessed to premeditating a murder. All the gray calm of minutes ago fled like a flock of birds after the hunter's first shot, and the world came into a painfully sharp focus.

Alex stopped Stunt's maintenance truck and put it into park before turning off the key. "Hang on a second," Alex commented as though they were friends and Stunt had a choice in the matter. He jumped out of the truck and then vanished.

Stretching upward, Stunt tried to look over the dash, but all he could see was the dark green tops of balsam firs, pitch pine, and red maple trees, and the rough tops of the mountains poking up into a cloud-streaked sky. "Great," Stunt muttered to himself as he settled back down, butt on his heels. The keys were there in the ignition and the radio hung from the roof of the truck, but both were hopelessly out of reach.

Helpless to even watch his captor, Stunt let his mind drift back to the first time anyone had ever tied him up. It'd been Howie LaMont, the victim of his kiss-on-a-dare scheme. Being raised in the country, most people understood homosexuality on a certain level. They'd seen some prize bull's value plummet because the idiot couldn't figure out to mount the cows instead of the other bulls… not to mention other bulls could get a mite unhappy about getting mounted. So it wasn't like

Stunt hadn't understood that he was sexually idiotic growing up, so the dare to kiss Howie had been more of an excuse than the true horror his friends envisioned.

He'd snuck up behind Howie, the class delinquent whose father had gone to prison for robbing clinics for prescription pills and whose mother turned tricks at the truck stop down by Chicken Creek. After tapping the older boy on the shoulder, Stunt had waited until he'd turned around and then kissed Howie right on the mouth before dancing backward, shrieking out, "It was a dare. It was a dare—blame them!" He'd pointed at his friends, who were all laughing maniacally. J.B. clung to Raelene like he might fall over without the support, and Robert Joe was red in the face and struggling to breathe through his howls. Howie had glowered for a moment, stalking off without a word.

It was going on three weeks before Howie got his revenge, snatching Stunt off the road and pulling him into the woods. Stunt had hollered up a storm until Howie had cuffed him upside the head, and at that point, Stunt had figured he was in a good deal of shit. He'd shut up.

Down in a dry creek bed, Howie had tied him with his hands behind a tree, and Stunt still remembered the rough bark against his bare arms. "So, you think you can take what you want?" Howie had demanded, his voice slurred. He'd leaned in and kissed Stunt back—an eye for an eye and a kiss for a kiss. That moonshine-stained, adolescent kiss had set Stunt's sexual appetites for the next ten years, not that Stunt had followed up on anything until he went off to the University of Tennessee. However, Stunt wondered if Alex and his gun were going to ruin his best fantasies the way Howie LaMont had fueled them. He hoped not. He really liked getting tied up during sex.

The truck door opened. "You ready to get out of there?"

"I don't know. Are you going to shoot me if I do?"

Alex gave another put-upon sigh. "You are annoying. I promise to not kill you. Okay?"

Stunt didn't say anything, but that promise had sounded more promising before Alex had gone explaining how he intended to kill a man. He cooperated as Alex pulled him backward out of the passenger side, stumbling and going to one knee with a pained hiss. The pain flared in his shoulders, and Stunt fell to both knees as he cried out.

"Fuck." Alex was next to him, squatting down at Stunt's side. "Come on, talk to me here. What's wrong?"

A rough laugh slipped out before Stunt could stop it. If he got out of this alive, he was taking up praying and therapy.

"What is it?"

"My shoulders," Stunt finally managed through clenched teeth. He could feel the sharp pain radiating down his back. Stunt didn't know what he expected, but he sure didn't expect to have the barrel of his own gun pressed to the side of his neck just under his ear. The metal was cold against his skin, making goose pimples break out all down his arms, and Stunt stopped even breathing.

"If you're trying to trick me into uncuffing you… if you plan on trying to attack me… you'll be sorry."

Stunt's mouth was dust-dry as he answered. "I'm all kinds of sorry already." He was also starting to wonder if Alex didn't need therapy more than he did, not that he had any room to go throwing around insults related to sanity.

"I wish…" Alex stopped. He rested one hand against Stunt's arm and the pressure of the gun pressing into his neck vanished. "I didn't want innocent people getting caught up in this, and you don't deserve to be in pain."

Stunt blinked, trying to figure out if that was genuine regret in Alex's voice, but then Alex reached down and started unbuckling Stunt's belt. His next words were back to business. "Facedown on the ground."

Stunt couldn't have moved if Saint Peter himself had appeared to give the order. He couldn't figure Alex out, and it was disquieting to have an armed and unpredictable man in the immediate vicinity.

Alex pulled Stunt's belt free of the loops. "Lay down on the ground, and I'll change the cuffs to take the pressure off your shoulders. If this is a trick, tell me now before we risk having a fatal accident out here." Giving Stunt a push, he pretty much tipped Stunt over. Stunt arched his back to keep himself from hitting the ground face-first, and then Alex was wrapping the belt around Stunt's ankles. "I'll get the rope, and we can rearrange your arms a bit."

Stunt figured that was a royal "we" because he sure wasn't getting a vote in the matter. Alex headed toward a dirty, brown truck with rusted wheel wells and an old camper bolted on the back. It was the sort folks might live in or run a mobile meth lab out of. The new crop of meth dealers didn't need much more than a soda bottle and a recipe for "shake and bake" meth, but the older dealers who preferred the big-batch cooking would use these types of trucks to haul their load, and then they'd blow up when they went over a pothole.

Alex's soft curses came from his truck. Maybe he didn't have any rope. Maybe he would decide to just let Stunt go, which was highly unlikely, but a man could hope.

"So, did this Michael Garrido do anything in particular to you, or did you go picking his name out of the phone book?" Since Stunt liked nice Alex, the one who talked to him and made promises about how Stunt would survive this, he decided to try and do a little playing nice himself.

Stunt frowned, suddenly wondering if asking someone about their murder plots qualified as playing nice. His grandmother had pounded a whole lot of manners into his head over the years. Open doors for ladies, always say "sir" and "ma'am" to older folks, avoid cursing where proper folk could hear, and never go to a dinner party without a gift. Those he knew, but polite conversations during a kidnapping appeared to have been left out of the moral instruction of his youth.

"He's a killer," Alex said as he climbed back out of the back of his camper. He dangled a rope where Stunt could see it. In the short term, Stunt's arms were going to get a little relief, and in the long run, his chances of escape had just gone up considerably. Unless Alex was a master of knots, Stunt would be able to squirm out of any ropes. At least, he could after the circulation returned to his arms. Right now they were a'hurting like a son of a bitch, and he wouldn't win a slap fight with a three-year-old.

"So, you're looking to join the murderers' club?" Stunt asked.

Alex looked honestly shocked for a second. "Killing Garrido isn't murder; it's a public service." He knelt down, his knee right on Stunt's ass. This guy knew something about controlling people, that was for sure. Even if Stunt's arms weren't nearly helpless with cramps, he wouldn't have been able to launch any sort of attack.

"No offense, but you don't seem the public service sort… or the type to murder folks," Stunt said, hoping that last part was true. If Alex was a cold-blooded murderer, he spent a lot of energy trying to convince a hostage he wasn't. Of course, Alex was looking pretty good for having one of those serious mental illnesses right now, so he might have one of those alternate personalities tucked away that had all kinds of homicidal rage going for him.

Alex unlocked the cuffs, and Stunt let his hands fall to either side, moaning in pleasure as the overstretched muscles in his shoulders could finally relax. Letting his arms lie limp, Stunt opened and closed his fingers to try and help the blood move again.

"You should have said something," Alex scolded.

"Right, because the guy who keeps pointing that gun at me and telling me how he's planning on killing someone would have cared?"

"I would have." Alex had an odd sort of determination in his voice. "I didn't mean to hurt you." Again, Alex's hand came to rest on Stunt's arm. "I admire how well you're keeping it together. A lot of men would have panicked by now."

"Your behavior is slightly contradictory to that particular argument, especially given the number of times you've pointed a gun at my head."

"I just don't want you to make a fatal mistake." Looping the rope around Stunt's right wrist, Alex quickly tied a rolling hitch. The universe must hate Stunt because a rolling hitch was going to be a bitch to try and work out of. Alex shifted so his knee was on the back of Stunt's thighs as he pushed the end of the rope under Stunt's stomach and pulled it out the other end to do a neat rolling hitch around Stunt's left wrist. Then Alex pulled both ends of the rope around to Stunt's back and finished so his hands were tied down to his sides. It was better than handcuffs, but Stunt didn't see how he was going to get out of the bindings.

"Trust me, I'm likely to do all sorts of stupid. It's in my nature. However, I'm not likely to argue with an armed man who appears to have some moral lapses going for him."

Alex frowned as he took a moment to work his thumbs in circles across Stunt's shoulders. The tight muscles cringed under the pressure, but as Alex worked his way across the shoulder blades, the massage eased the worst of the cramps. Stunt couldn't hold back a groan of pleasure as Alex soothed away the pain. He might be morally questionable, but he was good with his hands.

Just when Stunt was starting to feel pain-free, Alex stopped and slapped him on the shoulder. "Let's get into my truck and get moving before someone sees us," he said. He reached down and undid the belt around Stunt's legs before pulling him to his feet.

Stunt had any number of inappropriate remarks about how much he didn't give a rat's ass about what Alex wanted. He was proud of the fact that he managed to avoid saying them as Alex guided him into the camper and settled him onto a sleeping bag in the bed of the truck. As Alex tied the belt around his feet again, Stunt tried to figure out this man who clearly wasn't your average kidnapper.

Before he came to any conclusion, Alex pulled the tailgate up before closing the camper shell's back flap. Someone had modified the truck, using a welder to cut out a narrow door between the camper shell and the cab of the truck. That was a pretty popular trick with a number of people, including the hookers and meth cookers who didn't want to have to get out of the front to crawl in the back. It was definitely a local trick, and the fact a city boy had bought a local truck did seem to suggest he'd been stalking through the mountains a while.

It made Stunt wonder how long he was going to be tied up. Alex wiggled his way up into the driver's seat. Whoever had cut out the door didn't leave enough room for someone as large as Alex. "If you understood what I was doing, you'd probably help me."

"You know, I really doubt that. I'm pretty big on following the Ten Commandments. Or nine of them at least, but 'thou shalt not murder' is one of the nine I'm fairly consistent about." Stunt twisted around until he could see the front of the truck.

Alex settled into the driver's seat and looked back at Stunt with a sly grin. "Should I ask which one you're not good at following?"

The man looked far too amused, and Stunt could feel a little spark of true anger burning through his fear. The smug look turned that spark into a full-on conflagration. "I figure the fact that I'm spending so much time thinking on you and how you're a Goddamned son of a bitch who likes terrorizing people at gunpoint means that I'm not real good at showing respect for the Lord's name," he said, his voice tight with emotion.

Alex paled some. They sat staring at each other, and Stunt could feel his mouth go dry and his heart start to pound painfully hard. That would be fear showing up about two minutes too late.

Then with a jerky nod, Alex started the old truck without a word. The engine came to life with a roar, and Stunt rested his forehead against the musky sleeping bag, the anger gone as quickly as it had come. With nothing else to do, he called himself an idiot as Alex pulled out onto the road.

CHAPTER
4

BY THE time Alex decided to stop racing over every pothole in the state, Stunt had squirmed until he settled himself on his stomach and dropped his head down on a pile of semiclean jeans. It was better than having his tailbone bruised seven ways from Sunday.

"Okay, I need to stop for supplies," Alex said, his tone making it almost sound like he was asking permission. Stunt wasn't entirely sure why the man had decided to phrase that as a question. Stunt certainly wasn't in a position to argue. Alex turned off the truck and it died with a long series of spluttering coughs. "I'm really sorry about this part."

Stunt's stomach immediately twisted into a tight knot and he rolled onto his side so he could see Alex. "You have the power here. You don't have to do anything you don't want to," he said carefully. After calling Alex all those names, he sure didn't have much room to ask for mercy, but he wouldn't lie down and die easy. It left him in a bit of a quandary.

Alex turned and looked through the opening into the back. "I wish that were true," he said, and there was such a sudden sadness about him that Stunt wasn't sure how to handle the quicksilver moods. Then Alex cleared his throat and the emotion vanished. "I need gas and supplies, and that means I need to take the truck in close to people, and I can't risk you calling out for help."

Stunt's mouth went dry. "Not to sound like a broken record, but that's sounding a little like a threat. Or a lot like one."

Alex got up and angled himself through the narrow opening. "You do sound like a broken record, and at this point, so do I. I'm not going to kill you. I am, however, going to piss you off." Alex crouched down at Stunt's side.

Stunt frowned, not liking how that sounded.

"Let's get you turned around." Alex grabbed Stunt's shoulders and helped him up to his knees. Until this moment, Stunt hadn't registered how very strong Alex was, but the fingers holding him were steel. Stunt didn't argue as Alex got him turned until he was facing the back of the truck. Then Alex settled him back onto his stomach. Tugging on the sleeping bag, he slid Stunt down until his knees hit the wall that separated the cab from the back. "Let me know if this is too tight." Oddly, Alex was busy taking the belt off Stunt's ankles as he said that.

"Why are you doing this?" Stunt asked as Alex used a rope to start tying his left ankle before looping it around to tie it to Stunt's right ankle.

"Because I have to."

"No… no you don't. There's very little that people have to do. You know that old saying about death and taxes? I'm telling you, I know about a third of the folks on the mountains would shoot you if you so much as suggested they pay taxes, so I'm thinking dying is the only thing we have to do, and we spend our whole lives trying to not do that."

Alex paused, the trailing end of the rope in his hand. "You're a philosophical little shit, aren't you?"

"Not usually." Stunt made a face. He'd hated philosophy up until he'd gone and gotten kidnapped. "But whatever you think you have to do, you don't. And as long as you haven't hurt anyone, folks are less interested in tracking down a kidnapper than you might think. Oh, the police will put a warrant out there, but two years ago when Rabern

Woodstown tied me to a tree for two days while he moved his still, no one went out on any manhunt. The sheriff took a report and entered the arrest warrant, and then pretty much life went on like normal."

From the look of horror on Alex's face, he didn't appreciate the story much. "No one arrested the guy?"

Stunt snorted. "I think mostly people were surprised he didn't shoot me, and no one was going to press their luck by trying to track him down. One of these days he'll get appendicitis or jaundice and show up in a hospital where they can arrest him, but until then, I don't want someone killed trying to serve that warrant. Unsurprisingly, there is a dearth of folk signing up for that job anyway. So you wouldn't even be my first kidnapper to go free." Stunt tried giving Alex his most charming smile, the one that made all the Doms sit up and take notice.

It didn't work.

Alex shook his head. "You're fucking crazy. This whole state is full of crazy people. Personally, I figure I'm going to jail within an hour of finishing this job. And don't worry, when they drag me into the interrogation room, I'll tell them where to find you."

"Or you could avoid jail and just call this off now." Stunt felt an odd sort of discomfort at the thought of Alex going to prison. Compared to his first kidnapping, this one was downright comfortable. Terrifying, but comfortable. Hell, if he'd gone and lost his temper with Rabern the way he had with Alex, he would have been in a whole lot more pain.

"No, I can't." Alex leaned back on his heels and studied the truck like he was searching for the meaning of life, his eyes shining even in the dim light that filtered through the darkened back window of the cab shell. "Michael Garrido signed his own death warrant almost two years ago. It's just taken me this long to get around to serving it. That's my only goal here, to kill him. If I have to take out his soldiers, fine. If they kill me two seconds after I take out their boss, that's fine too." Alex's Adam's apple bobbed, and Stunt could feel the emotions swirling like a mountain storm. None of this made any sense, but Stunt was thinking something had happened to drive Alex past the point of caring for logic.

The silence continued with Alex just holding the rope leading to Stunt's hobbled ankles. "Why?" Stunt asked as softly as he could.

For a time, he thought Alex hadn't heard him or maybe he was ignoring him. It took a long time for Alex to move, and then he shook his head and seemed to force himself back into motion. Letting out a length of rope and tying Stunt's ankles to a rod way up high meant Stunt would have very little chance to try and work the knots. Alex might be all kinds of unstable, but he was good at tying a man down.

"He's a dealer. A big-time drug dealer like you see in the movies, and two years ago, he ordered one of his men to kill my brother."

All the emotion seemed to have leached out of Alex's voice, and he clenched his jaw so hard Stunt could see the muscle bulge. But Alex's hands gently ran over the ropes, and he rested his palms against Stunt's hands, holding them for a second before moving on to run his hands up Stunt's arms and then rest against his back.

Stunt had had a dozen Doms do some variation on the same thing. Alex was checking for cold extremities, feeling to see if the circulation was safe and the ropes weren't dangerous. Sometimes a sub couldn't rightly tell how tight things were because they were too caught up in their own heads. However, Stunt's body wasn't quite sure how to handle this particular ritual from a man who was on the unsafe and insane side of the consensual fence. He had to admit some small part of him was warming to this man, and that might be the fear speaking. It might also be the fact Stunt could understand the sort of Biblical retribution Alex had described.

"You could go to the police," Stunt suggested. Mountain folk would laugh themselves into a conniption at that suggestion, but folk who were raised off the mountain tended to see the police differently.

"Yeah. The police are going to kill themselves trying to solve the murder of a two-bit street dealer all on the word of an ex-con." The laugh that slipped out of Alex sounded a lot more like a sob. He rubbed a hand over his face.

"Damn it. I told him to not get involved with these assholes. I told him. I ordered him to steer clear, and he sold fucking drugs for that monster." Alex slammed his fist into the floor of the truck, and for a second, Stunt didn't dare breathe for fear of bringing that fury down on him. People this worked up could do some stupid stuff. Turning his back, Alex rummaged through a box on the other side of the truck. "Drop it, Stunt. This is one problem you don't want to go poking at."

Alex turned around again, and Stunt spotted the rag in his hand and knew immediately what Alex had planned. Shaking his head required an awkward arching of the back to get clear of the sleeping bag, but he made the effort. "You don't have to do this. You know I don't want to drag more people into this."

"Open," Alex ordered, and all the hot emotions of moments ago had vanished under a real brittle coldness.

Stunt was seriously buying the man psychotherapy sessions for Christmas, but given his current mood, arguing seemed likely to get Alex even more het up. Unhappy, but unable to see any other solution, Stunt opened his mouth and let Alex stuff the rag in. He'd dampened it, which made it a good sight more comfortable, since dry filling tended to soak up so much of the saliva it stuck to the inside of the mouth, but that didn't mean Stunt appreciated it.

"I'll be as quick as I can. Do not attract attention," Alex ordered as he wrapped another strip of cloth around Stunt's face to hold the gag in. "Now I suppose if you worked at that long enough, you could probably push some of that rag out. If I tie it tight enough to make that impossible, I think we both know what we'd be risking."

Stunt grunted through his nose. Push a gag in too far, and you made the nasal cavity swell up with the pressure and choked someone. Of course, Alex was assuming a lot by thinking Stunt knew that particular fact.

Reaching out, Alex rested a hand against Stunt's shoulder. "We may be together for a few days, so consider this a test. I expect you to lie there and not try anything, not wiggle, not use that tongue to try and get the gag out, not reach for knots with those nimble fingers. If I can trust you to do that, then I'll know we don't have to take the bondage to the next level. Clear?"

Stunt angled his head so he could look up at Alex as he weighed his options. He could lie, but not only was he uncomfortable with lying in general, but lying to a man who'd just revealed his own pain seemed impolite to say the least. He could refuse to go along, but Stunt figured Alex knew much more uncomfortable ways to tie a man. He was entirely too good with knots. The only men this good were Doms and woodsmen, and Alex sure wasn't the last.

Sighing through his nose, Stunt nodded. He'd play the good boy. Maybe while he was at it, he could convince his cock to be good—the damn thing had perked up and noticed a man with a whole lot of rope skills. *Idiot prick.*

"Good boy," Alex said with a smile as he patted Stunt on the shoulder.

Stunt would have woofed in response, but his mouth was packed full. Settling down onto the sleeping bag, he wiggled a bit to get a hip off a ridge in the floor of the truck as Alex went back to the driver's seat. Hopefully, this little supply-and-gas trip wouldn't take too long. If it did, Stunt was going to be very uncomfortable, and his cock was going to get so very confused. It wasn't like it was the brightest to begin with, but that crack in Alex's façade, that peek into an angry and hurt soul had definitely confused it more than usual. Stunt always had shown terrible taste in Doms, and his gut was starting to take an unhealthy interest in a man who was putting off every sign and signal that he knew his way around the scene.

CHAPTER
5

THE supply trip took longer than Stunt had hoped, but it did seem like Alex had moved as fast as he could. Still, Stunt's jaw ached from being gagged and his nose itched. It was weird, but every time his hands were tied, it started itching. Without the blind terror to distract him, it was starting to get right bothersome.

However, the trip gave Stunt time to think on the fact that Alex wasn't quite as unbalanced as he seemed at first blush. Oh, he was touched in the head, but more the normal sort of touched Stunt had dealt with before. Mountain folk had regular acquaintance with Biblical rage.

Alex pulled to the right, and Stunt could feel the change in the road as they left the blacktop and started bouncing over a rain-rutted road. He opened his mouth more and then tried to relax the muscle, but without being able to close his mouth, it didn't help much. He could feel a cramp threatening, and his mouth watered so much a thin line of drool slipped past the rag and out the corner of his mouth.

"We should be safe here," Alex announced as he parked the truck and turned the engine off. It rumbled roughly before falling silent. "I got trail supplies—food, more water, a second sleeping bag, and enough gas to make a clean getaway if I manage to do this without getting killed." He angled his body and crawled into the back. Immediately, he knelt beside Stunt. "Thank you for not making this more difficult." Alex worked at the gag's knot. It took a second, but he untied the rag and Stunt immediately spit it out.

"I didn't think I had a choice," Stunt said before using his tongue to poke the sore spots on the inside of his mouth. Alex reached down and started massaging Stunt's jaw. Strong thumbs pressed firmly into the muscle to work the soreness out, and Stunt's mouth watered even more.

"You and I both know you could make this a lot more difficult." Alex finished and then let his hands travel down Stunt's arms until his fingers wrapped around Stunt's wrists.

"Do we?"

"I think we're both more comfortable with ropes than most people."

"Speak for yourself."

Alex gave him an amused look. "You're the one who offered to find me a club or two where I could play like this, and trust me, if you weren't used to getting tied up, you'd be freaking out about me checking your circulation. You'd probably accuse me of feeling you up, which is why I had a whole speech planned for when you started panicking. I don't think you need to hear about the dangers of restricted circulation, though, do you? I think you're used to having a man or woman do this for you—used to having a partner tie you up."

Stunt closed his eyes. This guy was annoyingly insightful. "I prefer men, and that don't mean I appreciate you doing this."

Alex paused. "I know," he said, his voice serious. "I know that this has to be hard on you because of that preference. But I will keep you safe and clear of my mess. I promise. Now, is anything hurting?" When Stunt paused, debating whether or not to be honest, Alex's hand caught him by the back of the neck, fingers pressed hard into the flesh. "Don't play hero now. If you're hurting, say so."

"I have to pee, okay?" Stunt snapped.

"Oh." Alex closed his mouth. Stunt had finally found something to throw him off his game.

"I can hold it, okay?"

Alex sighed. "Not for two or three days you can't."

Stunt made a face. "I'm willing to try."

Alex laughed as he started untying Stunt's ankles. "I give you points for speaking your mind, but you have to piss, Stunt, and I'm not going to untie you to do it. So let's do this fast before it gets awkward."

Stunt was painfully aware of his cock. He wasn't hard now, or even half-hard, but he could feel that pressure in his balls, the cobwebs of desire clinging to him. One touch, and Stunt's cock was going to make this all kinds of awkward, especially given his cock's peculiarities. But on the other hand, he couldn't exactly hold it for two days. "Since we're getting along so well, maybe we can make a deal. I promise to not run, and you untie me long enough for me to water a tree."

"No," Alex said firmly, but the corner of his mouth twitched. Stunt had finally found a Dom who enjoyed Stunt's mouth instead of getting annoyed by it. The universe did have a wicked sense of humor.

"You could tie a bowline knot around my neck, use it like a leash to make sure I didn't go nowhere," Stunt suggested hopefully. Actually, that wasn't a half-bad idea.

"No." Alex had one of Stunt's ankles untied, but he left the rope trailing from his other leg as he started helping Stunt kneel up.

"It'd be safe. I mean, you've been real solicitous so far, so I'm not looking to get you riled."

"So, you're telling me that you plan on helping me—or at the very least, cooperating—while I kill a man?" Alex crossed his arms, the rope from Stunt's ankle dangling from one hand.

"If Sheriff Kennedy were standing out there with a bead on your forehead, I'd holler for help. Short of that, I'm not about to get any more civilians involved."

The humor vanished from Alex's face. "Really?" His tone dared Stunt to stick to that truth, and Stunt never had been one to turn down a dare.

"You keep talking to me like I'm ten pounds of stupid shoved in a five-pound burlap poke."

"Poke?"

"Bag, a five-pound bag. Stop interrupting me. The fact is, I'm not stupid. Now, I don't agree with what you're doing, but I also don't happen to think you're evil incarnate or some nonsense like that. You're a man twisted up over your brother's death, and that's making your judgment a little questionable...." Stunt fell silent when he saw the expression of pure rage on Alex's face. Clearly, this was a dangerous topic to be bringing up, but he didn't see a way to avoid it.

"Out." Alex slammed opened the back of the pickup shell with such force the top flew open, hit the end of the hinge, and then slammed back closed. He had to open it again, slower this time. Clearly, his willingness to be amused by Stunt's mouth had a very limited shelf life. If his sarcasm wouldn't work, Stunt would have to fall back on logic.

"You're telling me that a drug dealer has moved into my backyard. Trust me, all sorts of folks around here will sit up and take notice of that. You don't have to do this alone." Stunt talked fast, even as he tried to follow the guiding hands on his shoulders as Alex pushed him out onto the tailgate. The air was still and muggy, and a regular chorus of insects sang their hearts out as the sun started to sink behind the mountains.

"So, all these people who don't pay taxes and who don't enforce kidnapping laws are going to go after Garrido?" Alex gave an ugly laugh. "Don't treat me like I'm fifteen pounds of stupid in that five-pound bag of yours." Alex was a little less careful about helping Stunt off the back of the tailgate, and the second Stunt's feet hit the ground, he gathered up the rope that led to Stunt's ankle. Stunt was going to be leashed after all.

"You don't understand." Stunt tried to keep his voice calm. "Moonshiners... they hate drug dealers. They hate drugs. They hate that they've watched their mountains get turned into some sort of meth capital of the country, and they hate what meth does to the kids around here. They aren't exactly fond of marijuana growers either, but as long as the growers are small, they tolerate them. But the meth shacks...." Stunt shook his head.

Meth dealers didn't worry as much about the police as they did about their neighbors. He needed to explain just how deep the hate ran in this part of the country. Alex wasn't alone, and he wouldn't be alone in taking the law into his own hands, but if he kept trying to do everything on his own, he was going to get himself and Stunt killed.

However, Alex kept right on marching Stunt toward the trees.

"We had a shack go up about two years ago," Stunt explained. "It went up in one giant fireball and took out a couple that was doing the cooking. Now, the state police said the couple probably did something wrong, but I'm telling you that the Brennans had been cooking meth for years, and they weren't to the zombie stage that some of the users get to before dropping dead. I can't see them blowing themselves up, but their new shack was just a hair down the road from the Dwyer farm, and he's an old-school moonshiner who's had stills up yonder for going on forty years, and these days his two sons run them so much that the feds harass them on a semiregular basis. I'm pretty sure the Dwyers decided to take out that shack. So yes, I do think that folks would care if Garrido is some sort of big-time drug dealer. They don't want that on their mountain."

"So, I should go to the Dwyers and ask if they want to help me kill a man?" Alex demanded.

Stunt sighed. The word "frustrating" didn't do Alex justice. Stunt needed a word that was far stronger to describe this giant bullock of a man. At least that helped him avoid another problem, because Stunt did not find obduracy attractive. As Alex unzipped Stunt's pants, Stunt's cock was smart enough to not get hard under Alex's hand. Well, not much anyway. Stunt looked up at the trees and peed as fast as he could, squirming when Alex shook him off with a little more enthusiasm than strictly necessary.

"Don't try to play me," Alex warned as he zipped Stunt back up.

"You've got no idea how things work up here," Stunt warned in return. "You keep trying to use city logic, and city logic don't rightly work in the mountains. These folks… they aren't going to bother much about a man trying to take out a drug dealer in order to avenge his brother. If anything, they'd think you were less of a man if you didn't try."

"Of course," Alex said sarcastically. "I'll take out an ad in the paper and see if anyone wants to throw in with me."

"I wouldn't take things that far." Stunt pressed his lips together before he could curse the man out for his sheer obstinacy.

"No, you wouldn't. I have to say, you're smarter than I gave you credit for. Maybe we'd both be safer if I kept you gagged," Alex said.

Stunt studied the man. Even in the fading light, he could see the tight lines at the edges of Alex's eyes and the way his knuckles turned white where he held the rope leash tied to Stunt's ankle. Alex swallowed more than a man should have to, and his shoulders were set at an angle that reminded Stunt of a mule trying to haul a whole lot of weight.

"You wouldn't be the first Dom to think that," Stunt agreed softly, needing to say something to ease the tension that swirled.

Alex sighed and brought a hand up to Stunt's shoulder. "And I won't be the last. There will be plenty of Doms for you to annoy after this is all over." He smiled. "I get the feeling you're very popular with those Doms because you are a challenge. I bet you're a lot of fun to play with." Alex paused for a second. "I just need to finish this my way."

Stunt nodded without answering. He still thought Alex was all sorts of wrong, but sometimes you couldn't talk a man out of doing his own brand of wrong. Stunt thought about his grandparents, his father's folks. When Stunt was young, they'd take him to their church, at least until the state came along and said the snake handlers would get arrested if they brought any more children into the church. For some odd reason, the social workers weren't real fond of young'uns being around live rattlesnakes and cottonmouths. Imagine that.

His memaw had put down her foot and said she wasn't risking having Stunt taken by the state, and Stunt's parents had been equally adamant. They hadn't been exactly thrilled to hear Stunt had been there when the preacher brought his snakes out for the parishioners to handle, so they were just as happy to follow the law. But his peepaw never had accepted that maybe other folks had a point. Stunt respected snake handlers, and if they wanted to show their faith by picking up things that could kill them, he would defend their right to do so. However, he had to admit he came down on the state's side and thought children didn't have any place being in a room with poisonous snakes unless there was a real thick piece of glass between them. Real thick.

But Stunt remembered his peepaw's anger. He'd railed against the state and how they were interfering with his religion and endangering Stunt's soul by not letting Stunt prove his faith the righteous way—the Biblical way. As far as his peepaw was concerned, the state was holding a gun to his head and telling him to let his grandson go to hell.

The fact Stunt thought his peepaw was dead wrong didn't mean the old man had been any less adamant or any less sure of his own rightness. That was the weird thing about people—they were all convinced of their own righteousness. His peepaw thought he had a moral obligation to take a six-year-old boy to hold a rattlesnake. Stunt still remembered cupping a snake's belly as his grandfather held the head and described the nature of faith. He remembered the dry slide of snake skin over his small palm. And Alex was just as convinced he was justified in killing Garrido. Maybe he was. Maybe Stunt was the one in the wrong this time, because having a murdering drug dealer as a neighbor didn't feel real safe.

Stunt figured he had some time to stew on the matter, because this neck of the woods seemed pretty quiet and Alex was guiding him back to the truck. The worst part was that even if Alex was morally in the right, Stunt still didn't see how he was going to get his revenge without turning the mountain into a bloodbath. This was a real mess.

CHAPTER
6

STUNT squirmed on his sleeping bag and tucked his leg under him. His head ached, but it was a distant throbbing paired with an odd tickle in the scalp that hinted at dried blood. Alex spared him a look and then went back to studying his maps by the light of the kerosene lamp. Night had fallen, and Stunt could still taste the salt of Alex's hands from having to eat canned cheese crackers out of his hand. This would be a real good fantasy if not for all the uncomfortable bits and his slight case of terror every time Alex lost his temper.

"So, tell me about your brother," Stunt said when the silence grew too heavy.

Alex looked up from his maps and frowned as he studied Stunt real good. Yeah, it'd been a stupid subject to go poking at, but then Stunt hadn't earned his nickname by being conservative and careful. "There's not much to tell," Alex finally said slowly, as though looking for a trap. Stunt had been good and quiet for close to two hours, so that should have bought him some faith. Besides, if he tried being quiet anymore, his head was going to explode.

"Considering that you're out here trying to kill a man, I ain't sure I'm buying that."

Sighing, Alex leaned back against the opposite wall of the camper. "He screwed up. He screwed up, and that asshole Garrido had him killed."

"For screwing up?"

Alex gave a quick shrug and looked down at those maps as if waiting for an answer to jump out at him. Stunt figured that was about as likely as Garrido being polite enough to drop dead of a heart attack on his own. It'd be nice, but you couldn't count on the world being nice to you.

"While you were in prison?" Stunt guessed.

Alex's head snapped up. For a second, he just stared at Stunt. "You're smarter than you sound."

"Is that a crack about my accent?"

"Yes," Alex said without apology. "How did you...." He stopped and looked down at his arm. "The tattoo?"

"The tattoo," Stunt agreed. "Well, that and you already went and told me that the police weren't likely to believe you, seeing as how you're an ex-con." From the look of chagrin on Alex's face, he hadn't meant to let that bit slip. However, Alex didn't comment as he rubbed his arm. "Why did you have that done?" Stunt asked. "I never did get why folks would want to mark themselves like that."

"It's another world in there. Getting a mark...." Alex shrugged. "It's not really a choice. If I could have avoided it, I would have." His whole body seemed to coil in on itself. "It's not something I'm going to talk about."

"That's fair," Stunt rushed to agree. "I'm just wondering exactly what your plan is, or sometimes I'm wondering why this Garrido went after your brother, and mostly I'm just bored out of my mind." He pulled against the ropes. He wasn't used to spending this much time tied up, at least not when he wasn't getting sex.

That last forced a small laugh out of Alex. "You have a thing for honesty, don't you?"

"Yep. I suppose I do. I had a momma that would wash my mouth out with soap if she caught me using it to break the Lord's commandments... same as most folk in these parts."

The smile faded as Alex went back to staring at his maps. "I was in prison and my brother wanted money... needed money...." Alex rubbed a hand over his face. "Fuck, I don't even know."

"But he went to work for Garrido," Stunt guessed. Alex nodded. "And now you're trying to figure out how to get in there." Stunt nodded toward the map. Everyone knew about the big house that'd gone up on the land near the state park about five years back. The feds had confiscated and sold it after finding some big banker-type had built it with stolen money.

"That's the plan. It's why I was on that trail. It backs up to Garrido's land."

Stunt hunched up and squirmed around until he could use a knee to scratch his nose. "I bet that growing up, you heard Jack tales," Stunt said. His memaw always said that a man learned more from a story than from a hundred lectures, and maybe it was time Stunt started following her advice.

Alex raised an eyebrow. "I bet I didn't."

"Jack and the beanstalk?"

Alex crossed his arms. "That's a fairy tale."

"Folk tale, and it's part of a whole bunch of Jack tales."

"Actually, it's a fairy tale. So, is this conversation going somewhere?" Alex's voice had real aggravation in it.

"You're the one who didn't think to buy a radio," Stunt said with his sweetest smile. "I just thought you might like a little harmless entertainment. You see, Jack's daddy tried to make him do his chores, even whipped him when he didn't, so Jack slipped off and headed down the road, thinking he'd find some place where people appreciated him. Well, he wasn't even a mile down the road when he saw an ox a'bellowing up a storm, and when Jack asked it what was wrong, the ox said that its owners were planning on killing him because he was too old."

"The ox said that?" Alex demanded.

"It's a folk tale. Oxen in folk tales will talk your ear off," Stunt said before going back to the story. "So anyway, Jack invited the ox to come along with him. The same thing happened with a jackass and an old coon dog and a tomcat and a rooster so worn out with life that his coxcomb hung down like hair."

"There are a lot of really old animals in that town, huh?"

Stunt ignored the sarcasm. "When it got plumb dark, they found themselves at a little house in the woods, and no matter how much Jack hollered or the donkey brayed or the rooster crowed, no one came to the door, so they decided to investigate. It turns out that robbers owned that little house. So, they decided to sit a spell because they were so tired."

"Being old and all," Alex added.

Stunt gritted his teeth for a second. Alex's attitude was wearing thin. "Only they knew the robbers would be coming back, so they decided they had to be ready."

Alex sighed. "You're subtle like a freight train, you know this, right? I mean subtle like a freight train full of explosives. I'd hate to be the first person who ever pointed that out."

Stunt figured as long as Alex didn't gag him, that was the same as an invitation to continue. "So, they all made a plan to fight 'em. Come dark, they heard not one but seven robbers coming down the trail. One of the robbers volunteered to go inside and start up the fire so no one tripped in the dark, and the others waited for their friend outside at the gate.

"That man came inside and went down on his knees in front of the fireplace, planning on fanning the burning coals back to life. Only the cat was crouching in the ashes, and what the robber thought were coals were really its yellow eyes. He blew in that old cat's eyes, and it scratched him across both cheeks. Then, when the robber started caterwauling and heading for the door, the dog bit him. By now, the robber figured he had the devil himself on his tail, and he headed for the yard. That old donkey raised up and kicked him right in the gut, and while the robber was still stumbling around, the ox caught him up on its horns and threw him over the fence. And the whole time, that rooster kept on a crowin'—"

"Because many old farm animals working together can do what one man working alone can't. Got it," Alex cut him off.

"Didn't your mother ever teach you it was impolite to interrupt a story?" Stunt asked.

"If she were still alive, she'd probably be more upset about me letting my little brother get killed, me getting sent to jail, and the fact that I've taken a hostage. Her concern about my manners would probably slide to the bottom of the list right under the lack of vegetables in my diet."

"Well, it shouldn't. Good manners are real important," Stunt pointed out, although he did appreciate Alex's humor. In other circumstances, he would have gone out of his way to catch the man's eye. "Now, the other robbers heard all the noise, and they grabbed up their friend and demanded to know what had happened. The poor man started his caterwauling all over again, and he told them that a whole gang had taken over the house. One tore up his face with an awl, and when he tried to run, another knifed him in the leg, and when he finally got outside, some other bloke had hit him with a maul before using a pitchfork to toss him out of the yard. And the whole time, someone stood on the roof screaming for them to do more, so all the robbers ran away."

The look on Alex's face fell somewhere between weary and disgusted. "And Jack and his animal friends lived happily ever after. Yeah, yeah, yeah. That'd be fine if we lived in a fairy-tale world."

Stunt figured that maybe his memaw's advice worked better on sane folk, because Alex didn't look too impressed. "Actually, the story ends with Jack going home and cutting wood for his mother, which feels a little out of place because he didn't rightly learn the lesson of hard work from that particular adventure, but the Jack stories can be a little like that," Stunt said with a shrug. "But you do seem to have gotten my point."

"The one where you keep trying to verbally beat me to death with your suggestion that I get help?"

"Yep, that's the one," Stunt agreed. "That and the fact that folks in these parts are raised on Jack tales. The sheriff never solves problems in those stories. Hell, I'm pretty sure at least some of these folks will claim the Dukes of Hazzard was modeled after their families because they're proud of how well they can tell off the authorities... politely, of course. Folks 'round these parts don't use profanity. However, they ain't going to turn you down the way you assume. Not if you can show them that this Garrido is a dealer. I mean, they aren't going to help on some stranger's say-so, but if you have proof..." Stunt waited and let Alex think through the rest on his own.

"You'd provide the introductions?" Alex asked.

That made Stunt laugh. "Trust me, you're better off on your own. As a duly sworn employee of the federal government, my name is not the most trusted on the mountain." Stunt didn't add that his youthful indiscretions complicated his life about as much as his job did. Writing articles for the school newspaper on the subject of gay rights and gay marriage wasn't real high in subtlety. At the time, Stunt planned to leave town and never look back. That was before he had found living off the mountain was like trying to breathe without air. He didn't understand city folk. His whole time at college, he'd been the oddity, not because of his orientation but because he'd been raised on an alien planet. "I can tell you where to start and who's most likely to listen to you before shooting, but you'd do better without me, leastwise if you have proof."

"I have it." Again, a hard mask dropped over Alex's features as he reached for a backpack stuffed behind the driver's seat. He pulled out a fancy computer and hit the power button. He loaded one particular picture and damn near flung the laptop at Stunt.

Instinctively trying to bring his hands up, Stunt flinched as the ropes around his wrists burned a bit, but when he looked down at the computer's screen, he forgot that altogether. A man lay sprawled obscenely in the street, his neck blown apart so that it resembled meat. Stunt's stomach revolted. Dry heaves nearly brought up his whole cracker dinner.

"Whoa, hey, just breathe." Hands pulled him toward the back of the truck, and Stunt sucked in the fresh air as he fought down the nausea. "Fuck. I should have warned you."

"Please tell me that's not your brother." Stunt looked over, but Alex's face was devoid of all emotion. "Okay, then tell me why the police aren't tracking that man down."

Alex helped Stunt settle back onto his sleeping bag. "They did track the man down. Miguel Elis Acosta. They arrested him—the police had all these platitudes for me. The prosecutor told me he wanted me to feel good about the plea deal since I'm the victim's family. They gave him fifteen years and acted like they'd waved a magic wand. They thought it made everything better." Alex pressed his lips together and turned his head aside as though hiding the pain. Mind, it was a real poor job of hiding it, because Stunt could feel the anguish soak in through his skin.

"And Garrido?" He asked softly, feeling a little like he was trying to handle a cottonmouth, and a riled one at that.

Alex shifted away and started rearranging the maps. Stunt tried to breathe quiet as Alex slammed his hand down on top of them. "I raised my brother. My mother was sick with cancer so long, and I raised him. Before she died, I promised her that I would keep him away from men like Garrido, and then I had to be stupid."

Pulling his legs in close, Stunt curled into the corner as the emotional storm gathered. The agony and the fury swirled around Alex until Stunt wondered how the man avoided spontaneous combustion. Worse, Stunt had managed to get himself tied up at ground zero of what looked to be a full-on nuclear meltdown.

"Do you know why I was in jail?" Alex demanded. Figuring that was rhetorical, Stunt chose to stay quiet for once in his life. "I lost my fucking temper. I lost my temper in a bar and punched some asshole who fully deserved it. Drunk and disorderly, assault, and criminal fucking stupidity." Alex punctuated his words with several punches to the side of the camper. Something made a cracking sound, and Stunt hoped it was the old camper shell and not Alex's hand. "I got thirteen months for being a fucking idiot and punching some fucking moron who happened to have fucking important, fucking rich friends."

Stunt guessed Alex had left out a detail or two, seeing as how thirteen months was a mite bit long for a simple case of bar-fighting, but people off the mountain tended to get mighty riled about some stupid things. And after going to college, Stunt knew being rich bought you favors in most parts of the world. Around these parts, people mostly whispered about how the Bible said rich folks went to hell. Of course, that didn't stop them from wanting to be rich anyway, but Stunt figured every human walking the Earth had some sort of crazy going for them. Alex more than most, though.

Alex's jaw muscle bulged as he fought with his emotions. "Acosta worked for Garrido," he finally said in one of those slow, soft voices that generally meant a person was trying to avoid screaming. "I don't give a shit about Acosta going to prison. He pulled the trigger, but he didn't murder my brother. Garrido ordered it. Garrido runs that gang, and Acosta wouldn't take a shit without permission. I'm not going to stop until I see that man's guts decorating the floor."

CHAPTER
7

ALEX breathed fast and stared out at nothing, but other than that, all the emotions had mysteriously vanished. Or been buried, more likely. The volcano was ready to explode the second someone stepped on the wrong crack, and Stunt was entirely too good at stepping on cracks. Actually, Alex reminded Stunt of Howie LaMont. They both had the same careful and gentle nature that would explode into these storms of emotion that could scare a man out of a year's worth of life.

The world hadn't been kind to Howie. He had this goodness combined with a psychological wound that festered and burst every once in a while, like when he'd tied Stunt to that tree or when he'd thrown an ax through Richard Bowker's front window. And Stunt didn't like thinking of how often him and his friends had made Howie's life more difficult. Stunt had always regretted not mending that particular fence before Howie had gone and gotten himself dead. He'd missed that chance, and remembering Howie's sloppy kiss, Stunt sometimes wondered what might have happened if he'd tried apologizing.

Now, even in the face of Alex's anger, Stunt found himself wishing he could fix what'd gone wrong before he lost another chance. It didn't make a bit of sense, because he wasn't one for getting involved in people's personal lives. That got messy, and he was allergic to messy relationships. *Wham, bam, thank you, man with the big cock*, that's how Stunt tried to live his life.

An uneasy quiet filled the camper, and the weight of silence pinned Stunt down far more than the rope tying his hands at his sides. And he didn't understand the world off the mountain well enough to know which direction Alex was likely to jump. Up here, if you killed someone, you'd better be prepared to deal with that person's entire family—fathers, brothers, cousins, nephews, and the more liberated female members. It meant people mostly didn't kill. So Stunt wasn't real sure about the social rules for this sort of situation.

Not that Stunt's people were perfect. Hill folk shot at the boys creeping around the house, threatened strangers, died of overdoses and liver failure and diabetes at an alarming rate, and worshipped pickup trucks and Mountain Dew. But in the end, Stunt's world made a whole lot more sense than Alex's.

Alex finally spoke. "No one can help me. He has a helicopter and every luxury he could want on that property, including enough security to kill anyone who tries to help me." Alex turned the pad to show Stunt a picture of a man in a suit getting out of a helicopter. A dozen men stood nearby, some with guns visible on their belts and a couple with rifles. Fancy ones. And a little fluffy white dog that looked like a rabbit and a rat had gotten Biblically involved.

"Yeah, they're going to stand out. Land o'Goshen, they're going to stand out around here." Stunt tilted his head to the side. "Wait. You dodged the security systems of some big-time drug lord?" Stunt studied Alex, watching him shift uncomfortably. Alex stared back, not even trying to make an excuse for how he had learned that particular skill set. Well, it explained why the police had come down so hard on Alex for an assault—they'd been gunning for him already. "Uh-huh. Just to let you know, in these parts, people tend to shoot thieves," Stunt warned him.

"Just to let you know, I wouldn't steal from anyone who didn't have enough money to spare some."

"Then you ain't looking to start any trouble around here. Duck and his bar down on Highway 129 is about as close as we come to people who have money to spare. He can afford to get a new truck every three or four years."

"Duck?"

"Danny Joe," Stunt clarified. "We mostly call him Duck because of the time he tried chasing some girl, and he slipped on a hillside and went rolling into a pond. A real mean duck took after him, and he squealed like a stuck pig, and then when he got to his feet again, he ran like a little girl. A real slow and clumsy little girl at that."

"Nice."

Stunt shrugged. "We do tend to remind each other of our most embarrassing moments."

"So, is Stunt related to something embarrassing?" Alex pursed his lips and waited, and Stunt did truly hate how this man tended to put pieces together.

"Might be," he admitted, thinking about Howie and that tree. "But I tell you what, Elijah Pierpont has the property on the other side of that land. He runs stills up there, and he will not want a drug dealer sitting on his border. You prove to him that Garrido is a killer, and you'll have some help."

Alex shifted on the box he was perching on and scratched his cheek, which made Stunt real wistful for the days when he could scratch himself whenever he wanted. "What exactly do you think this Elijah is going to do?" Alex asked.

Stunt shrugged. "Help." Alex just waited. "I don't know what he'll do." Stunt's volume went up out of sheer frustration. "But Elijah is fifth-generation moonshiner. Trust me, if he thinks there's a problem in his backyard, he's going to want to take care of it, and his version of problem solving does not include calling the police."

For a second, Stunt thought he'd made some progress, but then Alex started shaking his head. "I'm not interested in getting more people involved in my problem."

"Well now, doesn't that sound a mite bit arrogant?"

Alex turned and looked at Stunt with incredulity, like he couldn't even understand the words. "Excuse me?" he finally demanded.

"You… acting like you're going to save all us poor folk from the big bad drug dealer." Stunt put every bit of disgust he could into his words. Good men never did like having their own shortcomings pointed out, but it was time to shove Alex's nose into a mirror so he could get a good look at himself.

"I'm not interested in saving anyone. I'm going to make him pay for what he did to my brother." Alex reached out like he might poke Stunt in the chest, but he pulled his hand back at the last second.

Stunt rolled his eyes. "And those of us who live in this community, we ain't invested in stopping a drug dealer from moving in and making himself at home. Not at all. We need to have you citified-types coming in to save us." Sarcasm was one of Stunt's favorite weapons.

Alex went deadly still, his voice almost a whisper. "That's not what I said."

"It seems like that's what you mean." Stunt looked Alex up and down, daring him to disagree.

A flash of surprise or maybe hurt crossed Alex's face, but then he narrowed his eyes. "Then you aren't listening well."

"Now that's possible. One or two people have commented on my lack of good listening skills," Stunt admitted. "But that don't mean I'm not right. This is our community, a community I love enough to stay in even if it ain't the most hospitable place for a gay man who likes to get tied up on a semiregular basis."

"I thought you staying around here had more to do with you being a masochist." Alex's dry humor nearly distracted Stunt from his goal.

"That too." Stunt couldn't argue that point. "But in these parts, we take care of our own business. If you get to Elijah and show him that a drug dealer has set up as his next-door neighbor, he's going to take care of his own business."

"So, if Elijah kills this guy, that's better than me doing it?"

"He's less likely to get all tangled in his own emotions and do something stupid."

"Are you calling me stupid?"

"From where I'm sitting, you're just all kinds of dumb. You can't do this. You can't, and getting yourself killed or arrested ain't going to make one thing better." Stunt could feel hot desperation crawling up from his belly. The idea of a good man getting killed over a drug dealer made the nausea roll through his gut. He didn't want Alex dead. He just didn't see another outcome if he tried taking on these men alone. "You're lying to yourself if you think you're handling this well." The second the words came out his mouth, Stunt knew he'd gone too far. He'd stomped all over that rumbling volcano.

"And you just have all the answers!" Alex roared, leaning close enough Stunt could smell coffee and the sour musk of Alex's unwashed body. Stunt froze, watching as that temper rose up. Alex's jaw bulged as he ground his teeth together. His hands clenched and unclenched. His whole body drew taut and all but vibrated.

Stunt knew plenty of Doms who had that edge, that temper. The same impulse to take control led them to push that control too far. The need to protect their own could warp into the desire to hurt others. The best Doms had a huge personality that filled every room. They could push and crowd until Stunt couldn't think about anything but how they demanded every bit of attention. He never had to figure out how to find his own off button around a Dom, because they always found it for him. But then that oversized personality would push too far, and Stunt would find himself scrambling to clear out of the way.

Problem was, he was tied up for the fair and he couldn't scramble away from this cold fury. Worse, he didn't want to. Even angry, Alex had a strength that made Stunt's cock think some mighty stupid thoughts.

For a long second, Alex stood, almost trembling as the emotions spilled over. Then he turned away. The sound of his heavy breathing filled the camper as he wrestled with his own emotions. "He was my brother. I raised him from the time he was nine. I did. I'm not going to let someone else get justice for him."

Alex's brittle words made Stunt wish for a gag. If he didn't have to talk, he wouldn't have to risk running afoul of that temper. But if he didn't talk, people were going to die, and Stunt had a feeling Alex didn't deserve that. "Dying won't get him justice," Stunt said carefully, feeling a whole lot like a snake handler picking up a foul-tempered cottonmouth but knowing he needed to show some faith. "But maybe asking for some help might. You go. You talk to Elijah, and at the very least, you're no worse off."

"Unless he turns me in." Alex's voice had gone all flat and emotionless again. The man either needed therapy for this streak of stubborn of his, or he was in need of getting laid worse than about any man ever born. This sort of foul mood just wasn't normal.

"The chances of that are exactly zero. Pierponts don't go to the law."

"Mountain logic?" Alex asked with a touch of his dry humor.

"Yep. There ain't a chance in the world that Elijah would turn you in, not unless the Rapture were on us and Christ himself appeared with divine orders, and even then Elijah would be asking the Lord why the Pierponts had to get involved with the police."

Alex rubbed a hand over his face, and Stunt could feel his indecision rising up like a tide.

"Worse thing he might do is slow you down by a day, and that won't matter in the long run." Stunt wanted to argue, to keep talking until he wore Alex down to a nubbin, but men like Alex generally didn't like getting pinned in a corner. Stunt held his tongue and waited, listening to the rustle of the trees outside as the wind picked up. Wicked John was riding the wind tonight, laughing at the mortal fools and all their games.

"So, we drive up and you introduce us?"

"Whoa. No," Stunt rushed to say. "I know I've mentioned that he doesn't like feds, and funny enough, I just happen to be paid by the federal government."

"So... I drive up there alone?" Alex sounded faintly horrified.

"And talk fast, unless he threatens to shoot you, then I'd recommend you skedaddle even faster."

Alex looked over with utterly dead eyes. "And meanwhile, you're standing by the side of the road, hitching a ride back to the sheriff."

"You got a streak of paranoia in you, you know that?"

"I took you hostage, shoved a gun in your face, and tied you up. Logic suggests you're going to go to the police sooner rather than later."

"Maybe," Stunt said. He didn't want to lie about this. "I mean, if I think things ain't settled, I'll tell Sheriff Kennedy. Feuding tends to lead to all sorts of innocent people dying. But I'm not going to go dragging the sheriff in if he can't help none. If I get him now, what's he going to do? Stand at this guy's fence line and ask him to leave real nice?"

Alex's features were growing harder, so Stunt's silver tongue was clearly failing him.

"We aren't going to test that loyalty of yours."

"It's common sense, not loyalty."

Alex reached out and caught Stunt's arm right above the rope. "I trust your common sense far less than I trust your loyalty." After pushing Stunt back onto the sleeping bag, Alex ran his hands up Stunt's arm and down to his hand. He repeated the process on the other side, checking the circulation, but the warmth from Alex's hands made Stunt's cock start to harden. Even gritting his teeth didn't stop the process.

Alex picked up the belt he'd earlier used to bind Stunt's feet and he paused, his thumb rubbing over the worn leather as he looked at Stunt's crotch. It was hard to miss the growing bulge, and Stunt could feel his face heat up. "I'm not going to hold this against you, Stunt. I know that our dicks don't always listen to the brain, and this has got to be hard for you. You're a player, and being tied up this long has to be screwing up some wiring in the brain."

Stunt didn't answer. He'd had the same thought, of course, but it wasn't a thought he wanted to go discussing.

"So your dick getting hard is pretty normal, and I'm not going to confuse it for anything other than an overload of adrenaline and the effects of being helpless."

Stunt still didn't answer, but Alex started winding the belt around Stunt's ankles. Sleeping wasn't going to be comfortable by a long shot, but nothing hurt. Alex knew how to secure a man without doing him any damage.

"Are you going to Elijah?" Stunt finally asked.

"We'll see in the morning."

"We could—"

Alex reached out and put a hand over Stunt's mouth. Falling silent, Stunt looked up at Alex. "Why do I have a feeling you have a whole lot of gags at home?"

Stunt huffed a little laugh. It was true.

Grabbing the cloth strip he'd used earlier, Alex started tying it around Stunt's face. Without the stuffing in Stunt's mouth, the gag didn't do much except press against the corners of his mouth and make him uncomfortably aware of the pressure. After running his hands over Stunt's face and under the cloth, Alex loosened the gag a little so it rested between Stunt's teeth.

"Now, you're enough of a player to know that when you've been gagged, you leave the gag in place and don't talk. If you don't play by the rules, I will find another way to make you be quiet, because I do not have any more patience for talking. Not tonight." Alex smiled and ran a finger over Stunt's cheek. "Next time, I need to find a quieter hostage. Actually, next time I might want to just hide better, because this whole hostage-taking thing… I didn't think it through very well."

Stunt snorted his agreement. Alex gave him a look, but Stunt wasn't breaking any rules, and he just blinked. Scooting back, Alex returned to his maps and his computer with all his pictures and his planning.

"We're trying something else first. If my plan doesn't work, maybe we'll think about yours. But the fact is that I'm going to have to be pretty desperate before I try something that dumb."

And as much as Stunt wanted to keep right on arguing his point, the loose gag told him that now was the time for being quiet. Alex had found his off button, so Stunt wiggled around and settled in for a night of frustrated silence.

CHAPTER
8

"THIS is the plan that's better than mine?" Stunt asked as he leaned against the old telephone pole. At least, Stunt assumed those were telephone wires Alex was messing with up at the top.

"Quiet," Alex hissed.

Stunt rolled his eyes. While he understood working the telephone lines this close to Garrido's property was dangerous, he figured someone would spot the man sitting on the telephone pole before they heard him. Alex had used a loop of rope to brace himself, and now he typed away on his laptop, a whole nest of wires connecting him to official state communications lines. Stunt was pretty sure there were federal charges with Alex's name on them. However, Alex seemed real focused on that laptop of his, so Stunt did not go pointing that out.

The bucket he'd pulled up with him dropped into the weeds next to Stunt. "Send up the drill and that brown box thing," Alex whispered.

"If I get charged with federal wiretapping, I'm blaming you," Stunt said too quietly for Alex to hear. Bending down was awkward with his hands tied at his sides, but Stunt managed. Unfortunately, he still couldn't reach the tools on the ground. "Cotton-picking stinking son of a—" Stunt eased himself down to his knees and reached out with fingers until he could catch the wireless drill and drop it in the bucket. The brown plastic box with all the wires followed.

Alex pulled it up, and Stunt took time to think about the sheer awkwardness of the situation. On his knees and tied up by a handsome man with a moral center that led him to want to avenge his brother's death—that sounded a whole lot like his fantasy life. What was wrong with him that he had fantasies that felt so dangerous in reality? Stunt didn't have an answer for that as he stared at a ladybug crawling her way across a blade of grass. She raised her wings and shimmied them before settling back down. The bucket thumped down to the ground again, and the ladybug flew away.

"Ladybug, ladybug fly away home, your house is on fire and your children are gone, all except one," Stunt whispered.

"Hey, you okay?" Alex dropped into the weeds at Stunt's side. His computer case was slung across his chest like Indiana Jones' leather bag.

"Peachy," Stunt said. He tried to struggle his way to his feet, but he was tired and sore. Alex got a hand under his arm and pulled him up. "So, did I just assist in a federal crime?"

"Under duress. They can't charge you," Alex said with a grin. "I'm used to doing things by hijacking wireless networks, but not all that many people use wireless out here."

"Imagine that."

"That's okay. I'm adaptable." Alex sounded very smug.

Stunt looked up at the pole and then back down to the bucket. The drill was there, but the brown box was missing. "It's still up there?" Stunt squinted as he tried to see the top of the pole.

"People have to connect their computers to the rest of the world somehow. If there's a wire, there's a way for me to get into their system. This time I'm just having to work a little harder."

"There's a skillset."

"It's useful," Alex agreed. He knelt down and started untying the rope that tethered Stunt's ankle to the pole. "I've earned a living since I was fourteen using my computer skills."

"I reckon there are a few people who might argue with your use of the verb 'earned'," Stunt said.

Alex grinned at him.

Frustration gathered in Stunt's gut. "What if Garrido's men had seen you sitting up there?"

"Are you worried about me?" Alex laughed like that was a joke as he went on winding the end of the rope leash around his hand.

"Yes," Stunt said firmly.

Alex paused and gave Stunt a surprised look. For a time, he stood there not saying anything. "That's... I guess that's not unexpected, given that I've taken you hostage, but you don't have to worry about me."

"I wouldn't if you didn't have such an all-consuming hate eating you from the inside. This ain't smart. This ain't even near smart," Stunt said with an abortive gesture toward the pole. "You're going to end up dead."

"I probably am," Alex said without any emotion. "But not until after Garrido."

"Lord a'mighty." Stunt turned away. He couldn't look at the man, not without suffering a need to punch him real hard.

"Let's get back to the truck," Alex said. Strangely, he spoke softly and rested his hand on Stunt's shoulder without any of his pushing or shoving.

Stunt didn't move. "What did you put up there?"

"A piece of tech I cooked up myself. It monitors the line until I redirect the signal and then I can take over the signal using my laptop."

"And this gets you closer to Garrido?"

"It gets me closer to Garrido's communication network so I know when he's coming and going. I'm hoping he'll take a trip into town, a very short and very fatal trip."

Stunt turned back around to study Alex. "You're all shades of crazy. We don't have anything he wants. Someone like him ain't interested in sitting down for a few beers or trying Sally's chicken fried squirrel."

Alex made a face. "Chicken fried squirrel?"

"It's good. But that ain't something Garrido wants to go experiencing. So I don't see how this is ending. I just know the second you took me, you started a clock to running. Sooner or later, someone's going to come looking, and while I freely admit that might be more later than sooner, I don't want to see people hurt." Stunt took a step closer. "I don't want to see you hurt."

Insects sang away the morning as Alex stared at him. "I'm starting to worry about your mental health. As your kidnapper, you're supposed to hate me."

"Maybe I would, but like you've already figured out, I've had one too many fantasies like this, and I do not want this ending in a visit to the coroner to identify your body."

Rubbing a hand over his face, Alex leaned against the pole. "I never meant for you to get mixed up in this. I can tell you're a good man, and you don't deserve any of this. However, what you have to keep in mind is that I'm not a good man. I mean, I've taken you hostage at gunpoint, I've lost my temper, yelled, scared the snot out of you, and when all else failed, shoved a picture of my mutilated brother under your nose to make my point." Alex let his hand fall to his side. "It worries me that you care about what happens to me. It suggests that you're having Stockholm syndrome."

Stunt had considered that, but he'd already decided it wasn't the case. "If I were, I wouldn't be spending so much time thinking that you're an idiot. I'd be identifying with you, not calling you names." He also never heard that lust was part of Stockholm syndrome, and Stunt was a little too aware of Alex's body. The man was fine, or he would be if he stopped going back and forth between emotional diarrhea and brooding.

"What do you want me to do?"

"I don't know. Something sane?"

"Like go to your friend?" Alex crossed his arms.

"Elijah Pierpont is not my friend. His brother served in the military with my grandfather, and Peepaw said they were cousins of some sort, not that I know how. Around here, anyone who's lived on the mountain more than five generations tends to call each other cousins. However, we aren't friends. He doesn't approve of sodomy, and he takes it as a personal affront that someone from the mountain would take a job with the federal government."

"You're a forestry guy, not an FBI agent."

"I'm a federal employee, and most of these contrary old boys who take a shot at me do it for that very reason."

Alex pulled the rope tight, and Stunt felt the tug on his ankle. "I don't know how much of what you say is real and how much is some mountain tale."

"Most is real. If I'm going to tell you a tale, I'll make Jack or Wicked John the protagonist." Stunt was about to say something else, but he tilted his head to the side as he studied the trees. A number of tiny warblers rose up, their soft voices trilling in warning. "Something's coming," Stunt said, already backing away from the pole.

"What?" Alex looked around like he could see the danger.

"The birds. They ain't going to leave their nest without that there's something disturbing them, and that something is coming right at us," Stunt said. Panic rolled through his stomach—panic for his own skin and panic for Alex. Right now, someone could kill Alex and claim to be trying to rescue his hostage. Now that Stunt thought on the subject, that would actually be a persuasive story.

Alex took a step closer to Stunt, and Stunt used it as an excuse to back away even more. "Maybe an animal wandered under their tree."

"They're warblers. They don't have many predators except hawks and men, and I don't see no hawks in the sky."

Alex looked up, and when he glanced back toward Stunt, his expression had grown infinitely more concerned. "Let's get back to the truck." Alex started down the narrow road, but taking the road meant passing by where those birds had gone. Alex had parked the truck off the road and behind a bend Stunt had shown him. If they tried going straight for it, they would get caught for sure.

"We don't have time," Stunt said in a rough whisper.

"Then hurry," Alex gave the rope leash a pull, but Stunt dug in and refused to move.

"We don't have time. We've got to head uphill and get in the brush."

Alex opened his mouth, probably to argue more, but then a sharp crack startled them both into silence. The sound bounced off the mountain, but the softer sounds of people pushing through the brush definitely came from the direction of the truck. Stunt doubted California boys would know where to find that truck, but it wouldn't be too hard to find two men walking down a road, or even running down that same road.

Reversing direction, Alex headed for the slope. "Hurry up," he said, his hand around Stunt's arm.

"There, head upslope there," Stunt said, nodding toward a spot where a tree had sent out massive roots that broke through the earth. It would give them an easy way to scramble up the steep slope.

Alex pulled a knife out of his pocket and flipped it open.

"No, they have guns," Stunt hissed. Panic had reached whole new levels at this point.

"So do I." Alex yanked Stunt closer and slipped the knife under one strand of rope. One good jerk and the rope separated. Stunt's right hand was free now. Thank the Lord his ankles weren't tied or they'd have a real problem. "Go, go. I'll cover," Alex said, shoving the rope leash into Stunt's hand. For a second, Stunt wanted to argue, but Alex gave him a strong push. "I'll follow, but not until you're clear. You're not ending up dead because of me."

At that, Stunt turned and dashed for the tree. Using the exposed roots, he clambered up the hillside and sprinted for a thick stand of low oak trees upslope. The trees were a good run off, and by the time Stunt reached their shade, he gasped for every breath. Turning, he waited for Alex to catch up. In these thick trees, a man could get turned around, and considering they were on the line between Garrido and Pierpont land, that wouldn't be safe.

Two seconds later, it occurred to him that he should escape. Right now, he had a head start and he had an understanding of the mountains that would make it impossible for Alex to catch up. The need to run circled his belly like an underfed cat. Despite the fear and the growing sense that he was an idiot, Stunt waited. It took several minutes, but Alex came crashing through the undergrowth without looking right or left.

Stunt's head told him to wait until Alex had passed and then head for the main road. He could avoid Garrido's men easily enough. But his gut told him he would feel guilty for the rest of his life if Alex vanished, and strangers did have a habit of vanishing in the mountains. Either Garrido would kill him or he'd stumble over Elijah's still, and that man was not reasonable when his moonshine was in danger. Given Alex was a full-grown man, Stunt should leave him to his own devices.

That thought lasted for less than a second, and Stunt stood up and waved his free hand. "Over here," he whispered. He didn't hear any of Garrido's men, but that didn't mean anything.

Alex stopped. Hell, Alex seemed trapped inside a moment and incapable of moving.

"Come on," Stunt whispered.

Shaking his head, Alex started toward him. "I thought you'd be heading for the hills."

"I'm more likely to head down the hills," Stunt pointed out, "but if brains were lard, you couldn't scrape up enough for a biscuit. Leaving you out here feels like cruel and unusual punishment."

Alex's mouth came open and then he closed it again without saying anything. He did snatch the rope leash back, though. "You're not the brightest, you know that, right?"

"Yep. We're two peas in a pod on that front. So, what were they doing?"

"Checking out the pole, but they didn't find my equipment."

"And you're not going up on another pole. They're going to take to shooting at you, and I don't care how fast you run, you can't outrun a bullet. Besides, you don't run fast." That earned him a dirty look.

"Most of the time, I try to be good enough at disabling security systems that I don't have to run." Alex ran his fingers over the cut edges of the rope that had held Stunt's right wrist. Because he had only cut one strand, a good deal of rope hung down.

"I hope you're good with computers, then."

"I am," Alex agreed. "But I think you're right that I can't risk that again. Damn. I've got seven of those up, but I haven't tapped Garrido's communication yet."

Stunt didn't say anything, but if he was a drug dealer, the first thing he'd do was invest in something that couldn't be tapped by an idiot hanging off a telephone pole.

"I guess we're going to have to try your plan, as dumb as it is."

"It's no dumber than yours," Stunt objected as he scratched his nose.

Alex grabbed his wrist and pulled it back down to his side where he used the remaining rope to secure it again. "Yeah, but my dumb plan depended on me. Your dumb plan depends on trusting someone I've never met. I'm not good with trust."

"No," Stunt said sarcastically while he watched Alex tie the final knot around his wrist. "I never would have guessed."

"Smartass."

"Hey, just you wait. Elijah is going to be on your side, that is assuming that you can explain your side before he shoots you."

"Assuming that," Alex said with sarcasm as sharp as Stunt. As long as Alex stopped trying to take on the world alone, he could be as sarcastic as he wanted. Stunt just wanted him to get through this in one piece, and surprisingly, Stunt found he wanted that more than he wanted his own freedom, at least right now.

CHAPTER
9

"THIS is a real bad idea," Stunt warned. Again.

"No, no, don't throw me into the briar patch, cried the Brer Rabbit," Alex mocked him. Maybe Alex realized he sounded like an ass because he sighed and tried again. "Look, I respect that you're trying to help, but I really can't see someone shooting you over your forestry job. I promise I won't let him scare you with his shotgun."

Stunt was starting to dislike Alex, or at least, he would dislike him if he hadn't already formed an unhealthy respect for the man. Alex kept assuming Stunt's rather vehement objections were designed to manipulate him. Personally, Stunt was just hoping Elijah was in a real good mood, because the man had a habit of inviting feds off his land at the end of a shotgun.

"Right there. That's the turnoff." Stunt tried to gesture with his hand, only to have the ropes stop him.

"That's not a road," Alex said.

"That ain't a good road. But then, not many people go visiting Elijah. Mostly, people just avoid him because he's a little on the cranky side."

Alex turned the old truck to follow the twin ruts farther up the mountain. Tall weeds grew between the tire trails, and they slapped at the grille of the truck until Alex slowed to a crawl. "They're going to know we're coming."

"Yep, they are. You know, if you cut me loose right here, you could go talk to Elijah and get back here in time to catch me before I got anywhere close to civilization, especially seeing as how I would have to circle around Garrido's property." Stunt gave Alex his best smile, but all he got in return was a blank stare. "I had a chance to run and I didn't. I think I earned some trust with that," he added. Of course, he'd said the same thing three times already, and all he'd gotten in return was a discussion of how Alex didn't trust easy. This was going to be so very ugly. Alex came around a stand of trees and an old, half-fallen shed made out of graying wood. Elijah's house had red flowers planted out front, his wife's probably. Stunt could see a roundish woman standing in the shade of one of the far sheds.

Elijah's wife didn't come to town much, but Stunt saw her most Christmases at the church. Teresa Ann Pierpont was a thick woman with gray hair swept up onto her head and one hell of a turkey-wattle neck, like most of the Hodges women. It'd been a bit of a scandal, a Hodges marrying a Pierpont, but Stunt had the feeling Elijah and Teresa hadn't been exactly conventional back in their day.

After pulling up in front of the house, Alex turned off the truck. The engine rattled for several seconds before finally cutting off with a sickly sounding *thunk*. Stunt wasn't real surprised to see the woman vanish behind the shed, but he was sorry for it. He figured his own chances of surviving this went up if Miss Teresa were around. Most men tried to avoid making a mess out of human innards when their wives were in the immediate vicinity.

Looking stupidly cheerful, Alex got out and came around to the passenger side to pull Stunt out of the truck. Stunt opened his mouth to lodge one more protest, but really, what was the point? The die was cast, and they'd all have to deal.

"Play nice," Alex warned as he slammed the truck door shut and pulled Stunt against his chest like some sort of hostage.

"This is me playing nice. You should see what a pain in the ass I can be when I put my mind to it," Stunt whispered back.

Alex started walking them toward the porch, but a voice from the right called out. "Get off my property!"

Stunt's eyes got big as he watched Elijah come out of his old shack, his gun at the ready. Alex's arm tightened around Stunt's throat, holding him like a human shield or a hostage, which technically he was.

"Get off my property!" Elijah shouted again when no one seemed to be moving. His voice had the sort of gravel that came from smoke and corn whiskey, but the end of the gun pointed at Stunt's middle was steady enough.

"Are you Elijah Pierpont?" Alex called. That seemed a mite strange to ask, seeing as how they were standing on Elijah's property, but Stunt wasn't in a position to complain.

"Stewart Folger, that you?" Elijah asked, raising his rifle. He looked older than the last time Stunt had seen him, and the salt-and-pepper hair that hung just past his shoulders had gone mostly white. The beard had been white for some time, but now it looked more straggly. "Why ain't you getting off my damn property?"

"Yes, sir. I'd love to, but I don't have a choice here," Stunt said, yanking at the ropes that tied his hands to his sides so Elijah would notice them. "So let's maybe take a deep breath and try and remember that the tied-up guy in the middle can't defend himself."

Elijah's eyes narrowed and he moved forward, probably to get a better look. The fact he was squinting as he pointed his gun didn't make Stunt feel any too good.

"He's not going to shoot you," Alex said, but at least he had a little worry in his voice. Stunt was more than a little worried about his own hide.

"Ain't you a fed now, boy?" Elijah demanded.

Well, crap. He would have to go remembering that part. "You might want to reassess that assumption that he wouldn't shoot me," Stunt whispered before he found himself pulled back toward the truck as Alex moved to cover him.

"You are, ain't you?" Elijah demanded, and Stunt figured he'd managed to join the list of people Elijah would like to shoot on sight. This was just not his week.

"I clean trails. I'm not some FBI or tax man," Stunt tried explaining, his voice growing sharp with desperation, but Alex pressed back into him so Alex's body covered his. It meant Stunt was tucked up safe behind him and he couldn't even see Elijah. Of course, if Elijah decided to shoot Alex, that wouldn't mean much. Worse, Alex didn't even have his gun out. Idiot.

"That big old Uncle Sam of yern pays your paycheck, don't he?" Elijah was getting downright worked up, and Stunt couldn't exactly deny that particular charge.

Alex jumped in the middle of the argument, pulling out his own gun. "That's not important. Drop the gun, old man," he ordered. Stunt cringed. Wrong tactic.

"Old man? I'll show you old man, you young idjit. I don't reckon I'm too old to aerate your hide." Whatever Elijah did, Alex took a step back, pushing into Stunt and forcing him back into the side of the truck.

"Sir, please," Stunt started, "Teresa is going to be put out with you if you go dropping bodies on your land."

"Not if they're feds."

"Do I look like a fed?" Alex sounded insulted.

"You went and came up here with a fed. You're either one or yer dumber than a coal bucket."

"With a tied-up fed," Stunt shouted. This was such a very bad idea… even if it was his. Sorta. He had warned Alex to leave him behind.

"Huh." Elijah paused. "There is that. So, what are you doing up here with a fed all tied up?" Oddly, he sounded more friendly-like now. Stunt wished he could see the man, to judge just how riled he might be. But Alex was playing at being a big brick wall—a brick wall that would bleed and die if he didn't start talking nicer.

Alex glanced back at Stunt before he lowered his own gun a little. "I'm looking for a man."

"Then get the hell off my property," Elijah suggested.

"We have a problem, sir," Stunt called out while glaring at Alex. He acted like he had all the time to stand around jawing with Elijah, but Elijah was going to lose patience too fast for that nonsense.

"Which I'll solve by putting buckshot through you."

"Elijah, just hear him out." Stunt was having some trouble sounding authoritative when Alex was smushing him up against the side of the pickup.

"I ain't listening to no fed."

Alex finally got the hint and decided to get to the point. "Then listen to me. Your new neighbor to the west—"

"The citified idjit with the fancy car?" Elijah asked.

Yeah, that had his attention. If there was anyone Elijah hated more than a fed, it was rich city folk. Lots of lost tourists thought the Appalachians were full of cranky, well-armed sons of bitches who liked to threaten any random soul that wandered down their bit of road. The truth was, it was mostly just the tourists in nice cars who got threatened. These old boys would help out anyone who showed up in some dirty old pickup or broke-down twenty-year-old car full of screaming young 'uns. But let one fancy SUV full of kids with iPods turn onto the wrong road, and someone would chase them off, often at gunpoint.

Alex took a step forward, and Stunt could finally peek around him. "Yeah, that's him," Alex agreed.

Elijah narrowed his eyes and moved to rest his gun against the crook of his elbow. "You got a beef with him?"

Alex looked back at Stunt as though waiting for some sort of assurance that this wasn't some trap. "He's more likely to be sympathetic than I am," Stunt offered loud enough for Elijah to hear. He didn't need the man thinking they were conspiring against him, not when Elijah was in a mood to shoot someone and Stunt seemed to be the nearest fed for him to shoot.

"I came up here to kill him," Alex said firmly.

That shocked Elijah enough the man took a step backward. "Then why you got Stewart Folger with you?"

"He saw me checking out the property, and I didn't want him running to the police." Alex sounded pretty disgusted with himself about that.

Elijah gave a huff of laughter. "Yeah, feds. They're all the same, sticking their noses in where they ain't wanted—and sure as God made little green apples, they sure as hell ain't needed."

"Elijah," Stunt protested.

"They'll turn you over to the law, even when you're minding your own business on your own land. This country is supposed to be free, not some land of regulations where feds get to tell you what to do."

Stunt was starting to take offense. "I ain't never told you one thing, Elijah Pierpont, so don't you start blaming me for something some revenuer in 1918 did."

"I wasn't even alive in 1918, you idjit. And you. Stop pointing your gun at me unless you're trying to rile me up." Elijah aimed that last part at Alex, and without waiting to see what Alex would do, he turned and headed for the porch. After one confused look back at Stunt, Alex lowered his gun and took a step forward, leaving Stunt to follow. Walking into Elijah's place with his hands tied felt a little foolish, but Stunt didn't have a lot of choice. Whatever litmus test Elijah used to separate folk he liked from folk he didn't, Alex had passed it.

Elijah settled himself down on a barrel set on its side with some boards nailed to the top and bottom to make a sort of bench. "So, what did this fellow do to you?"

Stopping at the first step, Alex seemed to think through his words, which was a first. He did seem more the sort to act first and think about how he'd backed himself into a corner later. "He ordered someone to kill my brother over a drug deal," he finally said. "The police think they've done their job because the man who works for him, the one that actually pulled the trigger, is in jail. And when I tried to get them to go after Garrido, your new neighbor, they told me to go away." The bitterness in Alex's voice couldn't be faked, and Stunt could see Elijah nod.

"But yer brother's dead and you're sure this fellow did the ordering?"

Alex swallowed. "Yeah, I'm sure."

"He has evidence, sir," Stunt offered. "I'm the one who told him to come up here, although I did suggest that I might want to stay anywhere else. But this Garrido… it looks like he's a big-time drug dealer from California. The papers wrote stories about how he controlled a big portion of the drug trade and the police couldn't get enough evidence. Alex showed me."

"Police." Elijah grunted, making it clear that he considered the police worthless. For some time, Elijah studied them. He took out a pipe and shoved tobacco into the bowl before pulling one leg up and propping his foot on the bench. "Seems like that's a serious charge. He know you're coming?"

This was some dangerous territory. Alex had just entered a sort of hill court, and he likely didn't know it. Worse, by taking a job with the federal government, Stunt had lost him every iota of credibility he might have once carried around here. Well, nearly every iota. He had a feeling Elijah was listening because Stunt had asked him to. Stunt's snake-handling grandfather and Elijah's older brother had served together in WWII, which still wouldn't keep Elijah from pulling the trigger if he thought Stunt would bring the federal government down on his head.

"He should," Alex said. "Years ago, I told him that the second I got out of prison I was going to track him down and put a bullet between his eyes if he didn't leave my brother alone."

"That ain't right, bothering a man's family when he's behind bars. That's the sort of trick a fed might pull." Elijah gave Stunt the hairy eye, but Alex shifted to the right, just enough to get in the way. It was a nice enough gesture, but Stunt was starting to think it wouldn't help much. If Elijah took personal offense to Stunt being on his land, Alex couldn't stop him. But something was going on, because Elijah was being downright solicitous. Elijah scratched his cheek. "So, can you show me this evidence of yours?"

"Yeah, I have it all in the truck." Alex took a step toward the truck before looking at Stunt. Great, now he was worried.

"I'll be fine standing right here," Stunt promised. He looked over to Elijah to see if the man was going to contradict him, but Elijah was smoking on his pipe and watching as if they were the morning's entertainment.

"I'll be right back." Alex headed for the back of the truck, and Elijah shifted in his chair.

"Not real smart of you, coming up here," he observed real quiet-like.

"I didn't have a choice, sir. You know I've never come near your property, but...." Stunt pulled at the ropes again.

"So, he really nabbed you?"

Stunt nodded. "Off one of the trails on the other side of Garrido's property. I was tending the trail when I stumbled across him."

Elijah grunted again and took the pipe out of his mouth before leaning back against the side of the house. "Is his evidence against this fellow good?"

Stunt took a deep breath. This was a hill trial, for sure. "It convinced me," he said. He didn't want to offend Elijah by trying to tell him what to believe. "Lots of folks out in California know this Garrido deals drugs and kills, but it seems like they're all worried about getting all their legal Ts crossed and all their Is dotted."

"Slack-jawed morons, the lot of them. Them and their laws is going to ruin this country, just you watch and see," Elijah complained. "And Alex there? What's he like?"

Stunt glanced over to see Alex coming back with a full backpack in his left hand. His right was hovering near his gun, so maybe he did have a clue.

"He's got him a temper," Stunt started, and Alex was close enough to hear because he started turning pink. "But he's careful to not do more damage than he has to, and he's real focused on avenging the brother he helped raise. He feels guilty about letting down his dead mother after promising to look after him." Stunt knew that up here, loyalty to a family meant a lot. That's what Elijah needed to know.

Elijah turned his attention to Alex. "You seem a little young for a dead mother."

"You seem a little old to be helpful," Alex shot right back.

Stunt flinched.

"Watch it, boy, or I'll teach you what it means to respect your elders," Elijah warned, but sounded oddly unoffended. Maybe he was mellowing with age. "But I'm wondering why you don't have any of your people helping you on this—brothers or cousins maybe. Did your folks tell you to let this one go, or maybe there's more going on here than you're telling?"

Alex stood with the sun playing through his dark hair and lighting up his eyes until they flashed bright blue. "My father vanished weeks after my brother was born. He liked the needle more than his family. And my mother spent most of her life after that dying of cancer. It took her seven years to finally pass. And me? Well, I've never been the type to settle down and get married, so that left me and my brother. And now my brother is dead. If you don't want to believe me, that's fine. We'll just leave. I didn't want to come here at all because I can take care of Garrido myself." Alex took Stunt's arm and pulled him toward the truck.

"They'll get you for kidnapping a federal employee," Elijah pointed out.

"You're assuming I care," Alex said. "As long as Garrido is dead, I'm fine spending the rest of my life in prison. Hell, I'm fine being dead."

Stunt sucked in a breath as Elijah's cold gaze settled on him. Crap, crap, and warm steaming piles of horsecrap. Why hadn't Stunt spent more time worrying about his own hide and less time thinking about Alex's? Why the hell had he not thought about the legal charges here?

Elijah leaned forward. "And you want my he'p with that?"

Stunt's heart pounded rabbit fast. Fear. No, terror. He was definitely feeling terror. Looking around like an animal caught in a trap, Stunt noticed one of Elijah's sons or grandsons leaning against the barn and another strolling up the road with the sort of swinging gait long-legged men had.

"Stunt seemed to think you could help," Alex said. "Personally, as long as Garrido ends up dead, I don't care who helps. But the fact is that I want him dead, and you don't want a drug dealer as a neighbor. At least, Stunt seems to think you don't want that."

Alex looked over, and Stunt felt like he was looking down a very long tunnel. Alex frowned at him and reached out to pull him closer. The brush of Alex's hand across Stunt's arm made a shiver go through his whole body. Stunt opened his mouth, but there wasn't one good thing he could say. If Elijah helped Alex, he was an accessory to kidnapping a federal employee. He'd go to prison, him and anyone who helped. And unlike Alex, Stunt didn't think he could talk Elijah around any corners.

But if he asked Alex to leave with him right now, Stunt suspected neither one of them was making it off the property alive. Federal charges and federal prison... those were two things moonshiners tried to avoid at all costs, and Stunt knew just how ruthless people could be when they were defending themselves and their families.

"Come on in and let's go through this evidence of yours," Elijah said. Standing up, he gave Stunt one long look, shook his head, and then headed into his house. The man coming up the drive was close enough for Stunt to see the rifle tucked in his arm. Oh, this was bad, this was so very, very bad.

"Okay, evidence I have," Alex said cheerfully as he gave Stunt a little push to get him going up the steps.

CHAPTER
10

ELIJAH leaned back on the sagging couch and looked at the pile of evidence Alex had laid out. Stunt had claimed a stool near the fireplace, and Alex perched uncomfortably on the edge of a rocking chair. One of Elijah's grandsons, a man about nineteen or twenty, leaned against one wall.

"Would anyone like anything to drink?" Teresa appeared beside her grandson, and they looked about alike as peas in a pod, except for Teresa's gray hair and the turkey wattle. The boy definitely had his grandmother's eyes and nose though.

"Mountain Dew," Elijah said as he lifted a newspaper article.

"Water, please?" Alex asked. At least he'd found his manners.

"Just as soon as you untie that boy. I won't have that in my house." Teresa braced her hands on the roll of fat around her middle and then stared down Alex. For a second, Alex looked confused, like he wasn't sure how he was supposed to react to a demand like that.

Elijah gave a huff of laughter. "You might as well give in now, son. Women always get their way in the long run. The good Lord told women to bow their heads to their husbands because he knowed that without that biblical command, they'd run us all over like out-of-control freight trains."

With a roll of her eyes, Teresa transferred her considerable glare to her husband. "Elijah, how you go on. I know you don't hold with keeping a grown man tied up any more than I do."

Elijah looked Stunt up and down, and Stunt knew full well that Elijah was just fine with it, even if Teresa wasn't. Elijah dropped the paper back down onto the coffee table and sighed. "It ain't like he can go anywhere. Cut him loose," Elijah ordered Alex. "You know better than to run, right?" he asked Stunt.

Stunt nodded. "Yes, sir." He figured if he tried running, Elijah and his boys would run him down and then kill him twice.

Elijah gave a quick nod before returning to the papers. "Looks like there's no real schedule here. It's going to be hard to kill a man when he doesn't come out of his house on a regular basis."

Alex had moved to a spot behind Stunt and he was working on the knots. From the length of time it was taking, Stunt guessed they were pretty tight. "I'll get to him." Then Alex sighed. "The real problem is that I don't know how to make sure he's dead and not wounded, and I sure as hell don't have a plan for getting back out."

"In other words, you ain't got no plan at all."

Alex made a face. "I don't have a good plan, I'll give you that." He finally pulled the knot free.

"And what is Stewart doing while you're off trying to take care of your business?" Elijah asked. His filmy gray eyes pinned Stunt with a real sharp gaze.

"I haven't figured that part out yet. The truth is that taking a hostage hasn't worked out all that well. He complains a lot." Alex finished untying Stunt's right hand, and Stunt pulled both hands in front of him so he could pick at the knots around his left wrist himself. It gave him something to do other than notice the way Elijah kept a'looking at him.

"It's a right awkward situation," Elijah agreed, and Stunt kept his eyes focused on the knot around his wrist as he ignored the one in his stomach. There wasn't much he could do right now, so gnawing at the fear wasn't going to do much good.

Teresa walked in, her steps quick little slaps on the old plank flooring. "One Mountain Dew and one water. Stewart, can I get you something to drink?"

Stunt looked up, and Teresa was giving him a look like one might give a particularly bedraggled stray mutt. "No, ma'am. Thank you anyways."

Before the silence went on long enough to even get awkward, Alex jumped in again. "If Stunt could stay here, I could take care of Garrido."

Stunt held his breath. Alex was about fifteen pounds of stupid all shoved into one real stretchy five-pound poke. If it weren't bad enough Elijah was an accessory to kidnapping, now Alex was asking him to be an actual kidnapper. And Stunt wasn't near smart enough to figure a way out of the trap he'd built for himself by asking Alex to come here.

"I can keep Stewart from falling into any folly," Elijah agreed. "Not sure what I'm supposed to do if you go and get yourself dead."

"I don't think it'll matter at that point," Alex said.

Stunt closed his eyes. Yeah, this was pretty much as bad as it could get. If he had a chance to come back in another body—to be reincarnated—he was showing up on Alex's doorstep and kicking his ass. He just had to make sure he came back in a pretty good-sized body, because Alex was a fair-sized man.

"I'll make sure Stewart isn't afflicted with any distress," Elijah said mildly. Unless Stunt had badly misjudged something, it sounded like Elijah had just offered to kill him quick and easy. His grandson shifted from one foot to another. It seemed like he wasn't quite as comfortable talking on killing as his grandfather.

"I said I'd let him go as soon as I had this taken care of," Alex said in a voice that sounded a whole lot like he was agreeing. He'd moved to sit near the window, and Stunt shifted around to look over toward the man.

"So, I've seen the way you look at Stunt, and I got to ask. Why are you hauling him hither and yon?" Elijah scratched his beard.

Alex frowned. "I told you. He saw me on the trail."

"I think he's asking why you haven't put a bullet in my head," Stunt translated. In college, he'd been annoyed when surrealism stuck its head up in some book he had to read, but he was developing an appreciation for it.

"I'm not going to shoot Stunt. I'm not going to shoot anyone who hasn't done anything to me." Alex was working on a good head of steam, but Elijah just nodded with a real thoughtful look on his face.

"Thou shalt not kill," Teresa said quietly from the spot near the door where she stood hovering. "It's a good rule to live by, seeing as how the Lord gave it to us." Her voice was quiet, but she was looking at Elijah.

"Exactly," Alex agreed, and Stunt was pretty sure he was still missing most of the point. Teresa was arguing for Stunt's life, and right now, Stunt was starting to think he should take up some serious praying.

"Bible's full of men who did what they had to in order to protect their family or their way of life, just like Alex there is doing." Elijah didn't sound convinced, but he was talking, so Stunt was holding on to some hope.

"Defending yourself and your family's not the same as revenge or killing a man who hasn't done anything to you." Teresa kept her voice quiet, but she clearly wasn't ready to give up. Hill women were about as stubborn as their men, and right now Stunt was putting a lot of stock in that simple fact. "Vengeance is mine, sayeth the Lord."

"You can't want a drug dealer—a murderer—setting up at your doorstep," Alex jumped in. He gestured toward a set of wooden toys in the corner. "You can't want that kind of evil near your family."

"Cursed be he that doeth the work of the Lord deceitfully, and cursed be he that keepeth back his sword from blood." Elijah's voice took on a solemn, almost lilting quality.

"What?"

"It's from Jeremiah or Isaiah," Stunt explained to Alex. "I think he's saying that if you're going after Garrido, you need to get blood on your sword."

Stunt wanted to explain more. He wanted to tell Alex what other death they were debating in this room, but how did you explain to someone who wasn't from the hills just how seriously these folks took their killing—or how good they were when they decided they had a moral cause? Most of the men Stunt knew who'd gone into the military had ended up in special forces because they'd grown up with a gun in their hand, talking about times when a man had to kill. Sexist? Maybe, but hill folk didn't shy away from ugly truths the way the rest of the world did.

"It's Jeremiah," Teresa corrected him. "And Moab had sinned."

"So has Garrido," Alex argued. "He ordered my brother killed. He's killed dozens of others, and he sells drugs on the street."

"We all know the suffering that follows drugs." The look Elijah gave Teresa was long and full of meaning. Their grandson shuffled his feet again, and Stunt started mentally tracing the Pierpont family tree as he tried to figure out who they were talking about.

"I'm aware," Teresa agreed. "But there ain't one reason any innocent blood's got to be spilled."

"When Joshua came to the aid of Gibeon, he killed those who weren't his enemy."

"But they had sinned, Elijah. It ain't a good thing, what you're thinking."

Elijah snorted and sat up, and one way or another, Stunt knew he'd made up his mind. "Go tend your own business. This is ours." Elijah sounded uncompromising on that point, and after a second, Teresa turned and headed toward the back of the house. She might try and argue for him later, but Stunt had the feeling she had lost the fight, and if she couldn't change Elijah's mind, no one would. Stunt was looking at his own death there.

"If I could get into the back part of the property, I could set up with a rifle here," Alex said, turning immediately back to his computer with the satellite image of Garrido's land.

Stunt tuned them out as they talked logistics and lines of fire, and at one point, they even discussed an actual fire, as in setting Garrido's house on fire. Stunt didn't have the energy to care much though.

"You okay?" Alex nudged Stunt's shoulder, and Stunt blinked as he realized he'd been drifting in and out of awareness.

"Yeah. Tired." Running a hand over his face, Stunt realized he was more than tired—he was exhausted.

"David, set him up in your room," Elijah told the lanky young man who had taken the seat near the window.

"Sure," he agreed with an awkward smile. "I'll show you where it is," he offered Stunt.

Stunt should probably thank Elijah for even caring at this point, but he couldn't come up with the energy for that sort of irony, so he just nodded at the man and stood. David gave him an odd look and started down the hall into the house while Stunt followed.

The room was the one closest to the kitchen, a fact Stunt could tell from the mighty banging Teresa was making in there. If she kept that up, she was going to put a pan right through some appliance. David opened the door and held it as Stunt passed him.

"Do you need anything?" David's voice sounded strained from emotion… either that or his voice was changing mighty late.

"I'm fine," Stunt said as he headed for a solid-looking rocker. The window looked out onto the mountain, and with the glass up, nothing stood between him and the deep green he loved. He could smell a stream somewhere near, and something that felt a lot like peace settled in.

"I could get you some food. Memaw's cooking up some cookies." David sounded almost desperate to do something nice, and on any other day, Stunt would have wanted to ease that discomfort.

"I just sort of feel like sitting for a time," Stunt said, keeping his face toward the window. David took a step into the room, his boots sharp against the wood floor, but Stunt didn't bother turning. For a time, they simply existed in the silence. Then David turned and left, pulling the door closed behind him.

That left Stunt in private. Scratching his nose, he rocked and watched the wind catch at the limbs of a yellow poplar. It wasn't a poplar though. It was a liriodendron. Some folks called it a tulip tree, seeing as it had big yellow flowers, but it wasn't even related to the tulip. He'd spent his life learning stuff like that. He knew which trees to expect in the cove forests you found on the lower mountains and which you'd find when you got right up near the peak, and now not a bit of that mattered. And other than his life tending the mountain, all he had to show was a long line of encounters with men whose names he couldn't even come up with.

Dan. That'd been one. Dan had been some sort of lawyer or paralegal or something, and he'd thought the stories of Stunt's sexual prowess were slightly exaggerated—a tall tale made up to make fun of the city folk. Stunt had left Dan sexually satisfied and a hundred dollars poorer. And next time, maybe Dan wouldn't assume every man had the same abilities. Thaddeus had been a mountain kid like Stunt, but he'd moved down to Tallahassee and never looked back. They'd found each other at a leather bar, each smiling at the other's deep hill accent. He pretty much had the life Stunt had once wanted for himself, but even now, Stunt couldn't imagine himself living or dying anywhere other than his mountains.

His thoughts weren't as pleasant as the rustle of leaves, so Stunt shoved all failure aside and watched a scarlet tanager with her yellow breast and olive-brown back hop from branch to branch, her *chuck-kurr* call going out into the woods.

It was a nice place to be.

CHAPTER
11

THE sun was setting, and the long shadows made shapes across the ground before Stunt heard the click of the door. However, a balsam woolly adelgid was making its way across the windowsill, and Stunt didn't want to give up watching the small ball of fluff. The white feather-like body and tall wings made it look like a flying bit of cotton or an escapee from some fairy tale. If he were on the job, Stunt would call this in and schedule a time to bring up some pesticides, seeing as how one of these little immigrants from Europe could decimate a stand of fir trees. But he wasn't on the job, and he was just enjoying the sight of those gray legs carrying that fluffy body.

"Stunt?" Alex called a second before a hand landed on Stunt's shoulder. Stunt looked up and saw Alex—his face shadowed and creased in confusion. "Hey, are you okay? You've been in here hours."

"Have I?" Stunt blinked.

"I thought you were sleeping."

Stunt looked over at the bed. The quilt lay folded near the foot, and the sheets were unwrinkled. David Pierpont was a neat, neat man. "I was looking out the window."

"At what?" Alex walked over and peered out into the dusk.

"A scarlet tanager is looking to make a nest in that tree, and it looks like Elijah might have some bug trouble round these parts."

Alex turned away from the window, looking even more confused when he crouched next to Stunt. "Are you diabetic or something? Do you need medicine?"

Stunt blinked. "What? Why?"

"Because you just turned into happy, quiet little pod-Stunt, and it's kind of freaking me out." Alex rested his hand on Stunt's knee. "What's going on with you? Is this some alternate personality you had tucked away in a back pocket for when you weren't trying to annoy me?"

His tone was teasing, but Stunt didn't rise to the taunt. Closing his eyes, he rested his head against the back of the chair.

"You're scaring me here, Stunt."

"I guess I've decided to just stop fighting."

"Okay." Alex said the word slowly, like he was still trying to figure out exactly what that might mean. "You don't have to look like someone shot your dog." Again the tone was almost teasing.

Stunt looked at Alex, disbelief temporarily robbing him of the ability to form words, even in his own mind. "How exactly should I feel about dying?" he finally asked. If he was going to die, he figured he had a right to feel the way he wanted to on the subject.

Pulling his hand away from Stunt's knee like he'd touched a hot stove, Alex stood up. "Don't start that again. I told you, I won't kill you."

For a second, all Stunt's thoughts scattered in the face of such stupidity. "You're not half as scary as Elijah. Even if you wanted to kill me, I figure Elijah's going to beat you to it."

"What?" The confusion was unmistakable.

Closing his eyes, Stunt forced down the anger that made him want to scream. Alex had as good as killed him, and he didn't even understand how. And Stunt could either let Alex go do his plan in blissful ignorance, or he could explain a few facts of life. If he were nice, he'd do the first, but Stunt didn't know anyone with that much milk of human kindness in 'em. "Elijah's going to take care of me while you're gone," he said bluntly.

"Yeah, which he seems to think includes feeding you rabbit stew and hot chocolate. At least, that's what he said was for dinner when he told me to come 'fetch' you."

Stunt let his breath out and tried to find some way to have a civil conversation with the world's stupidest kidnapper. Or maybe Alex wasn't stupid as much as he was a cultural idiot, thinking everyone in the universe acted like people from California. Stunt supposed that out there folk weren't so nice before murdering you and hiding the body, but this wasn't California. "He won't risk no federal time for kidnapping, not for me, not for any government employee. I figure as long as I'm real polite, he'll make it quick and easy, but sure as God made little green apples, as soon as you're gone, he's going to take me out and kill me."

"He wouldn't—" Alex stopped. Maybe it finally dawned on him that Elijah would. Stunt figured these old moonshiners would do most anything to steer clear of the hoosegow. "He knows you. He likes you." His voice sounded distant, like he was too caught up in his own thoughts to say the words.

Stunt nodded. "Which is why he'll make it quick and easy."

"No. No, I won't let him. I told you that you could go free as soon as Garrido was dead, and I meant it. I'll tell him he has to let you go." Alex's spine stiffened.

"Great. We can share a narrow grave." Stunt gave a laugh. "In case you've failed to notice, folk around here ain't real fond of strangers. Elijah's not going to take kindly to you telling him what to do. After all, he's the one who cares about keeping his neck out of federal prison, and he's not going to care if you're signing up for the electric chair."

"Then you have to run." Alex looked around as though searching for an escape route. It was amusing, in a dark and bitter sort of way.

Stunt could feel his face ache as he smiled widely. "You, I'd run from. Elijah? I'm not that stupid, and you getting all het up about this ain't going to change it."

"You have to run. I'll stay here and distract them."

Stunt blinked at Alex, wondering where that bit of stupidity came from. "No, I don't. Elijah knows these woods better than anyone else out here. He'd track me down inside an hour, and then I'd make the man who was planning on killing me upset. Now, I don't know how you think this works, but generally, I try to avoid pissing people off when they have that kind of power over me."

Alex crossed his arms over his chest. "You never avoided pissing me off."

Stunt figured there was some truth to that. Even when fear curled in his belly, his mouth had run full speed around Alex. He shrugged helplessly. "Maybe my wires got crossed. You're cuter than Elijah."

"I'm...." Alex sat down on the bed heavily, like his legs had just gone and stopped working. "You're mouthy because I'm cute?"

"Fact is, you remind me of more than one ex-lover. Now Elijah... he doesn't remind me of anyone but a moonshiner who'll do anything to protect himself, his family, and his still. Out here, after God and a good pickup truck, those three are the holy trinity."

Silence fell on the room, and Stunt could almost see the truth finally penetrating Alex's thick skull. Although to be fair, coming here had been Stunt's not-very-bright suggestion. Clearly, they were both dumber than a coal bucket.

"Oh God," Alex finally whispered.

"I don't think he's likely to get involved."

Alex started breathing faster as the panic kicked in. "We can take the truck, get out of here before Elijah notices."

Stunt had thought about that, but he figured it was too late now. "I'll bet you anything that Elijah had one of those boys pull something important out of the engine. He'll want to control when you go and know where you're going to. In case I haven't mentioned it in the last five minutes or so, folk up here ain't fond of strangers."

"You're annoyingly repetitive."

"Yeah," Stunt laughed, "I am. But you won't need to worry too much about it. I feel a nice long spell of quiet coming on."

Stunt had a heaviness in his stomach that didn't sit well. It wasn't fear, not exactly. He'd felt fear plenty in his life. Hell, he'd been shot at more than most men twice his age, but considering he wandered remote trails littered with moonshiners and meth shacks and marijuana growers, it wasn't exactly surprising. Every time he heard the crack of a gun, that unique echo as the sound bounced around the mountains, he felt his legs tremble with the need to run. He'd gotten singed by a bullet once, a long, low crease along one hip. He'd been so preoccupied with fear he hadn't even noticed until he'd gotten out of his truck in town and seen all the blood. Only then had it started stinging like a nest of wasps had taken after his whole leg.

But what he felt now didn't have the same desperate edge to it—it didn't fill him with the overwhelming urge to move. Right now, Stunt figured he wouldn't be able to run if someone paid him. He'd sooner sit in this chair until Elijah came in with a soft voice and told him it was time.

"How can you be calm?" Alex's voice had an edge of desperation, and his fingers clasped his own knees tightly enough the knuckles were turning white.

"Don't really see any other choice," Stunt pointed out. "If you have any real smart ideas, I'm open to suggestions, but seeing as how your plans so far have gone, I'm not counting on you to fix this." He felt a flash of guilt as pain twisted Alex's features. "And I ain't counting on me either, seeing as how I encouraged you to come up here in the first place. Face it. We ain't got but one brain cell between us, and neither of us has been using it lately."

Alex stood, his lips pressed into a tight line. "I'm sure he didn't mean to make it sound like he'd kill you. This is all a stupid misunderstanding." He practically charged out of the room. Part of Stunt was grateful. He really did just want to sit in the quiet and do a bit of praying. If he told Elijah he needed some time with a Bible, he figured Elijah would give him that. It was funny how a man felt real close to God when he came to the time to meet him. However, if Stunt didn't do something, Alex was going to get himself killed and dropped in the same grave.

"It'd serve him right," Stunt said quietly, even though he didn't believe it. Alex wasn't a bad man, just turned around a bit. "Not that I owe him. He started all this by kidnapping me." Stunt stared at the open door. He could sit here and let Alex stir the pot, and that would be a sort of biblical justice—an eye for an eye, a stupid death for a stupid death. Or he could use Alex as a distraction and start a'running. He didn't know how far he'd get, but if he was real lucky, he could die on his feet and never feel the bullet hit him. Or he could get shot in the gut and have Elijah leave him to bleed out.

With a sigh, Stunt pushed himself to his feet. "I guess I should get the idiot out of this mess." He steadied himself on the edge of the door, his legs weak under him. Knowing he was looking at the tail end of life had taken a lot of the starch out of him, but he didn't plan to lie down without doing what he thought was right. He was dead, and he didn't see any way around that, but Elijah didn't have to kill Alex. Alex had more cause to hide from the police than Elijah, so he wasn't a threat. Of course, that was assuming the moron didn't turn this operation of his into a suicide mission.

He wasn't even halfway down the hall when he heard the raised voices. "You can't be serious!" Yep, that was Alex—diplomatic as ever.

"I ain't doing no twenty years for kidnapping."

"I can convince him not to talk." Alex sounded so sure Stunt took a second to worry about just what the man had in mind.

"Can you? He ain't exactly real tractable."

"I can handle him." Stunt reached the end of the hall and watched Elijah and Alex go nose-to-nose in the middle of the living room. Alex fisted his hands at his sides, but Elijah had his shotgun tucked under an arm. "I promised him I'd let him go after I killed Garrido."

"You are letting him go, but I'm picking him back up. He's seen too much. I ain't about to let him go singing to the police." The way Elijah said it, it was perfectly clear he thought his logic was real sound, but Alex pressed his lips into a thin, angry line.

"I'll take him with me… keep him quiet."

Elijah took a step back and studied Alex up and down. "He ain't your kin."

"I promised him that he would be safe."

"And you ain't the one killing him."

"And neither are you."

Stunt didn't like the thoughtful look on Elijah's face. Sometimes his grandfather would get that look, the one that said he'd been pushed just a little too far and someone was about to be in for a world of hurt.

"You two can stop bashing into each other like rams on some damn nature show," Stunt said, jumping into the middle of the mess with a piece of profanity sure to catch Elijah off guard. Sure enough, he turned his unhappy look toward Stunt. "Neither of you want Garrido on this mountain, and neither do I. This place is meth central, and even if he ain't noticed yet the built-in market for his product, he will eventually. Folk make their own meth in Mountain Dew bottles and set fire to themselves more often than I care to think on. So what sort of market will there be for Garrido's sort of cheap, mass-produced stuff? I won't watch my home go to rack and ruin, and I sure won't watch more young people killed by some poison that's so common they can pick it up on the street corner. Elijah, you and I both know we've lost too many people, more than most others realize. And Alex… you ain't got one say in this. Not one. We're in Elijah's house, and you ain't about to go challenging him to a game of chicken. You'll lose, and then there won't be anyone to take care of business, so both of you stop this damn posturing because you look like idiots."

Stunt turned to leave and nearly walked right into Teresa. "Menfolk do like their posturing," she said kindly, patting him on the arm before nudging him back into the room with Elijah and Alex, which was about the last place he wanted to be right now. He wanted to go back to David's room and watch the mountain, not deal with human irrationality.

"Teresa," Elijah said in warning.

"You've had your say, and now I'm having mine. It's a sin, killing Stewart, and his grandfather is turning over in his grave that you're even thinking on it, Elijah James Pierpont."

"I'm not having this family put in the crosshairs of some police warrant."

"Then don't. I swear, men don't think outside their narrow boxes." When Elijah opened his mouth to protest, Teresa poked a finger in his direction. "When my father called you a foot-washing, lard-eating horned toad, you didn't take that as an answer. You came down and got me, and my daddy would have called that kidnapping if we hadn't been married before he caught up."

Elijah stepped back, an almost alarmed expression on his face.

"You've seen how the boys look at each other. And now each of them's trying to keep you from killing the other. If that ain't love, then I'm too old and too blind to see the truth that's right in front of me. Either that or you are." Teresa nodded sharply as though convinced she'd just come up with the right answer. "Now you solve this, and it better not include bloodshed, Elijah." Turning on her heel, Teresa strode out of the room.

For a second, time stood still. Then Elijah snorted. "Womenfolk," he complained softly. "Not that I hadn't noticed you were a sodomite," Elijah said, looking at Alex. "And Stewart made a right fool of himself at school so the whole county knows he's one."

"He... what?"

"Long story," Stunt interrupted before Elijah could break out into a description of Stunt's antics on the school debate club. Defining sodomy in front of a group that included ninth graders hadn't been one of his finest moments. "But you can't be considering a shotgun wedding, Elijah. We're both men."

Elijah looked from one of them to the other. "From where I sit, you're willing to give up your life without even a fight to keep Alex safe. It sounds like you've already made a pretty serious commitment. 'And Ruth said, entreat me not to leave thee, or to return from following after thee: for whither thou goest, I will go; and where thou lodgest, I will lodge: thy people shall be my people, and thy God my God'." Elijah spent a long time looking at Stunt. Maybe it was the slim chance of not dying, but Stunt couldn't bring himself to deny any of it.

His judgment had been pretty much compromised from the time Alex had cleaned the mud off his face with that handkerchief.

"Wait," Alex said, "you don't mind that we're gay?"

Elijah shrugged. "I figure you'll go to hell, seeing as how the Bible calls that one of those abominations. But until you get yourself dead, it ain't none of my business. Actually, it ain't my business even after you're dead, seeing as how I don't intend to be down in hell with all the fornicators and such." It was perfect hill logic, but Alex looked a little like a man who'd just seen the sky and earth switch sides. "But if you make a commitment in front of God, that means something in these parts. That's not to be undertaken lightly."

Maybe it was standing in Elijah's house that made things so clear, but Stunt understood exactly what he meant. Alex didn't, but maybe it was time for Alex to start trying to understand hill logic. "If I vow to obey you, and then turn you in, there isn't a person on this mountain who will talk to me. I couldn't convince someone to throw a bucket of water on me if I was on fire," Stunt explained. "Betraying God… it's just not done. Ever. If I turn on you, I'd have to leave the mountain."

"And you won't do that," Alex finished. "I mean, if you're a big enough idiot to stay in the middle of homophobia central when you could move anywhere, I have to assume you're illogically fond of this place."

"You might say that," Stunt agreed. "This is my home."

"And if'n you're kin to Alex, you won't do anything to turn on him."

A puff of laughter slipped out of Stunt. "I never was going to turn on him, Elijah. He's an idiot, but he has a good heart, and he's doing the right thing, even if I am questioning his reasons for it." And on the practical end of things, Stunt was already so turned around in his own head, he couldn't even imagine how he'd explain any of this to Sheriff Kennedy.

"You sound like a wife already," Elijah joked, and for the first time, the old man smiled at him. Stunt knew Elijah never wanted to kill him, so this was feeling like a real good solution on all sides.

"However, seeing as how I'd like things official to protect myself and my own family, I suppose I'll be getting Reverend Carswell out here."

Stunt knew the name, but Carswell was from a couple of counties over. He had to be one of those liberal city ministers if he was the sort to marry two men.

"But…." Alex sounded completely lost.

"Unless you're saying no to marrying him," Elijah offered.

Stunt's stomach knotted, his lost fear making a sudden reappearance.

"What? No. I mean, I'm definitely not saying no. Yes, I would marry Stunt. There's nothing to even ask about, because I'm not letting him die for my mistake." Alex seemed to be flailing a bit, which wasn't exactly the proposal Stunt had dreamed of—not that he dreamed of proposals at all.

"Well, seeing as how you two are going to be making a public vow in front of God and Reverend Carswell, I guess you two can share David's room." Elijah reached out and caught Alex's arm. "This ain't for show. You need to take Stunt as a wife and consummate this relationship in front of God. And don't go thinking that you can act like one of them city folk by marrying him and then getting some divorce a month later. If you turn on Stunt, I will personally hunt you down and beat you like a rented mule. Clear?"

"Yes, sir," Alex managed. He was blinking fast, but then Stunt figured hill logic did that to brains that weren't wired for it.

Elijah nodded. "Just you keep that in mind," he warned. "Now, Teresa's made stew, and we're going to have a nice family meal." With a wide smile that showed off a couple of gaps, Elijah slapped Alex on the arm. "I'm glad that's settled."

CHAPTER
12

"THAT was a good dinner. I can't believe I like rabbit," Alex said as he stood in the middle of David's room looking intensely uncomfortable. "I'm just going to try hard to avoid thinking about Thumper."

While Alex talked about things that didn't rightly make a whole lot of sense, Stunt sat on the bed and started pulling his boots off. "Teresa's a good cook." Dropping the boots down beside the bed, Stunt wiggled his toes out of sheer happiness to get those damn things off. He glanced over, and Alex still stood in the middle of the room looking like a deer about to have a head-on collision with a semitruck. Maybe this wasn't a good idea right now. Maybe Alex needed some time to ease into the thought of marriage.

Scooting up so his back was against a metal headboard that looked like it had come through the Civil War, Stunt pulled a leg under him. "You know, Mother always said she'd swept under my feet once too often for me to ever get married."

"Is that supposed to make any sense?"

Stunt shrugged. "Maybe. It's a saying we have in these parts. If you sweep under someone's feet, they won't ever get married."

Alex laughed darkly. "And here I thought it was because you were gay and this state doesn't have gay marriage."

"That too."

Running a hand over his face, Alex walked over and sat on the end of the bed. It was a start. "Your logic is a little rusty, you know that, right?"

"Says the man who came out here with no plan and who just earned himself a first-rate shotgun wedding, including a shotgun," Stunt pointed out.

That seemed to require some thought on Alex's part. "So we're both illogical."

Now Stunt laughed. "It's a good thing we can't have kids. Anyone who inherited our genes would be a complete moron."

Alex rolled his eyes, but Stunt noticed he didn't disagree. After all, facts were fact, and they'd both been all kinds of stupid on this one.

"People have to get divorced up here. It can't be as simple as Elijah makes it out to be," Alex said softly.

Stunt sighed. This was dangerous territory, especially if Elijah caught them talking about it. "Divorce happens," he admitted. When Alex tried to say something, Stunt lifted a hand to still him. "That's because people grow apart after years of living together and having life beat on them. But like I said before, if I stand up in front of God and vow to love, honor, and respect you, and then I turn you over to the police before the next full moon, I'm done. There won't be one person in this world that trusts me, including myself."

"So, this is for real?" Alex looked into Stunt's eyes, the blue of them nearly black in the low light of an old lamp with peeling paint.

"I suppose it is," Stunt agreed. "I won't deny a vow I make to God. I have more than one superstitious bone in my body, and they all ache at the thought of even trying anything that dumb."

"So, do we do this…? Now?" Alex looked a whole lot like a nervous virgin.

"I reckon Elijah's not going to trust the vow until he knows the consummation took place. Most people around here think that until the sex has happened, the marriage isn't official. Plenty of fathers have tried to undo a hasty decision on the grounds that no sex means no marriage."

"Great," Alex said with a wry grimace. "I don't like performing for an audience."

"It's not like he's going to ask to watch."

"Nope, just eavesdrop. Shit, it's hot in here. Why do none of these people have air conditioning?" Alex complained, and before Stunt could point out poor people cared a little more about food than comfort, Alex turned to him with wide eyes. "Oh shit. Do you have any condoms?"

That was about the last thing Stunt was worried about. As much as he was a proponent of safe sex, Elijah sitting in the next room with a shotgun negated any part of this being safe. "I am a sexually uninhibited, healthy gay man who intends to stay healthy. Of course I have condoms," Stunt offered. "I have a rainbow of colors, your choice of latex or my favorite, polyurethane, plain or studded or ribbed, and I think I might still have a Santa-hat condom from last Christmas. I even have female condoms for when I bottom, and while they're a right pain in the ass—no pun intended—once they get up there, they are a real improvement over the regular kind. I got me a regular cornucopia of condoms." Stunt waited until relief made Alex sag. "Back at home," he added.

Alex glared at him. "Great."

"Yep. Life's just determined to kick us in the teeth," Stunt agreed. Someone had put out a fresh new quilt that covered David's bed, blue-and-yellow with interlocking rings. Stunt was fairly sure it was a wedding design. He ran his finger over the quilted cotton. He supposed it was Teresa's way of giving her blessing. This was one seriously strange situation.

"What the fuck do we do now?" Alex asked softly. He'd retreated to the window.

"We could try being honest and up front, and when I say that, I mean brutally, coldly honest. Because this whole situation is about as safe as snake handling."

"Handling a snake? A literal snake or some weird metaphor?" Alex demanded.

"Never mind that. The point is, how likely are we to give each other some disease, because I figure we're safe from pregnancy. I mean, if there's some reason to avoid penetration, we could trade blowjobs or hand jobs. I don't suppose Elijah has thought on the subject long enough to define what gay sex might look like, even if he is going to expect the consummation."

Alex's mouth fell open. "You want to have unprotected sex?"

Sitting on the edge of the bed, Stunt crossed his arms. "If you keep looking at me like that, you're not getting any sex at all. But face it, Elijah is looking for us to prove we're married."

"So we bounce on the bed for a bit and lie," he whispered.

"And if he catches us?" Stunt gave the metal rails of the headboard a good pull. They were as solid as the mountains. Whoever had built this thing either meant it to last a few centuries or needed a good place to tie down a partner. Either worked for him.

"How is he going to catch us?" Alex demanded. He had his arms crossed as he frowned.

Stunt shrugged. "I have no idea. I just know that old coots like Elijah do have a way of smelling out a lie, and I'd rather not lie when it's my hide on the line."

"You're being paranoid." Even though Alex said the words, Stunt could practically see the wheels turn in his head as he looked at the door. Yeah, if Elijah caught them lying, this was going to get so much uglier.

"Funny enough, I'm pretty sure that's what you said when I pointed out that bringing me up here to Elijah's place was all kinds of stupid," Stunt said.

Alex clenched his jaw hard enough to make a little knot of muscle under his ear.

"I'm just saying, maybe we can be honest and see whether this would be worth taking a risk."

"God, you're pushy."

"Suck it up. You're marrying me. Besides, me asking for sex from my husband is not exactly a shocking request."

"Husband," Alex echoed, his voice suddenly distant. Yep, it was still sinking in for him. Stunt had come to terms with the idea a little quicker.

"So, I know I've had more than my share of partners, but I have always used condoms on all sex acts, oral and anal, since I turned nineteen. Seeing as how I'm twenty-eight and I've passed a half dozen health checks since then, I think I'm pretty safe. My last blood work was about two years ago, but I haven't had any condoms break or done anything adventurous since then." Stunt frowned. "Well, maybe adventurous is the wrong word, since most people would rank my every sexual encounter as adventurous and abnormal, but I haven't had anything happen that would threaten my health. I have been part of some whipping scenes, but nothing heavy and nothing with blood drawn. Most of the time I'm just into a lot of heavy bondage and a little mild humiliation and pain." Stunt could feel the blush start just from making that confession, and the heat travelled right to his cock. While he might not appreciate some big scene that made him look like an ass in public, a little forced confession and a few eyes watching him always had added a little spice to the encounter.

Alex blinked at him, those dark eyes seemingly unfocused.

"Alex?"

"Yeah, okay." Stunt might have taken offense, only Alex's cock was making a bulge in his pants, and he kept opening and closing his hands like he wanted to grab something. Unless Stunt was mistaken, Alex wanted to grab him. Eventually, he did seem to focus his eyes. "You expect me to be that honest, don't you?"

"It'd be nice," Stunt agreed.

Despite the constipated expression, Alex took a deep breath. "I haven't had sex in almost two years." He blurted the words out so fast, Stunt had to mentally rewind and review them. Two years. He couldn't imagine a man not having sex for that long. He knew Alex had this whole lack of common sense going for him, but that was taking things a little far.

"Don't look at me like I'm some sort of freak. I spent over a year of that in prison," he snapped. "And watching men sell their asses for a little protection… I'm just a little soured on power games."

Stunt figured Alex still did like playing those games, even if he didn't allow himself to do much playing anymore. If he had decided to turn vanilla, he would have found himself a nice boring vanilla boy. But Stunt knew full well that caretaker Doms, the ones who liked to play with their toys and then clean them up all pretty and pet them, rarely had much patience for the sort of abuse that sometimes happened in the BDSM clubs. No doubt it happened even more in prison.

"I should also point out that I'm a little unusual in the bedroom," Stunt offered.

"You mean other than being kinky, getting off on humiliation, and enjoying being tied up and forced to finally stop talking? You're somehow unusual in some way other than those?"

"Yep." It was all true, so Stunt couldn't exactly get all riled. "I'm popular with the Doms because I can generally come twice… three times if you make me suffer and work for the first two orgasms."

"You… what?" Alex's voice went up into the tones of disbelief. He'd learn quick enough, though. Stunt found most men didn't truly believe until they'd watched it.

"Men like making me come and then watching me squirm because the later orgasms are a lot harder because, face it, I'm a whole lot more tender. There are plenty that like to fuck me hard and then—"

"Stop," Alex said firmly. Stunt opened his mouth, but Alex held up his hand. "This is me telling you to stop. One more word about a previous lover and you're going to be wearing a gag for a good long time. Clear?"

Stunt nodded. Very clear. And very hot. Alex had that rough tone, that commanding voice that made Stunt's cock sit up and take notice. "Just don't get all weird and think you have to call 911 or something because my dick's broken. There's a nice little warming sting of humiliation, and then there's having a doctor stick something cold up your prick as he asks what drugs you've been taking. I may like one, but the second is an experience I ain't looking to try again."

Alex laughed. "Deal. I won't call 911, and you won't mention what you've done with other men." He took a step into the middle of the room and sat on the end of the bed, his hand coming down to rest on Stunt's ankle. "Pushy bottom—that's a bit of a stereotype."

"A Dom who isn't pushing—that's a bit of an oxymoron," Stunt challenged him. Alex's eyebrow twitched and the emotions flowed just under his skin. Muscles flexed. His pupils dilated and his fingers tightened around Stunt's ankle.

"I know how to push, Stunt. You have no idea how hard I can push, which is why I try to be careful about not pushing unless I'm sure. I don't want this to be something we both regret."

"I don't plan to… not unless you're trying to warn me that you're real bad in bed. If that's the case, I may do some regretting." Stunt pursed his lips and pretended to think.

Alex reached out and caught him behind the neck. He pulled him in for a kiss, and Stunt ended up bracing his hands on Alex's thighs as the kiss grew deeper. Alex thrust his tongue in his mouth, forcing Stunt to open wider before he caught Stunt's lip and sucked gently. Even without ropes, Stunt's cock sat up and took an interest. Stunt was a little out of breath by the time Alex pulled away and gave him a firm push back onto the bed.

"What's your safeword?"

"Popcorn."

"Oh." Alex frowned, but then he seemed to get back in the groove, crawling up the bed toward him, so Stunt skipped any discussion of old Popcorn Sutton and his still.

"You gonna tie me up?"

Alex laughed. "I thought you'd had enough of that already."

"I've had enough of being tied up by an idiot out for revenge. However, I'm inviting my lover to play."

"So, if I stripped that shirt off and tied you to the headboard?"

"I'd point out this is my only shirt right now, and I'd rather look halfway presentable for Teresa and the preacher tomorrow."

"Oh." Alex sat up. "Okay, let me get something else."

Stunt opened his mouth to say he was a moron and getting sex was more important than a shirt, but Alex was already out of the room. "Smooth, you idiot," Stunt insulted himself before reaching down to pull his socks off. He shoved them under the bed and hoped the smell didn't rise up and kill them. Before he had time to do anything more, Alex was at the door again. The length of rope he'd used to tie Stunt in the truck trailed from one hand while he closed the bedroom door with the other.

"I think we can find some use for this." Alex stalked closer to the bed. He had a rolling gait that reminded Stunt of a predator closing in on its prey. Alex had done found his inner Dom.

"Are you planning on schooling me?"

"I plan to tie you up and gag you so I don't have to worry about you saying things I only half understand."

Stunt opened his mouth, but with a smile, Alex pounced on him. Grunting from Alex's weight landing on him, Stunt couldn't catch his breath before Alex pressed his mouth against his. This time, his tongue forced its way in and teased with fast flicks before he nipped Stunt's lip. At the same time, he ground his body down onto Stunt's.

Gasping for breath, Stunt grabbed for Alex's broad shoulders, but he found his hands pushed away as Alex pulled Stunt's shirt off. The armhole got caught around Stunt's elbow, and Stunt squirmed to get free, but Alex pinned his shoulder to the bed before yanking the shirt off and tossing it to one side.

"Lord a'mighty," Stunt whispered.

Alex laughed. "This is supposed to be shutting you up."

"Try harder," Stunt suggested.

"Oh, trust me. I haven't even gotten started." Alex caught Stunt's wrist and pulled it close. As he wrapped the rope around it, he rocked his body against Stunt's. Stunt's trapped cock got harder and harder as Alex undulated slowly against it, rubbing it, teasing it.

"Does the peanut gallery feel like saying anything now?" Alex asked as he captured Stunt's second wrist and tied it.

"Cain't think of nothing."

"You can still talk. I'll have to find a way to fix that." Alex leaned down, and this time the kiss started slower. Pressing his lips against Stunt's, Alex teased with featherlight brushes of his tongue that left Stunt straining upward, but then Alex pulled back and pressed Stunt's arms to the mattress over his head. A needy whine slipped out of Stunt before Alex was back, soft brushes of lips against lips even as the rope around his wrists tightened. Stunt had to admit, words were mostly scattering to the wind at this point.

Sitting up, Alex looked down at him with a hunger that made Stunt's body twitch. Then Alex efficiently stripped off his own shirt and tossed it to the side. Stunt couldn't reach out to trace the muscled stomach or explore the faint line of hair leading down to the front of Alex's jeans. He was well and truly tethered to the headboard, and with Alex sitting on his legs, he was about as helpless as a man could get. A little whine slipped out before Stunt could stop it.

"That's what I like to hear," Alex teased before running his hands over Stunt's chest. He pressed the pads of his thumbs against Stunt's hard nipples and gave them a little tug before rubbing the sting back out. Stunt hungrily gasped for air, unable to think about anything else. And then Alex was gone, his weight just gone and Stunt felt like he might fly apart.

Alex straddled his knees, his hands on Stunt's hips. "Breathe. I don't need you passing out," he said before he gave Stunt's jeans a good pull. He couldn't even remember Alex undoing the zipper, but Stunt found himself stripped. "I don't want you passing out before I test this ability of yours." Alex wiggled his eyebrows and leaned down to place a kiss on the end of Stunt's cock.

Now, in Stunt's defense, it did normally take more than that to make him come, but feelings had been running a little high. With a strangled cry, he came. A flood of white pleasure washed over him, and he sagged back onto the bed, panting.

"I'll take that as a compliment."

Stunt recognized Alex's voice, but he floated in and out, his half-hard cock still sending shivers of pleasure through his system. Warm, calloused hands ran up and down his sides as Alex's weight settled on his thighs again. After cracking his eyes open, he watched as Alex seemed to consider him with some curiosity.

"Wondering how it can do that?" Stunt asked as his cock continued to stand at attention. He wasn't anywhere near done, but he did know most men reacted with a bit of concern the first time they saw Stunt's quirks.

"I'm wondering where to start if I want to leave you truly speechless," Alex said. Letting his weight fall forward, he braced his hands on either side of Stunt's shoulders and leaned in to claim another kiss. The whole time, he made these little thrusts that sent his sweat-slicked stomach rubbing against Stunt's cock.

Stunt arched his back, his body straining against the rising need and the lack of control that left him blissfully, helplessly limp. He wanted to touch Alex, but with his wrists tied, he had limited choices. After lifting his leg, he ran his foot up and down Alex's body, feeling the strong muscles and the sheen of hot sweat.

Cupping Stunt's balls in one hand, Alex placed a kiss against Stunt's neck. "You are beautiful, wife of mine."

Sucking in a breath, Stunt pulled back to grace Alex with a tirade about how he wasn't a woman, but then he spotted the smirk. "Dork," he complained softly. He brought up both legs and wrapped them around Alex so he could hold him tight. He tried to keep him captive, but Alex was stronger. A lot stronger. Alex braced his hands on Stunt's hips and pushed himself up.

"I can be. Oddly, you seem to like me anyway," Alex pointed out. And then, before Stunt could come up with a retort, Alex slid his mouth down around Stunt's cock and sucked hard. Stunt thrust his hips up and gave a wordless cry.

When Alex kept sucking, sliding slowly up and down on Stunt's cock, Stunt found words. "Alex. Oh God. Yes. Oh God." Alex played with the cockhead before sliding down the length of the shaft, and Stunt pressed his head back into the pillow, struggling against the wrist bindings. Alex was good. Hell, Alex was great. If not having sex for two years meant being this good… actually no, Stunt still wouldn't go two years without sex.

Alex pulled back. "I have missed this," he confessed, "a lot." Then he took Stunt in his mouth again, this time letting his cock slide down the back of his throat so the tightness nearly sent Stunt flying. He would have come again, only the hint of a balls-deep ache and the first orgasm had left him on the razor edge of coming without allowing him to. It was a painfully delicious moment to get trapped in.

"Hmmmm. Clearly, I'm a little rusty. I'll need to try a little harder."

Stunt opened his mouth, but he couldn't arrange enough brain cells to form a response. Alex ran his nails over the inside of Stunt's thigh, each trail leaving a hot line that sent tingles through Stunt's body. After one orgasm, he shouldn't be this primed, this ready to go off with just a touch, but Stunt started squirming, his rising need threatening to overwhelm him.

Alex let his weight fall on Stunt, and Stunt oomphed as the air left his lungs, leaving him a little light-headed as Alex ran a series of kisses up his collarbone to an exposed shoulder. Stunt squirmed more, and Alex held him down, trapping him. Then Alex paused as he looked down. Stunt felt the moment settle around them.

Slowly, Alex started rocking, undulating against Stunt. Completely trapped by Alex and the heat of his body, Stunt could only moan as Alex ran teeth over his shoulder. Stunt pulled against the restraints so hard he could hear his shoulder pop, but the rope held. The feeling of being so utterly trapped under Alex's large frame made Stunt cry out softly.

"Too much. Too much," he finally gasped out, the words strangled.

"Stunt?"

"Just give me a second. Oh God. Yeah, that hurts," Stunt complained as Alex moved against his over-sensitized cock. "I just need… just a second."

Alex slid to the side, his hand running up and down Stunt's chest. The motion made Stunt aware of how much his chest was heaving. He couldn't catch his breath, and when Alex leaned close to his ear, Stunt's heart pounded even harder. "Do you want to stop?" Alex asked, his voice teasing and his hot breath sliding across Stunt's hot skin. Stunt shivered. "Do you want to stop, or would you like something to amuse yourself for a while, a little something to suck on?"

"Oh God, yes. Hell, yes." Stunt dug his heels into the mattress and thrust up.

When Alex straddled his chest, Stunt licked his lips and then opened his mouth, waiting for his prize. Alex shifted up so Stunt could reach the tip of his cock. He sucked it hungrily. Humming, he ran his tongue along the underside, opening wider when Alex inched closer. The feel of a cock in his mouth and hearing the desperate sounds of a satisfied lover were two of the best feelings in the world. Fisting his hands in frustration because he wanted more, Stunt struggled to lean up and claim more of his prize, but then Alex was moving down, the head of his cock brushing the back of Stunt's throat before withdrawing.

Stunt grunted and tried to follow Alex, but Alex was moving back down into him. Trusting that Alex wasn't pulling away, Stunt settled back onto the pillow and let him sway, his cock moving in and then sliding out. Stunt shifted his humming into a lower tone, making Alex shiver and jerk. Stunt would have smiled if his mouth hadn't been full. Alex's thrusts grew stronger, one hitting the back of Stunt's throat a little harder than he expected, but before he could even cough once, Alex's cock was out.

"God, I want to fuck you." Alex's voice was breathy and rough.

"Do it. Fuck me." Stunt didn't realize he'd said it so loud until Alex's hand was over his mouth. Alex's gaze went to the door. It was like being a teenager again, trying to have quiet sex so no one heard. Stunt started laughing silently, and then Alex was covering him, his mouth next to Stunt's ear as he struggled with his own laughter, little grunts escaping as the body that pinned Stunt to the bed shook with the effort of containing his own amusement.

"Fuck me," Stunt repeated in a whisper.

Alex's laughter tapered off, and he ran his hand over Stunt's arms. "Pushy."

"When I desperately need sex, yes."

"I could fix that, you know. Keep you nice and stuffed down there."

Stunt groaned, his whole body jerking with need as he fought the ropes. He could hear himself whimpering, although he would never admit to making that noise. He moaned and wailed and when there wasn't someone in the next room, he screamed, but he did not whimper at the thought of some Dom forcing him to wear a butt plug. Nope. Not him. He was way too sophisticated for... the rest of Stunt's thoughts scattered like dry leaves in a stiff breeze when Alex cupped his balls and rolled them gently.

With a knowing smile, Alex shifted down, his hands moving over skin slippery with sweat. Stunt arched up, thrusting into the air the second Alex's weight was off him. His cock was still hard and sore, the need to come battling with the pain to keep him on a keen edge. Alex braced his hands on Stunt's hips and forced him back down to the bed, and for one second, Stunt's entire brain whited out, the haze of need and pleasure wiping out every thought that didn't start and end with his cock. Mouth open, he writhed against the bonds holding him, both the knots and the hands.

"You are beautiful," Alex said in a near-reverent voice, and Stunt opened his legs, silently begging for more. The finger against his ass was slightly cool, and Stunt angled his hips, gasping for air as two fingers pushed into him.

"Yes. Shit. Yes." Stunt kept his voice down as Alex worked his fingers back and forth. He wasn't some virgin who needed prepping, but a little part of him suspected Alex just liked to reduce his partners to a puddle of goo, so he endured. He struggled to thrust down onto those fingers, and he jerked his legs until Alex sat on one, but he impatiently accepted as Alex invaded his ass. Stunt tried to use his one free leg to push himself up, but again he was reminded of how strong Alex was. He couldn't budge the man or make him speed up as fingers thrust lazily in before pulling back just as gently.

"Fuck me," Stunt begged in a whisper. "Please, do it. Please, Alex." His voice broke, but as long as Alex sat on his leg, he couldn't do anything. He could only lie there and suffer as Alex crooked his fingers to press up into Stunt's prostate.

Stunt panted, the heat pressing down on him. He threw his free leg out to the side, opening as far as he could, and Alex shifted so his knees were on the bed between Stunt's legs. Alex grabbed his thighs and thrust in. Stunt tried to scream, but Alex let his weight drop down and covered Stunt's mouth with his own, silencing him with a kiss, and all Stunt could do was whimper as he started with slow, small thrusts. After Stunt was crying in need, Alex pulled back and slammed forward until he buried himself in Stunt's body. Then he pulled out and slammed in again with a slap of flesh against flesh.

"Yes. Lord A'mighty, yes," Stunt gasped out as Alex pressed deep into him. Alex's hand wrapped around Stunt's cock, and Stunt whited out again as he came with a shudder of pleasure that rocked his whole body. He was still jerking in the aftermath as Alex used him, pounding him and grunting each time he buried himself balls deep. Being used after coming added a bright edge of pain that left Stunt's body buzzing with tingles as Alex finally came inside him. Then Alex let his weight fall down onto him and Stunt let his eyes fall shut. With no condom to worry about, Alex left his half-hard cock up Stunt's ass, and Stunt took care to not tense up. He didn't want to push Alex out too soon because the feeling of having his lover still in him was a rare one, one he enjoyed.

"You're going to break me," Alex said. "You're still hard."

Stunt cracked his eyes open to look down his body. His cock was still sitting up some, but it wasn't begging. "It just takes some time for me to downshift the engine," he explained. "But I am feeling well-used and sated." He felt more than sated. He felt like he'd been used hard by a man who needed him, and that did make for some mighty good sex.

Alex collapsed next to him, his hand trailing up and down Stunt's overheated body. Hell, they were both putting off the heat like stock car engines right off a race.

"I'm feeling like I should find out just how many times you could come if we pushed things." Alex whispered the words into Stunt's ear, each puff of air from his breath stirring the little hairs.

Stunt shivered. "Is that a threat?"

"Yep." Alex started working the knots around Stunt's wrists loose. It took a little time, but meanwhile, Stunt lay looking up at a rain-stained ceiling, feeling mighty good about the world. Considering he was still in a mess of trouble, he shouldn't feel this okay with their situation. But he did.

"Oh geez. Look at your wrists." Alex ran a thumb over the red, abraded skin. Little red dots of blood sat right under the surface, and deep red circles around each wrist were definitely on their way to some serious bruising.

"Next time, don't make me come so hard and I won't fight so much," Stunt suggested. "They aren't bad."

"If I make marks on you, they shouldn't be accidental ones." Alex continued tracing the damage with his thumb as he held Stunt's arm. Studying the bruising, Stunt had to admit it looked like someone had hung him by his wrists. If he hadn't been so worked up and lustful, he probably would have noticed they were hurting. "Next time I'm using suspension cuffs so you can fight without doing this." Right after Alex said it, he stopped. He didn't breathe, and his hand seemed stuck to Stunt's arm. It didn't take a genius to figure out why.

Instead of giving Alex a pass, Stunt came right out and asked, "Next time?" He watched while Alex pressed his lips together into a thin line and swallowed several times. "I hope next time you leave me a few marks you're proud of," he finished. He wouldn't apologize for enjoying this, and he sure didn't plan to make this a one-time event.

Alex studied him. Slowly, he brought his hand up, watching as though he expected Stunt to flinch away, but that wasn't going to happen. Cupping Stunt's cheek, Alex promised, "Next time I'll be more careful."

"Just make sure that careful includes being that rough. I like a little rough with the tender," Stunt said. He wouldn't have Alex start confusing whatever shit he'd seen in prison with the passion they'd shared.

"You need something to keep that mouth of yours busy— something that does not include talking."

Stunt smiled. "I ain't arguing with that."

Alex leaned in and kissed him again, this time threading his fingers through Stunt's short hair to hold him still, and Stunt truly did like the way Alex's mind worked.

Eventually, he eased back, his intensity trailing off into a series of little kisses along Stunt's jaw. "Now, stop complaining or I'll gag you with whatever smells so bad under this bed."

With a smile that had just enough devil in it that Stunt wasn't entirely sure Alex was joking, Alex leaned over Stunt's body to turn the lamp off.

CHAPTER
13

"BOYS, the preacher's coming. Get yourselves decent and get to the breakfast table before I come in there with a hairbrush to motivate you."

Stunt groaned. For a half second, he almost thought his mom had come back from the dead to threaten him. She was the last woman to come after him with a hairbrush. "Yes, ma'am. We're getting right up," Stunt answered when he realized it was Teresa. Blinking, he frowned as he noticed that Alex was already awake, sitting on the edge of the bed. "You're up early."

He shrugged. "I have trouble sleeping in strange places. Are you doing okay?"

Stunt ran a hand over his face. "Thought for a minute my ma had come back to chase me out of bed, but yeah." Swinging his legs over the edge of the mattress, Stunt paused as he got a bit of a head rush. Alex's hand rested on his arm for a moment to steady him, and Stunt smiled at the overprotective gesture. "I haven't been eating the best. I'm okay. Teresa's like to have cooked an entire pig's worth of bacon with company in the house, so I'll be fine."

"I feel a little like I just fell into some fifties sitcom with Mom cooking in the kitchen… only I don't remember any sitcoms that involved shotguns."

"*Green Acres* did. But I think Teresa's a better cook than Eva Gabor was on the show." Stunt grabbed his pants off the floor and made a few ineffective attempts to brush the wrinkles out. "Wasn't your mom one for cooking?"

Alex shrugged. "Before she got sick, she could do things with cheese. Grilled cheese sandwiches, macaroni and cheese, cheese crackers—that was her version of cooking, but she always made up for that by being the cool mom, the one who would dance with you in the middle of the store when you were four and everyone else glared because you weren't being some good little boy."

"She sounds nice."

Alex laughed. "She was loud, wild, and fun." The smile vanished, and it was easy enough to figure out what he was thinking on.

"My mom was the sort who would make sure your butt and the flat side of a ruler had an up close and personal meeting if you made a fuss in public, so I'm imagining how she would have frowned at a woman dancing with her little boy. That just wasn't done." As Stunt stood to put on his pants, he wondered what his mother would be saying about him marrying a man. "But you know, when I decided to tell the whole world I was a homosexual, she was right there telling the world if they wanted others to respect their choices that meant respecting mine, even if I was making an ungodly bad decision at that particular point in time. It was a complicated sort of support she showed."

"She sounds like an interesting woman."

Stunt nodded. "I wish she could be here. A heart attack took her about two years back."

"And your father?" Alex asked. "And feel free to tell me to mind my own business at any point," he quickly added.

"Not much to tell. I mostly stopped talking to him after I went to college. He has Alzheimer's, and I just visit twice a year so he can get all confused and think I'm his brother, and one time he thought I was a cop. That was a real fun visit," Stunt said sarcastically. Sadly, the staff said he was a happier man when Stunt didn't show his face. Of course, even without the Alzheimer's, Stunt suspected his father wouldn't have gone out of his way to show up for this particular wedding.

"You two have three seconds to get out here!" Teresa called.

"Crap." Stunt snatched his shirt, gave up on his shoes, and headed for the door.

"Coming!" Alex answered for them. He didn't have shoes on either, but he was trying to pull on his socks. Personally, Stunt wasn't taking a chance at having a personal experience with a hairbrush. There was fun spanking, and then there was having a woman take after him with a hard object. Shoving his arms in his shirt sleeves, he got his butt moving toward the kitchen.

He found Teresa in the kitchen with David and another young man who looked about as much like David as a person could get without being mistaken for a twin. Brother, most like. A young woman with a gaunt face that suggested drugs stood at a counter cutting out biscuit forms while Teresa stood at a stove with a big cast iron pan.

"Stewart, you know David, and I'm sure you remember Eli from Christmas services," Teresa offered. Stunt didn't remember anyone, seeing as how he didn't go to church, even at Christmas, but he smiled and nodded at Eli. "And this is Beatrice." Teresa nodded to the woman.

"Good morning," Stunt offered politely. Beatrice wiped her floured hands on a towel and picked up a plate full of food before holding it out toward him. With a smile, Stunt took what he was offered without commenting on the sheer volume of pig fat on the plate. He liked bacon and gravy as much as the next man, but there was such a thing as too much of something.

"Where's Alex?" Teresa narrowed her eyes as if she was holding Stunt personally responsible for Alex's absence. At the mention of his name, David and Eli both shoved the last of their food in their mouths and skedaddled out of the kitchen. Stunt didn't take no offense. Around these parts, most people were uncomfortable about homosexual couples, and silence was about as polite as they could come.

"He was looking for his shoes, ma'am," Stunt said, and taking a fork, he shoved a whole load of biscuit and gravy in his mouth before she could ask him anything else.

"I'm here," Alex said from the door. "I was just—"

"Late for breakfast," Teresa finished for him. "You ain't got much time, and the day's going to be a long one, so get your fill now." She took the bacon out of her pan and added it to the second plate of biscuits and gravy sitting next to the stove. "Bea, get those cat head biscuits in the oven," she ordered before offering Alex the plate.

"Why don't we have much time?" Alex asked all suspicious-like.

"Preacher's here. Elijah is having a conversation with the man."

Stunt cringed. "The preacher doesn't want to marry us, does he?" This could be a wrinkle in old Elijah's plan.

"Bea, go get them eggs from the chickens, and mind that you get them all this time."

Bea nodded. "Yes, ma'am." With that, she was out the door, and now would be the time for adult talk.

Sometimes Stunt wondered if folk didn't invent chores just to get the younger generation out of the room before anyone talked sex.

"If he wants his apple brandy, he does," Teresa said firmly. "And if he doesn't, he can go explaining to all of Buck County why they can't get no fresh lightning. Elijah's not one to make money off people he don't agree with morally. And as he's told the preacher, refusing to marry you is adding the sin of fornication onto the sin of homosexuality. He might have to put up with the one, seeing as how you two are stubborn, but he sure isn't holding with the general concept of sex outside of marriage. So don't you worry. What the preacher wants isn't half as important as what Elijah wants."

Alex frowned. "I would ask about the logic in that, but I think I'm done asking anyone to explain mountain logic."

Teresa smiled at him and patted him on the arm. "Some days it's just best to smile and go along. Now eat up so you can get out front. The preacher's brought his Bible, and then Elijah has called for a meeting at a nip joint."

"Nip joint?"

Stunt answered that one. "A place where they sell illegal booze, trade guns, and talk cars." Out of respect for Teresa, he didn't mention how many women sold their bodies at those places.

"It wouldn't be illegal if the government weren't trying to control what free people do on their own land," Teresa complained. Turning to the stove, she muttered some choice comments about government-types and then poured coffee out of an old-fashioned stovetop percolator before returning to the table. "We don't bother no one, but the government tries saying that our moonshine makes people go blind. Can you see Elijah ever cooking, much less selling, a load of bad whiskey?" she demanded.

"No, ma'am," Stunt agreed, although he could see Brett Millham doing exactly that. He might have, only last time he'd tried setting up a still, the store had refused to sell him the sugar. Brett had turned to meth and set his own truck on fire.

"People always trying to tell each other how to live." Teresa huffed in disapproval. "It's not that I hold with what you two were very enthusiastically doing last night, but you have a right to do it as enthusiastically as you like." With a firm nod, she made it clear the subject was closed, but Stunt could feel his face heat up something fierce. Land o'Goshen, she had heard them. He couldn't even bring himself to look at Alex. Instead, he shoved more food in his mouth and tried to not choke on it.

After several long and very awkward moments, Teresa got up and wandered out of the kitchen. Only then did Stunt risk looking at Alex.

"I thought we were being quiet," Alex said, the apology clear in his voice.

"Me too," Stunt agreed. But when he looked down at the purpling bruises around his wrists, he had to admit his judgment might be a little skewed. "So, happy wedding day." Yep, if there was awkward anywhere in the vicinity, Stunt was going to stick both feet right into it.

"Happy wedding day," Alex echoed the words, but he sounded almost enthusiastic about it. Satisfied maybe. Definitely sounded on the good end of feelings. "Are you okay?"

He shrugged. "A little tender. I usually insist on no marks."

That made Alex cringe.

"But mostly that's because I don't want to explain things at work. I don't reckon I'm going to be showing up in the office for a bit. Fact is, I'm not sure how this is going to work."

"I'll make sure you get back to your life," Alex said firmly.

"And you? What will you be doing?" Stunt knew one thing: Elijah wasn't kidding about hunting Alex down if he pulled a runner. For a long time, Alex stared at him. Stunt could almost taste the uncertainty that clung to the air between them. "You're a good man. I don't want you to leave, especially when your world ain't even a little sane," Stunt said. "I don't want you to get yourself killed."

"I can't let Garrido get away with what he did."

"I ain't saying you should."

That said, they sat and looked at each other, and Stunt wasn't quite sure how to smooth out the wrinkles between them.

"You boys ready?" Elijah asked, his gravel voice shredding the silence as he strode into the room. After walking over to the open shelf, he pulled down a cup and poured himself some coffee.

"Yes, sir," Stunt answered. He was still feeling a little twitchy, seeing as how Elijah had been thinking on killing him.

"We shouldn't be forcing Stunt to do this," Alex said.

"It weren't you that thought to come up here. It weren't you that went and suggested this, and it ain't you that's going to clean up the mess if you don't marry him," Elijah said sharply. Clearly, his patience had done run out.

"And it ain't me saying no," Stunt pointed out. "I'm starting to wonder if you're having second thoughts with all the stupid that keeps falling out your mouth."

Alex opened his mouth again, but Elijah caught Alex under an arm while holding his coffee in the other hand. "Have your first spat later. We got a preacher waiting." He pulled Alex out of his chair and propelled him toward the hall.

Stunt got up to follow, and Elijah stopped and looked down at the floor. Stunt followed his gaze down and realized he was still barefoot.

"If you try getting pregnant, I'm going to get real worried about you, boy," Elijah said.

Stunt's face flushed with heat. "I should go get—"

"You ain't getting anything. Get yourself out front before the preacher takes it in his head to argue more. I ain't seen a man that ornery in a good long time." When Alex stopped, Elijah gave him a push in the right direction, and Stunt followed.

"Barefoot and pregnant. After the ruckus last night, I suppose I wouldn't be all that shocked if you managed it," Elijah muttered as Stunt passed him. Stunt was officially in hell. It was like getting caught by his parents having sex. Worse… kinky sex.

The cool morning air felt good on his red face as he headed out into the shaded front yard. The preacher was a youngerish man who stood clutching his Bible like he expected the devil to come after him. David stood near enough that he sort of loomed over the preacher. Stunt somehow didn't think that was an accident. And Teresa stood right between the preacher and his car. Yep, more than one person was at the end of a shotgun here.

"Right then, let's get this started," Elijah said. The dappled sunlight drifted through the trees as they stepped off the porch. Come noon, the light would fill the yard, but right now, the morning light slanted through a hundred shifting leaves, making a carpet of dancing colors. Stunt hurried so he stood beside Alex.

Alex didn't look over, but his hand moved to Stunt's back and rested there. It would take a blind man to miss the disapproving stare of Reverend Carswell, but Alex didn't move one bit. He did pin the preacher with a look that could strip paint from the side of a barn.

"The Bible says—"

"That you should tend your own sins and not go talking on others'," Elijah interrupted. "And seeing as how Stewart's grandfather would never stand for this boy having sex outside of marriage, I ain't going to go talking on any sin other than that one." Elijah rested his hand on the end of the pistol he wore on his hip. "So start to reading verses."

The minister looked around wildly. Maybe he expected Jesus Christ or a big old bolt of lightning to save him from having to do this. When nothing happened except Elijah clearing his throat real loud, he opened his Bible. He took some time thumbing through the worn pages before he settled on one.

"The fool foldeth his hands together, and eateth his own flesh. Better is a handful with quietness, than both the hands full with travail and vexation of spirit."

The preacher definitely wasn't going for a traditional vow.

"Then I returned," Carswell continued, "and I saw vanity under the sun. There is one alone, and there is not a second; yea, he hath neither child nor brother, yet is there no end of all his labour. Neither is his eye satisfied with riches. Neither saith he, for whom do I labour, and bereave my soul of good? This is also vanity, yea, it is a sore travail. Two are better than one; because they have a good reward for their labour. For if they fall, the one will lift up his fellow. But woe to him that is alone when he falleth, for he hath not another to help him up. Again, if two lie together, then they have heat, but how can one be warm alone? And if one prevail against him, two shall withstand him, and a threefold cord is not quickly broken. Better is a poor and a wise child than an old and foolish king, who will no more be admonished. For out of prison he cometh to reign; whereas also he that is born in his kingdom becometh poor."

Carswell paused, and Stunt stood listening to the wind through the trees and wondered if Elijah had mentioned Alex's time in prison or if Carswell had chosen that verse on his own. If the second were true, Stunt's superstitious nature was working overtime.

"Preacher?" Elijah prompted when Carswell seemed to pause a little too long.

Clearing his throat, Carswell started speaking from memory. "Wilt thou have this...." His eyes went large as he looked toward Stunt. Yep, the preacher would definitely have to change the words, because if anyone started calling him a woman, Stunt would kick them. He'd likely break his own toe, seeing as how he didn't have on shoes, but he'd do some kicking anyway. He liked his dick, thank you very much.

After trying to hide the awkward pause under the world's phoniest cough, Carswell started over. "Wilt thou have this man to thy wedded… husband, to live together after God's ordinance in the holy estate of matrimony? Wilt thou love him, comfort him, honor, and keep him, in sickness and in health; and, forsaking all others, keep thee only unto him, so long as ye both shall live?" Carswell should have addressed that to either Stunt or Alex, but instead he seemed to mostly be talking to some spot off in the air. He finally had to look at Alex for an answer.

"Um, yeah," Alex answered. This was turning out to be a mite bit awkward.

Carswell cleared his throat again. "Wilt thou have this man to thy wedded husband, to live together after God's ordinance in the holy estate of matrimony? Wilt thou obey him, and serve him, love, honor, and keep him, in sickness and in health; and, forsaking all other, keep thee only unto him, so long as ye both shall live?" The preacher looked like he might pass the world's biggest piece of poop any time, and Stunt wasn't too much happier at being given the woman's vow, but he sure wasn't going to go arguing with Elijah standing right there.

"I will," he agreed. That should have led to the whole giving of the bride and about a half hour of more preachifying and rings and the first kiss. However, Reverend Carswell cut to the chase.

"Forasmuch as Alex and Stewart have consented together in holy wedlock, and have witnessed the same before God and this company, I pronounce that they are married. May God the Father, God the Son, God the Holy Ghost, bless, preserve, and keep you from sin." On that note, the preacher gave both of them a hard look. Stunt was surprised when Alex reached out to catch his hand and hold it. Eventually, Carswell sighed. "May the Lord mercifully with his favor look upon you, and fill you with all spiritual benediction and grace; that ye may so live together in this life, that in the world to come ye may have life everlasting. Congratulations."

Stunt was still kind of blinking when arms caught him in a big hug. "Now you make sure you take care of that idiot of yours," Teresa whispered in his ear as she embraced him with a fierceness that startled him.

"I'd invite you to kiss your bride, but I think you covered that bit last night," Elijah teased.

"Now don't you go embarrassing them on their day," Teresa chastised them. "It's not like you didn't break a bed inside our first week."

"You don't have to go telling that tall tale again," Elijah said, but Stunt could swear the old man was blushing. "So, preacher, is they all set?"

"The Bible is clear on—"

"If the wrong word comes out of your mouth, I'm shooting the tires out of your car all accidental-like, and you can walk home over two counties," Elijah warned.

"I'm just pointing out that morality isn't negotiable."

"Point it out on someone else's wedding day as you drink my moonshine. We got us some work to do, so if you'd be kind enough to go elsewhere—"

"Elijah. That ain't hospitable. Me and Bea are getting a good lunch together," Teresa argued.

"So go work on that lunch, but the preacher has to leave."

"I really should go home," Reverend Carswell said as he started sidling toward his car. "Elijah… Teresa. It was nice seeing you."

Teresa opened her mouth, but Elijah cut her off. "We both got work. Let's have to it," he said. Teresa gave him an unhappy look, but she did leave off trying to invite the preacher to lunch. "Alex, you get yourself settled with Stunt and then we're heading over to the nip joint."

"Without me?" Stunt blurted out.

Elijah gave him an amused look. "Are you suggesting that I take a duly sworn federal employee into a place featuring illegal activities?"

"Elijah, I've never said one word against moonshining, and as long as you ain't planning to sell guns to Garrido or some random ten-year-old, I don't care much what you do with your own guns. But you can't leave me out of this. Not after all this."

"I can't, but your husband can. And I'm advising him to keep you far from anything illegal, seeing as how eventually the police will be asking you uncomfortable questions."

"Oh no." Stunt stopped when Alex wrapped an arm around him and started pulling him off to the side. "Alex?"

"Let's go do some talking," Alex suggested. "We'll be back in a bit, Elijah."

"We can talk right here," Stunt protested.

"And we can talk over there." Without even a simple by your leave, Alex tugged him toward a path leading back into the woods.

"Where exactly are we going?" Stunt demanded.

"Somewhere else. Somewhere we can talk without an audience," Alex hissed in his ear. "I tried starting the truck, and it won't start."

Stunt snorted. He'd already predicted that one. But rather than make a fuss, he let Alex usher him through the trees. The wind was playing, stirring the air enough to keep the heat from getting uncomfortable. After stepping on a sharp stone, Stunt yelped and hopped on one foot for a second.

"Crap. You need shoes."

"Are you kidding? No, I don't. I grew up running mountain paths barefoot." Stunt rolled his eyes and took off down the faint trail. With his luck, he was about to run into Elijah's still, but Stunt trusted the old man had it disguised, and he planned on not looking. The trees on the south side of the path thinned, and Stunt headed into a small meadow. Something had been here, something big enough to keep the trees from growing up in the area, but it was gone now. Long grasses swayed, and weeds and wildflowers struggled to stick their leaves up high enough to catch the sunlight.

Alex followed and caught Stunt's arm to pull him around so they faced each other. The man had an intense look, and Stunt could feel his cock start to take an interest. Alex had married him. Now, it might be Alex was feeling a mite bit guilty about putting Stunt in the middle, but guilt meant he wanted to protect him. That was more than most of Stunt's dates felt for him. Leaning closer, Stunt waited for his wedding kiss.

"Is Elijah really going to help?" Alex blurted out in a rough whisper.

Stunt nearly lost his balance he was so caught off guard by the question. "You're asking that now? You city folk just ain't got the sense God gave a goose, not even a real stupid goose."

Alex gave him a dirty look. "Okay. Then explain this to me the way you'd explain to a stupid goose. Why are you so sure that Elijah is going to help? Maybe we should take off." Alex looked down at Stunt's feet and frowned.

"If he wasn't planning on helping you, he would have grabbed me and chased you off at the end of a gun. It would have made him a genuine hero—local man saves idiot ranger who got his sorry ass kidnapped," Stunt pointed out. "The only reason for getting rid of me is because he has to participate in the kidnapping for you to take care of your business. Therefore, Elijah has a vested interest in helping you. Now, do I understand what that interest is? Nope."

Without even really listening, Alex had started shaking his head. "Murder is a more serious charge than kidnapping, especially when he would only be an accessory after the fact."

"Popcorn Sutton got eighteen months for getting caught with a big old load of moonshine. He killed himself rather than serve that sentence." Stunt crossed his arms and dared Alex to debate that logic, but mostly Alex just looked real confused.

"Eighteen months is nothing. He would have been out inside a year."

"That's a year of living with someone else telling you how to live. He chose to go out controlling his own life."

For a second, Alex stared at him like Stunt had grown a second head. "He chose to kill himself," Alex said in this exasperated tone. "There's no way that I would ever call that anything but stupid."

"I don't rightly hold with committing suicide, and most people will call it a sin. However, he made his own choices. Around here, making your own choices as a man ranks pretty high."

"He's dead. There's no choice there."

Stunt sighed. "I don't suppose we could put this up there with mountain logic, could we?"

Alex ran a hand over his face, but then he surprised Stunt by reaching out and pulling him close. "Sometimes it scares the snot out of me that I can't understand you. How am I supposed to make sure I'm not doing something monumentally dangerous when I'm in the middle of some backward land where good is bad and suicide is a choice and killing someone you've known since they were born makes sense?" Alex's voice was tight with emotion.

Slipping his arms around Alex's waist, Stunt leaned into him. Alex wasn't worried about himself—the man didn't rightly care if he died on this quest of his. But still, it was hard to believe he was so worried about Stunt. It was the only thing that made sense though. "I'm safe now."

"But if I'm dead?" Alex stopped breathing.

Stunt tightened his arms around Alex's waist. Fact was, Elijah was counting on Alex to keep Stunt quiet. "I guess that's one more reason for you to not get killed," he said quietly.

A shiver went through Alex and he tightened his hold until it was almost painful. "He's not touching you," Alex's voice had a fierceness to it that made Stunt's insides feel about as sigogglin as when he got his first kiss. "I promise you that. I promise I will stop fucking this up and dragging you in the middle. You don't deserve it."

"And here I thought I'd annoyed the world enough that I had a little coming back my way through sheer karma," Stunt tried joking.

Alex leaned back a little and looked in Stunt's eyes. "From where I'm standing, you've put me and my brother ahead of your own safety. I'm not going to pretend to understand why—"

"Because you aren't a bad man. Because I like you." Stunt suspected it was more than just a case of liking at this point, but he was too much of a coward to say the word first.

Resting a finger against Stunt's lips, Alex silenced him. "I don't understand why you think I deserve your help, because it's been a long time since someone backed me unconditionally, but I promise you this—I will not get myself killed. I won't leave you alone to clean up this mess."

Stunt blinked as his emotions threatened to overcome his manly good sense. Men didn't cry, not unless their mommas or their dogs died. He nodded, not trusting his voice. Slowly, Alex leaned in. Stunt could feel the warmth from Alex's breath against his cheek, and then Alex pressed his lips against Stunt's in a long kiss. When Stunt sighed, his lips parted, and Alex teased him by letting teeth graze across Stunt's lower lip. Then he pulled back, and Stunt stood with his mouth still open.

"So, since I'm not the expert in hill logic, do you think this is safe, me going to this place with Elijah?"

Stunt resented Alex asking him a reasonable question. He didn't have any brain cells left to answer. He'd had men put three times more effort into it without affecting Stunt half as much.

"Uh...." Stunt cleared this throat. "He's likely just tryin' to get more help. I can't see him starting trouble for you after going to all the trouble of making it easier for him to get involved in your feud without ending up in jail."

"So, we play along." Alex said it firmly, his mind clearly made up. "I guess we don't have time for me to take care of that, huh?" Alex used his hip to bump into Stunt, and even that was enough to make Stunt's cock ache.

"Not fair."

"Oh, I have all sorts of not fair plans. But we will not be indulging in any of them under Elijah's roof."

That cooled Stunt's cock some. "I second that. It's downright embarrassing having folks hear the sex."

"This coming from a man who announced his gayness in front of an auditorium full of students."

Stunt felt his face heat. "How...." He let his head hang. "You'd already been awake for a while before I got up this morning."

"Yep. I tried to start the truck and then had a long conversation with Elijah. He thinks highly of you, and he's hoping that if the fear of God fails, I can keep you from going to the police. I'm not sure, but I think he offered to help me build a cabin far enough up the mountain that I could keep you tied up until you were utterly in love with me."

Stunt groaned. "That sounds like something Elijah would offer. However, you can reassure him that the fear of God and the vengeance of most of the moonshiners on this mountain is plenty enough to make me keep quiet."

"Too bad. The idea of keeping you tied to my bed in a secret cabin sounded pretty good." Alex gave him a wicked grin.

"Yeah, yeah. You say that now, but you ain't seen the winter storms yet. You'd be whining about having to cut wood inside a week." Stunt started wandering back toward the path. If he wasn't getting sex, he needed to get a little distance before his cock well and truly embarrassed him. Stunt always did have a real soft spot—or in this case, a very hard spot—for caretaker Doms. Thinking of Alex tying him to a bed and feeding him by hand wasn't exactly helping him lose his hard-on. So instead, he focused on the feel of the long grass as it caught between his toes. The sun hadn't burned off the morning dew, so the damp earth smelled fresh, and the bottoms of his pants clung to his ankles as he walked.

Something drifted across his face. "Look at that," Stunt said, watching the little puffs of white floating toward them on the breeze. Reaching out, he caught one.

"Did you just catch a bug in your hand?" Alex's hand came to rest against the small of his back.

"A thistle seed."

"A what?"

Stunt opened his hand to show Alex the tiny seed with its plume of featherlike white fluff. "If you can throw it up and catch it again, you get a wish."

Alex looked a bit less than impressed. "Or a sprained ankle when you stick your foot in one of these holes while chasing that thing."

"You're a pessimist. I married a pessimist," Stunt complained before he blew on the seed, sending it spinning into the air.

"I married a lunatic."

"Bitch, bitch, bitch," Stunt said with an eye roll as he followed his thistle seed. The grasses caught at his feet and ankles, and the mountain smell rose up as his tripping dance ripped at the grass that caught at him. The seed flew up out of reach before dipping down again, and Stunt caught it between his fingers. He held it up in triumph. "Ha! I get my wish."

Looking at the white plume caught between his fingers, Stunt realized he wasn't real sure what he wished for. He wished to keep Alex, but he wished for Garrido to magically disappear. He wished to steer clear of Elijah, but he wished Elijah would help get Alex out of this trap before it closed in around him. In the end, he could only wish things would work out the way they were supposed to. Closing his eyes briefly, he felt the dappled sunlight across his face and sent up his prayer. Then with a little puff of wind, the seed was gone, whirling into the sky.

CHAPTER
14

STUNT sat on the porch and whittled on a stick with a borrowed knife. Most days he wasted time with the television or Internet porn, but as a kid, he'd been a good whittler. His grandfather had given him his first knife, and then his father had pointed out whittling wasn't good for anything but dulling a good tool.

"You look like you're thinking on deep thoughts." David walked up and leaned against the porch rail.

"Worrying is more like it," Stunt admitted.

David gave a little wince and looked out over the mountain.

"I'm worried that Elijah and Alex are going to get themselves hurt," Stunt clarified. He didn't want David thinking he was expecting to die.

David jerked back around and pinned Stunt with a shocked look. "You're worried about them? Really? But didn't Alex kidnap you?"

"David Gilbert Pierpont," Teresa's voice snapped, out of nowhere.

Stunt's hand went right instead of left, and he yelped as the knife cut through the meat of his hand. He dropped the stick and the knife.

"Stunt." David jumped forward and grabbed Stunt's hand. "Memaw! I need a cloth. Stunt cut himself."

"Well, crap." Stunt flinched as David put pressure on the flesh below his thumb. "Ain't that just special? I can't even whittle a stick without making a mess." Stunt could feel the stickiness of his own blood, but he couldn't tell how much damage he'd done.

Teresa came out the front door with a bowl draped in white rags. "How bad is it?"

"Don't know," David said. He moved aside so Teresa could get in. Stunt had to sit still while she rinsed the cut and wrapped a bandage around it.

"It'll heal," she announced. "But no more playing with knives for you, young man. And you—" She turned to give David a sharp look. "—don't get next to his business. I swear. I raised you better than to go poking that nose of yours into every nest you can find."

"Yes, ma'am," David said meekly. "I didn't mean anything bad by it."

"No, you're just implying that Stunt's husband is violent and evil, but you ain't meaning anything bad." Teresa's look would scare a skunk out of stinking, and David shrank back some more. "Stunt's a mountain boy, born and bred. If he wanted loose, he coulda got loose without your help, and if he didn't want loose, then it's because he's decided that backing Alex is the right choice. So don't think that with your seventeen years of life experience you can go second-guessing your elders, because you are not too old to put over my knee."

With a huff, Teresa collected her bowl of bloodied water and tossed it out into the yard. "Stewart, this has been a real poor wedding day for you so far, but don't you worry. Bea and I are fixing you up a proper meal for when Alex comes back. And if David gets too big for his britches, feel free to use a switch on his backside." Teresa pinned David with a nasty look, but he was busy studying the boards making up the porch. With another huff, she collected her supplies and went back inside the house.

Stunt was left picking at the bandage and feeling embarrassed for David—and not the good sort of embarrassment either.

"I'm real sorry," David said quietly. He inched closer and sat on the chair next to Stunt.

"Apology accepted. Most of this time, I'm not sure why I'm doing what I'm doing, so I can't blame you for questioning me a bit." He picked up the pocket knife and wiped the bloody blade on his jeans. Blood had dribbled onto his shirt, but the Pierponts were poor folk, and Stunt wasn't going to ask Teresa for a new one. Moonshine paid well, but more and more, the moonshiners and bootleggers had to dump their loads and lose their investment as the government types pushed farther and farther into the mountains.

"I can tell Alex cares about you. I didn't mean to go implying he didn't."

Stunt nodded. It was weird. He'd always kept his male lovers as far from the rest of his life as possible. He'd assumed people would shun him even more if he went shoving his homosexuality in their faces. And given some of his experiences in those last couple of years in high school, he had some evidence for that belief. But so far, the Pierpont family had been real supportive for fundamentalist folk.

"I'm worried too. Peepaw says that the government is coming closer every year. He says I should get a college education and make sure I have something of value because the mountain ain't valued like it used to be."

"It's sad, but he's probably right," Stunt agreed.

"I don't like school much. I mean, I'm good at it an' all, but I can't say I like it, you know?"

Stunt gave a rough laugh. "No one likes high school, not unless they're shallow enough to think popularity means something. College is different. You learn about what you want to know—like how to tend the trees so that people don't kill them with their stupidity."

David wrinkled up his nose. "But folk at college… they're okay with people being…." David hand waved the next part of his sentence away.

"Gay?" Stunt asked.

He nodded.

"Lots of folk are gay. Heck, livestock can get a bit confused on the gender thing, and you and I have both seen that. It makes sense there are some people wired the same. Some people in the city see that as normal, and some are more cruel than anyone up here could ever dream of." Stunt remembered one particular preacher who stood in the center of campus and screamed such horrible threats against sinners, he made Stunt's grandfather look like a sweetheart of a man.

"Folk at the nip joint… they may not be real fond of Alex if they know that he's…."

"Gay," Stunt supplied again. "And Alex ain't exactly one to announce it to the world."

David shrugged. "He pretty much announces it every time he looks at you. You two are not real subtle."

"Really?" Stunt humphed. "I thought we were."

"Not even close. You're about as subtle as a cat in heat. So if the men come back here…." David stopped again, and Stunt was starting to think he had a real problem finishing his sentences. Actually, it was kinda cute the way he was trying real hard to not be offensive while suggesting some pretty offensive realities. Sighing, David started over again when Stunt let the silence drag out uncomfortably. "Peepaw ain't been real happy with some of these men lately. A couple of them have been looking for something that's easier than moonshining, and he's set against doing certain things."

Stunt guessed that would be drugs. "Are you saying I should avoid being seen if the others come back here?"

David chewed on his lip. His manners were probably warring with his common sense.

"David, I don't want them to see me. Even if I weren't gay, being a federal employee tends to make men with guns a little twitchy, and I'd like to avoid any more shooting. Given that this isn't even my first kidnapping, I do know that I'm not the most popular man on the mountain."

David smiled and seemed to sag as relief hit him. "I like you fine," he offered up like an apology.

For the most part, Stunt didn't keep up with mountain politicking, so David was offering up a new insight. The war between drug runners and moonshiners had been going on ever since the seventies, but an old moonshiner like Elijah should be on the side of the angels here. The idea that Elijah and David were worried had Stunt a little discomforted.

"How bad is it, David?"

His gaze skittered around the yard. "Been a few incidents."

"Incidents?"

David looked over. "Some of the younger men, they think they should make money however they can."

Stunt's guts turned to ice. "Meaning?"

David shrugged uncomfortably. "Peepaw keeps me out of it mostly, but there's been some threats, and there's more drugs going through the school than I've seen before. I ain't so sure Garrido's just holing up here. It could be he's here for business."

Stunt groaned. That would imply Garrido had local contacts, because strangers sure didn't make inroads into this community without help. Someone here had probably found Garrido, since he sure wouldn't know who to call. The game was a good deal more dangerous than Stunt had thought. "Well, ain't that a kick in the teeth." He leaned back and just let the frustration wash through him for a second.

"I don't know anything for sure," David quickly added. "I mean, Peepaw says that I'm imagining things and that young people don't know trouble from a gopher hole."

Stunt didn't say it, but he figured old people didn't want young people getting involved in hill feuds, which made for one very good motive for not mentioning what they knew. It also explained why Elijah had been quicker to offer some help than Stunt expected. Stunt had figured if Alex came alone, he'd have a small chance of getting himself some assistance, but Alex had clomped in with a hostage in tow and had still managed to talk his way into Elijah's good graces. Alex was a charmer, Stunt knew that. But if there trouble on the mountain, that did more to explain Elijah's uncharacteristically cooperative nature than any charisma on Alex's part.

"I guess they ain't talked to you either," David said sadly.

"Nope," Stunt agreed. He assumed Alex hadn't said anything because he didn't know what Garrido had been up to. Alex didn't have the good sense to know how ugly mountain feuds could get when folks felt they had the high ground. Stubborn people and an endless supply of guns and moonshine did make for some drama once violence actually broke out. That was the main reason violence almost never broke out.

"I suppose I should get to work," David said. "Peepaw says that if I'm not at school, I'd better be working or dying, because those are the only two excuses."

Stunt smiled at him. David looked like a grown man capable of intimidating most anyone, but the fact was, he was still an overgrown kid looking to his grandparents to set the rules. But if he was right that there was some feud going on, David and every other half-grown kid in the feuding families would get sucked right into the middle of it. Hell, after the Hatfields and McCoys, most people in these parts had learned their lesson. And now Alex was out there in the middle of it, and he had the instincts of a lemming when it came to hill folk.

Great.

By the time Elijah's old blue truck rumbled up the drive hours later, Stunt had all but worn himself out with pacing and worrying. As they bounced over the rough road, Stunt retreated to the side of the house and stayed in the shadows until he saw Elijah and Alex were alone.

Teresa appeared on the porch, wiping her hands on her apron before pushing a stray gray hair behind her ear. "Everything all right?" she called as soon as Elijah got out from behind the driver's side.

"Near enough to," he answered before pulling his shotgun out from behind the truck seat. That was not an answer. That wasn't even close to an answer, and from the way Teresa's lips tightened into a straight line, she knew it.

Stunt moved forward, and Alex offered him a weary smile.

"Are they going to help?" Teresa pressed.

"Woman, you go on too much."

"Man, you ain't telling me much at all."

Elijah rested his shotgun against the crook of his arm and ignored Teresa as he clomped past her into the house.

"Alex?" Stunt asked quietly. Teresa looked from Alex to Stunt for a second before she turned and headed into the house after Elijah. "Did something happen?"

Alex rubbed a hand over his face. "I'm not sure. I think most of the men were in favor of minding their own business, but a couple seemed angry that Elijah wanted to get involved at all. And can I just say right now that taking a gun to a conversation is never a good idea."

"It is if the other side has a gun. Who was angry?"

"Do you really think I could keep track of anyone? Random scruffy guys thirty-three and thirty-four." Alex snorted in disgust.

"Young or old?"

Alex crossed his arms. "You do know that between the tooth decay and the lack of skin care, everyone around here starts looking old at about twenty-five."

"Seeing as how I'm twenty-six, I'm thinking I'm offended by that."

"But that's what I mean. You look like a baby compared to most of these people. The angry guys weren't young, but whether they were thirty or fifty was hard to tell." Alex's body seemed to sag, and he moved over to sit on the wide steps up to the porch. "A couple of white-haired older guys came up to us in the parking lot and offered to help, but I get the feeling we're on our own here."

Stunt plopped himself down next to Alex. "Great." Resting his elbows on his knees, Stunt let his head hang down. What a mess.

"It gets better."

"If it gets too much better, I'm divorcing you and moving to Siberia," Stunt warned.

Alex gave a dark laugh devoid of any humor. "Well, apparently I suck at hiding trucks."

"What?" Stunt sat up.

"The sheriff found your truck. People are out looking for you in the woods, and apparently the sheriff sent a group up the mountain to find some guy named Rabern Woodstown."

"Well shit." Stunt closed his eyes and silently cursed the world. "He's the last guy to kidnap me, but if the sheriff's guys find him, he's going to take a shotgun to them. Why would they go after Rabern?"

Alex shrugged. "Between the accents and the generally mangled English, I only caught every other word. But it does seem like most of the county is looking for you, and even the FBI is involved because it's a case of kidnapping a federal employee."

"Shit, shit, shit. I seriously hope you didn't leave any fingerprints behind."

"I was careful, and no one mentioned the sheriff was looking for an outsider, so I think we have some time."

"Some time." Stunt snorted. Some time to do what, exactly? Alex had promised to not go off on some suicide mission, but without help, Stunt couldn't see any other way to bring Garrido down. And now the feds were searching for Stunt's kidnappers, and that was not going to end well. Not even a little bit. He ran his hands through his hair and flinched as his fingers found the big lump on the side of his head from where he'd hit a stone when he and Alex had gone sliding down that slope to avoid getting seen by Garrido's men.

Stunt was starting to wish the other side had kidnapped him. Sitting up straight, he ran that thought through his brain a second time.

"What is it?" Alex asked.

"I've got a plan," Stunt said, rolling the idea around in his head.

Alex sounded less than impressed. "You have a plan?"

Stunt glared at his husband. "Considering how well your plans have gone, I couldn't do any worse."

Alex returned his glare. "Your last plan led us up here."

"It all worked out."

"It nearly got you killed," Alex shouted, but Stunt got up and headed into the house.

"Come on. Let's find Elijah."

He didn't have far to go. Elijah had set up in the living room, his feet on the coffee table and a glass of moonshine in hand.

"I know how to get him." Stunt blurted it out as Alex caught up to him.

"We could walk up to him and shoot him," Elijah suggested dryly.

"Don't say that. Seriously, I do not want either of you getting that close."

Elijah slowly sat up and put his glass down on the table. "I don't need no federal employee telling me what to do." Looking toward Alex, Elijah said, "Keep the wife in line, boy."

"I'm not the wife," Stunt muttered, even though he knew he'd lost that battle. Alex didn't exactly help by slipping his hand into place at the small of Stunt's back. "But we all want to get rid of Garrido, right?"

"Seems like," Elijah answered all careful-like.

Stunt kept going, his voice getting faster with each word. "That doesn't mean we have to kill him. How about if we let the police do our dirty work and arrest him? If he's in jail, he's even more miserable than if he's dead. Maybe. I guess that depends on if'n someone believes in hell, but still, seeing him powerless and locked in a Tennessee jail would be a mighty fine thing, yes?"

Immediately, Elijah looked unhappy, but Stunt had expected that. He focused on Alex. "If he's arrested, then he gets to suffer in jail and you can avoid being arrested again. Win-win."

Alex frowned. "He's too smart. The police in California spent years trying to pin something on him, but his lawyers always had excuses and alibis lined up in advance."

"Yeah, but they were trying to catch him for something he actually did. I'm thinking we set him up for something he didn't do. His fancy lawyers aren't going to have any contingency plans for a kidnapping charge."

Elijah shifted around to better face them. "Did you hit your head recently?"

Moving into the room, Stunt smiled. "Actually, yes, but that ain't got nothing to do with this plan. It could work. The police know I'm missing, and the last place in my log book is that trail that leads past the Garrido place. What do you want to bet that they've already had a stray thought or two about whether Garrido is involved? If we can drop a trail of breadcrumbs and then make sure I'm found on the property, how's that going to look?"

"Like he kidnapped a federal employee, which is a really, really stupid thing to do," Alex said, joy blossoming across his face. "Garrido and his men would go to prison for something that stupid. No question."

"And if Garrido figures out what we're trying?" Elijah asked. "You're looking to put Stunt in the middle of this fight." Elijah's voice made it pretty clear he disapproved heartily. Then again, he had been ready to quietly put Stunt in a grave in the name of this battle, so Stunt didn't take his disapproval to heart.

"I'd stay close enough to cover him in case Garrido's men found him before the police did. I wouldn't put him in danger." Alex stepped forward, his hands clenched at his sides, and his whole body radiating fury. "No one is going to hurt him. No one. We clear on that?"

Stunt held his breath as he expected an explosion. Instead Elijah smiled. "Good for you, boy. A man takes care of his own, but if you put Stewart in the middle, things could get mighty rough."

"I can take care of us both."

"I'm not exactly chopped liver. I've been shooting a gun since I was five," Stunt pointed out, not that anyone was listening to him. Worse, Stunt's submissive streak definitely didn't mind Alex stepping up and playing big dog, but then that was leading to a new problem. Stunt moved behind a chair. Seriously, his cock hadn't been this riled since he was fifteen and his math teacher, who coached the cheer squad, dressed up like a cheerleader every Friday in some sort of show of support. Even gay, at fifteen that had been enough to confuse his cock mightily.

"A couple of those old boys could make a distraction," Elijah said thoughtfully, "especially if they didn't have to get involved directly."

"And I'm going to stay near enough to Stunt to make sure that the police find him safe and sound."

"Which might mean they catch you," Elijah pointed out.

"Then I'll confess to trespassing. One fingerprint check, and they're going to know what I'm doing there, and kidnapping Stunt wouldn't be part of my plan. I'll claim that I was searching for a way to kill Garrido when I ran into a kidnapping victim." Alex raised his chin as though daring Elijah to argue.

"Well, tarnation. That leaves the worst of the work for me. I'll have to lead the sheriff to the first breadcrumb." Elijah made a powerfully unhappy face. "No man worth a haet goes to the police. I hope you 'preciate the sacrifice I'm making for you, Stewart Folger."

"Yes, sir," Stunt said.

"You'd better," he threatened. "So now we need to figure out how to get on that property without you fools being seen, and how to lay a trail wide enough for that idiot sheriff to follow it to the end."

CHAPTER
15

STUNT took the plate of fried apple pie from Teresa and tried hard to hold back a groan. If he ate anymore, his insides were going to pop like an overripe boil and end up on the outside.

"Bea, get Peepaw some more coffee," Teresa ordered.

Dinner conversation had revealed that Bea, Eli, and David were the children of Elijah and Teresa's second daughter, a girl who had gone and gotten herself into drugs. As the oldest, Bea had done drugs with her mom after her father left home, and she wasn't exactly thrilled to be living with her grandfolks. However, both boys seemed to prefer their grandparents' house to the shack where they'd lived most of their lives. David had been twelve, Eli fourteen, and Beatrice seventeen when Elijah had come down from the mountain and taken all three of them.

Bea poured her grandfather some coffee and then took the pot back to the old stove before taking her seat again. David and Eli had both gone through a terrifying amount of ham, fried potatoes, greens, buttermilk biscuits, and tomato gravy, but both started tucking away the fried apple pie like they were starving.

"I'm not sure I can eat this," Alex said.

"'Course you can," Teresa said without blinking an eye, and the matter was closed. Stunt could have told him saying no to a woman's cooking just didn't happen. Stunt started eating real slow.

"It's a good plan," Elijah said as he started in on a smaller serving of pie. "Or at least, it ain't a bad one."

Teresa sighed loudly. "The boys haven't even had an evening to themselves, and after being married just this morning. You can't rush them off like that. It ain't polite."

"The longer we wait, the more dangerous this is for everyone," Elijah pointed out. "The last thing we need is a whole lot of feds running around like fools. They're like to find things they shouldn't."

"Will they find the still?" David asked.

"David! Don't go talking on that over your meal," Teresa chastised him.

"Yeah, idiot. Stunt works for the government," Eli added.

"When I need your help, I'll go asking after it," Teresa said with a cold glare for Eli.

Stunt was so very happy Teresa wasn't his grandmother. She scared him.

"Both of you hush up. This is adult conversation, and if you can't hold your tongues, you can take them out of the room before I tan yer hides," Elijah said firmly. Both boys went back to eating their pie, and Bea mostly pushed bits of crust around on her plate.

"The sheriff won't go onto the property unless he has some pretty good evidence," Bea said quietly. "Someone has to claim to have seen something."

Elijah snorted. "And that'd be my job."

Teresa froze with her fork halfway to her mouth.

"You're going to talk to the sheriff?" Eli demanded, shock making his voice rise like an adolescent boy's.

Slowly, Teresa lowered her fork back down to her plate.

"Maybe I should do that part," Bea offered. "I could help out... I could say I was wandering around and I saw something."

"I ain't having my own granddaughter do something because I ain't man enough to take care of it myself," Elijah snapped, and Bea's shoulders hunched some.

"Now, Peepaw, she never said you couldn't handle it. And I have to say, I'm scared that you're going to give the sheriff a heart attack, showing up at his place offering up evidence," Teresa pointed out.

Elijah snorted.

"Sheriff Kennedy knows that Elijah wouldn't come for help unless it was the end of the world. He's real likely to listen," Stunt pointed out. "Not that I don't appreciate your offer, because it's mighty kind of you to risk your neck like that," he told Bea.

She didn't quite meet his eyes, but she did start eating again.

Stunt was starting to understand why Elijah would do anything to strike back at the drug dealers moving into the area. The fastest way to rile a mountain man was to hurt his family, and now that Stunt had removed his head from his own posterior long enough to look around, he could see the rest of the world was having some troubles of their own. He wasn't entirely sure Bea was as far off the drugs as her grandparents thought. It was ungodly easy to get meth or prescription pain pills in these parts. Then again, maybe she was still just dealing with the after effects.

Alex spoke up. "I have everything I need to get us onto the property without being seen."

"Stunt can handle himself in the woods," Elijah said rather dismissively. It was an awkward, backward sort of compliment.

That earned a derisive snort from Alex. "Not when Garrido has installed Axis Q1921-E thermal network cameras on an overlapping grid to protect the perimeter and track local traffic, he can't." That was followed by some intense silence.

"What in tarnation are you saying?" Elijah demanded.

"For once, I'm not the confused one," Alex said a little too gleefully. When Elijah narrowed his eyes, he rushed to explain. "There are night-vision cameras set up on a wireless network. Luckily, I'm good with hacking networks and security systems."

"Real good from what I hear," Stunt added. He didn't mention Alex's crazy scheme to hijack all the phone lines in the county. That particular story didn't reflect well on his husband's intelligence.

"Good enough that the cops never caught me doing it, and trust me, they were trying," Alex agreed.

Elijah looked at Alex with a new expression of admiration. "Well now. It seems our Alex has some skill other than being in the wrong place at the right time," he said with a smile. "Any man the government takes a dislike to cain't be too far off the path of the righteous. So, if'n there's that much security, Garrido's going to have a real hard time convincing anyone that you just walked in."

"And you're going to have a hard time convincing the sheriff you saw anything standing outside his property line," Teresa pointed out.

"Details." Elijah waved her concern off with a hand. "We'll sort that out. I probably saw them through my rifle scope when I was hunting deer."

"You're lucky to even see a deer at fifty feet," Teresa said.

"Well then, maybe someone told me what they saw. Stop hunting up trouble. We'll make this work." Elijah was still smiling as he put a big forkful of apple pie in his mouth.

"If you lot go and get yourself killed, I'm following you to the next world and giving you all a piece of my mind," Teresa threatened, but then she settled in to eat her own dessert. Stunt almost felt like he was home with his parents issuing random threats on a fairly regular basis. It'd been a long time since dinner was anything but a quick meal eaten in front of a television or computer. Of course, it'd also been a long time since he ate so much he felt faintly ill.

"Can I be excused?" Eli asked as he pushed his plate back.

"Where are you headed?" Elijah asked.

"Upslope. I figured to pull down a few bushels of early apples and check on the hogs. David, you want to help?"

"Sure," David agreed, looking at his grandfather.

"David, you get back here in time to do that homework. If I get another call from a teacher, you ain't going to be sitting for a week. Go on, both of you are excused."

"Thank you."

"Yes, sir."

The boys took their plates to the counter before heading out the back door. Stunt sat at the table feeling weirdly unsure about whether he should ask for permission himself. He hadn't socialized much with mountain folk—as opposed to town folk—since going away to college, and back then, every adult had felt free to threaten him with a switch. The rules for adults and kids were so very different. Actually, Stunt felt a little sorry for Eli, who would be a man in any other world, but unless he was married or running his own home, he'd be stuck asking permission to leave the table.

"Well, you two deserve some time to celebrate your marriage." Teresa gave Elijah a look that just dared him to disagree.

"Yep, tomorrow is soon enough for this plan of ours," Elijah said. "And I, for one, plan to avoid the house, so you enjoy yourselves."

Teresa sucked in a shocked breath big enough to make her turkey wattle jiggle. "Elijah!"

"What? Just speaking the God's honest truth."

Stunt could feel his whole face turn brilliant red.

"I swear. Some days I think you were raised in a barn, Elijah Pierpont."

"Maybe they'd prefer to go up to the winter barn," Bea said as she stood and took her grandparents' plates from the table. "I'm guessing they'd prefer a little more privacy."

Teresa sat up so straight she looked like she had an iron rod up her backside. "I ain't having guests sleep in the barn."

"Actually, I think Alex and I would appreciate having a little… um… well, privacy." Stunt gave Teresa his best puppy-dog look. He didn't want to piss the woman off, but he sure wasn't having sex in this house again. Never. Not if the world was ending and it was his last chance before the whole kit and caboodle caught on fire.

"I'd feel better if we weren't pushing David out of his room, and after living in the back of that pickup for a month, a barn sounds like heaven," Alex added his voice to Stunt's.

Teresa frowned and pushed her gray hair back behind her ear.

"I could take out blankets and quilts so the old ticking mattress is comfortable," Bea offered.

"And it ain't like it's cold out. They'll be fine," Elijah chimed in.

Stunt could tell the moment Teresa realized she was outnumbered and surrounded. "Fine," she said rather gracelessly. "Bea, get out the winter bedding. That ticking is old, and I won't have guests poked to death with straw stuffing. Elijah, make sure that the boys did a good job of cleaning it out, and I'll get the batteries and the storm lantern. There's no electricity up there." She looked around. "Well, go on." She made shooing gestures toward them before she turned and started digging in one of the cupboards.

"Come on, I'll show you where you'll be bedding down," Elijah offered. "I swear, that woman gets bossier by the year." He gestured for them to head on out.

"I heard that," she called after him.

"You were meant to."

Stunt noticed Elijah left the kitchen mighty fast after that. He might be the head of the household, but Teresa wasn't exactly a faded wallflower. "Alex, put your foot down now, or this one's going to start getting that mouthy before he turns thirty." Elijah poked a thumb in Stunt's direction.

"Hey!" Stunt didn't appreciate the fact that Alex looked like he was trying real hard to not laugh.

"A marriage needs one head. That's the way it's meant to be," Elijah said firmly. As they stepped out into the afternoon sun, Elijah moved up to stand next to Alex, leaving Stunt a step behind. Seriously, this was starting to piss him off.

"A marriage that has two people trying to lead is like a cart with two horses hitched on different sides. You need to have one person deciding which way to pull the cart." Elijah kept right on pontificating as he walked around to the side of the house where a wide trail led up the slope.

"I ain't sure that's exactly right," Stunt said, but he knew he was losing some authority, seeing as how he was trailing behind Elijah and Alex. "This is the twenty-first century and women have equal rights, you know. They even get to vote." Stunt frowned.

Wait. That made it sound like he was womanish.

Elijah turned around. "I never said that women aren't equal. I'm just saying that a marriage needs a head of the household, and from what I've seen, that ain't you."

Stunt crossed his arms over his chest. "I never did say I wanted to be the head of anything, but I'm not a doormat."

Alex was spending considerable time looking at the clouds, and Elijah laughed. "Have you met Teresa? She ain't exactly a pushover, but that don't mean I'm not the head of the household." Elijah shook his head like Stunt was a particularly not-bright child. "You got your hands full with this one," he told Alex before he headed to the right, away from the little clearing Stunt and Alex had found earlier. "You might want to reconsider that cabin I offered you. A winter snowed in and obeying you might do him some good."

Stunt glared at Alex, and Alex held up both hands in surrender. Nearly growling, Stunt stomped after Elijah. A whole lot of his good feelings for the old man had just gone right up in smoke.

The winter barn had streaks of rust-colored paint that hinted at its previous color, but for the most part, the two-story structure was bare wood. Times hadn't been good lately. Considering moonshiners could make thousands of dollars with one good batch, Stunt wondered how long it'd been since Elijah had gotten a load of whiskey out to a top-paying market. Stunt felt sympathy push in through the cracks of his aggravation.

"Here you go." Elijah pushed open the side door to the barn. The air inside was stale, filled with dust and the smell of old hay. Under all that was a hint of animal, a certain musk that clung to the walls. However, the barn was empty except for hay bales stacked high on the north side. Empty stalls stood waiting, some with their doors hanging open. Ropes and chains were draped over rafters, and motes of dust floated through the sun that spilled through a few cracked boards. "It airs out good," Elijah said as he pushed the door open wider. Sunlight poured in, and now the air looked almost smoky with the drifting dust.

"Got a cot back there." Elijah gestured toward a small partitioned-off corner. "And Bea will be up soon with bedding, and most likely a heap of food from Teresa. If'n you want dinner, we'll be eating right after sundown, so come on in." With that, he turned and headed back out the barn. Stunt looked around, feeling a little like he was caught in some photographer's frame. Between the rusted hinges and the frayed rope hanging from a hook on the wall, it looked like some artistic version of an Appalachian stereotype.

"About being the head of the household." Alex cleared his throat. "I don't have trouble telling the difference between someone who wants to be dominated in bed and someone who wants to be dominated all the time."

Stunt frowned. "So, you think you know me all that well?"

"Yes," Alex said firmly. "You couldn't stop yourself from telling me what to do when you were a hostage, so I don't think you're going to stop now that we're married. Hell, if a man is going to shut up and go along, when he has a gun in his back is a good time to do it. So I already know you're physically incapable of simply letting things happen."

"I am not," Stunt protested, even though he knew full well Alex was right. It was the reason he loved bondage. He just couldn't get his brain to shut up long enough for him to enjoy anything unless he didn't have a choice.

"Keep telling yourself that," Alex said with more humor than the situation warranted. "Besides, I've had my time making all the calls, and it's not as much fun as Elijah makes it sound like." There was an edge of pain there that drew Stunt closer. He followed Alex until he stopped to lean on the rails making up one of the stalls.

"You don't like being in charge? You could have fooled me."

Alex turned to look him up and down with an open hunger that made Stunt get hard immediately. "You know I like being in charge in some ways." He stalked closer, using his larger body to crowd into Stunt, to lean into him so Stunt was pinned between his strength and hundred-year-old timbers meant to cage thousand-pound animals. Leaning closer, Alex whispered in his ear, "I love controlling certain parts of you." He ran his hands down Stunt's arms and then rested his palms on Stunt's hip bones. Stunt's cock was sitting up, begging, and ready to start baying at the moon.

With a smirk, Alex backed away, leaving Stunt nearly panting with need.

"But I don't need to make every decision. I did that once. It didn't work out."

"With a lover?" Stunt felt an unexpected flash of hot jealousy. He'd never been jealous before, mostly because he never chose the same Dom two nights in a row. He was on all kinds of new territory here.

"With my mother," Alex said dryly. "After she got sick, I had to take care of the home, be the man of the family so to speak, and when you're a kid, that's not easy. It's harder when you're trying to keep a little brother out of trouble. Every time I did something stupid, the weight of it came down on me, and when I managed to make all the right decisions, no one appreciated how much time I spent agonizing over those decisions. I was trying to figure out how to pay electric bills and which medicines I could give my mom half doses of without her getting more sick... all before I was sixteen years old. Trust me, I know what it is to be the head of the household. As far as I'm concerned, you get an equal voice in this household, which means you are equally to blame if something gets fucked up and you get to spend equal amounts of time worrying."

"When you put it like that...." Stunt grimaced.

"Yeah, well you aren't the sort to sit on the sidelines anyway."

Stunt shrugged. "True."

"Unless I tie you up and stuff you so full of cock you can't think and then leave you there," Alex said in a low voice that made all the little hairs on Stunt's body stand straight up.

"I brought the quilts," Bea called from the barn door.

Alex whirled away, but not without giving Stunt a wink that made it so very clear he'd known they had company. "Thank you so much. Those are beautiful. I hate to get them dirty," he said in a bright and friendly voice as he trotted to her. The pile of bedding came up to her nose, and he took the whole stack out of her hands. Meanwhile, Stunt moved to try and hide behind a strategically placed timber. Alex was a sadist. A serious sadist. He had to be, because giving Stunt a giant hard-on before making him deal with Bea was about as sadistic as they came.

"Do you need anything else?" Bea asked as she put a tin pail on a barrel.

"No, we're okay." Stunt struggled to keep his voice even. "Thanks for that."

Bea looked at him strangely for a moment, and he could almost see the very moment when she realized what she'd interrupted. Looking from Alex to him and then back again, she started smiling. "I guess I'll be leaving you to your business, then." Ducking her head, she turned and hurried out of the barn.

Once she was gone, Alex pulled the door closed so that it felt like twilight. Lines of soft light seeped in around the old boards.

"That was unkind," Stunt said with a huff.

Alex turned and propped the bedding on a crate next to the door. "Well, someone told me that he didn't mind a little humiliation. I guess I'm just testing the waters, and you definitely seem to be swimming just fine." His smile turned into a smirk as he stretched his head from one side to the other. By the time he started a long-legged stroll back toward Stunt, Stunt's cock was starting to get painfully hard.

"You embarrassed her," Stunt said weakly.

"If she was all that innocent, she wouldn't have recognized that adorably stunned expression on your face." After closing the distance between them, Alex caught Stunt by the shirt and pulled him closer. However, with the timber post between them, it meant Alex pulled him up tight against the wood. Stunt shivered as Alex used enough strength to trap him good.

"So, how are we going to spend our afternoon?" Alex asked. When Stunt opened his mouth, Alex quickly cut him off. "I would ask your opinion, only this is one area where I am definitely in charge. So you can just sit back and go along, because this is where you don't get to vote for the crazy-ass plan that puts you in the center of trouble. This is where I get to take care of you." He moved around the center post, and Stunt swallowed, all his words scattering like leaves in a good wind.

CHAPTER
16

ALEX took one of Stunt's hands in his and traced the line of Stunt's fingers, following the muscle down to the bruised wrist. "I'm getting leather. Well, after I get a job or make a big score, I'm buying you leather," he amended himself. "That way you can strain and struggle without doing yourself so much damage. But today I'll just have to get creative." He gave him a salacious grin.

"Creative... that doesn't sound half bad." Stunt's mouth was dry as a summer field.

"And you still have the ability to talk. We have to work on that." Alex used his body to pin Stunt against the side of the stall. One of the horizontal boards pressed into Stunt's back, and Alex slipped a knee between his legs. The restraint made Stunt even harder. "So, what do I do with you? Clearly, you can't be trusted with tied wrists. Much more bruising and you're going to look like a chew toy." Alex had a teasing tone in his voice.

When Stunt tried to make a suggestion, Alex silenced him with a predatory kiss. Hot lips moved against his, teeth nipping and tongue invading, and it all happened so fast, Stunt didn't have time to react. He reached up to grab Alex only to have his wrists caught and pinned against the worn wood.

Eventually, Alex stepped back and looked Stunt up and down with a hungry expression. "Good. Now strip."

"Strip?" Stunt's voice kind of cracked in the middle, which was embarrassing. It wasn't like he was some half-grown colt.

Alex leaned closer, his voice a rough murmur. "Strip."

His heart pounding hard enough to fill his hearing with the sound of drums, Stunt toed off his shoes and pulled his shirt over his head as fast as he could. After tossing it in the general direction of a stool, Stunt moved on to his pants. With his fly open, he looked to see Alex still standing in his camouflage pants and a short-sleeved black shirt. With his arms crossed over his chest and his intense expression, he was a wet dream right from *Soldier of Fortune* magazine.

"Are you losing some of those clothes?" Stunt asked.

Alex smirked. "Nope, but if you don't finish stripping, I'll have to think of some way to punish you."

Sucking in a fast breath as his cock did a little jig, Stunt got back to work. His pants and then his underwear and socks all followed his shirt, leaving him standing naked and a little uncomfortable in front of a fully dressed Alex. Luckily, he liked uncomfortable. A lot.

"So, I need to keep you out of trouble without risking those wrists of yours." Alex made a show out of thinking that problem through, but from the way he slowly grinned, Stunt figured the man had a plan. "You, stay here," he ordered, poking a finger in Stunt's direction. He walked to the corner and gathered up all Stunt's clothes, and with a wink, headed for the back room.

"Where are you taking those?" Stunt called after him without moving.

"I like the thought of you nude and too embarrassed to leave the barn," Alex called back. "It's almost as nice of a thought as you chained by one leg to a big old bolt in the middle of the main floor."

Stunt's cock twitched a mite, and he had to work hard to keep his hands off his cock. Only fear of Alex—of disappointing Alex—kept his hands at his sides. This is why he preferred bondage to orders. He sucked at taking orders, and not in the sexually fun way.

"Looky what I found here," Alex said as he walked back out into the barn proper. He held up a long coiled length of rope. "Now what can we possibly do with this?" He ran his hand over the coil as he meandered back toward Stunt. "It's nice and soft. Old. Worn smooth." He stroked the rope so sensually, Stunt felt a little twinge of jealousy, which didn't make even a lick of sense, but with most of his blood in his cock, he wasn't thinking real clear.

Alex moved closer, but then he kept right on walking past Stunt and headed into the next stall.

"What the devil are you—"

"Hey, stay put," Alex ordered when Stunt started to move. "You really aren't good at taking orders, are you?" he asked.

"When they don't make no sense... no." Stunt really wasn't understanding what was going on. Then Alex reached between the horizontal slats separating the two stalls to brush his fingers over Stunt's bare skin. Little teasing touches made Stunt squirm, but with only so much space between the boards, Alex couldn't touch enough to really fill Stunt's need. "Feel free to come on over here," Stunt suggested.

"I planned something different," Alex said, and a shiver went through Stunt at the dark tone in his voice. "I have something totally different in mind." Alex threaded the rope between the wide slats and stroked the soft fibers across Stunt's flank. The gap left enough room for him to reach all the way around Stunt.

The feeling of being held, of being pulled up against the wood, made Stunt's cock harden. Another shiver hit Stunt so hard his whole body twitched.

"I'll take that as a compliment," Alex said as he reached up so the rope crossed diagonally across Stunt's body. With one tug, Alex pulled him tight against the wood.

"I could compliment you even more if you came back here," Stunt suggested hopefully.

"Hmmm. You can still talk. Clearly I'm not getting the job done." Alex made little tsking noises with his tongue as he kept working.

After slipping the rope around Stunt's body, Alex worked through the slats, winding the rope through the stall rails and crossing Stunt's body with each loop. Whistling the theme to *Pocahontas*, he let his hand run across Stunt's back until Stunt was ready to explode, but still Alex kept his methodical pace. He tightened the loop that went from Stunt's right shoulder to under Stunt's left arm, and he tightened it around the slatted wall until Stunt could feel the pressure, feel the warm wood pressing against his back.

Careful layers of rope encircled Stunt's body before Alex finally stopped and announced, "There. That's better."

"It might be if you weren't in another room," Stunt said. He tugged, but the worn rope held firm. Alex had tied him tight up against the wall, and he couldn't reach any of the knots. It was enough to make a man swoon, or at least Stunt would consider swooning if Alex would get his ass back over to this side of the barn.

"You are begging for a gag," Alex said dryly.

Opening his mouth, Stunt started to make a smart-aleck response, only he knew what sort of dusty rags Alex might find in a barn like this. Discretion being the better part of valor, Stunt closed his mouth, sharp retort unsaid.

"Now I guess we can get to the distracting," Alex said. He came back around the partition and studied Stunt's nude and helpless form, and Stunt's cock was getting harder by the second.

Alex unbuttoned his shirt and paced the stall as he considered Stunt the way a hungry man considered a fried-chicken dinner. Pausing right in front of him, Alex took a second to run a thumb over Stunt's nipple. Then Alex gave it a hard tug.

"Land o'Goshen." Stunt breathed the words out, not able to get much volume what with all the lustful panting he found himself doing. He reached down, wanting to grab his cock, but the rope harness forced his arms away from his body just enough that he couldn't reach anything. He could only cling helplessly to stall slats and shift as his hot cock bobbed in the cool air.

"You do look good all tied up," Alex said. "And now I think it's time to play with my toy's little toy." He looked down at Stunt's cock. "Or not-so-little toy," he corrected himself. Reaching out, he ran a finger along the underside and then ended by playing with the slick head. "So, since coming doesn't seem to slow you down, let's have a little fun, shall we?" He wiggled his eyebrows like some nineteen-twenties villain. Give him an upturned mustache to twirl and he'd be all set. Before Stunt could get himself in trouble by making that comparison out loud, Alex wrapped his fist around Stunt's cock. His slicked fist. Alex had come prepared.

"Someone was a boy scout," Stunt said. The words came out sounding a little like the soundtrack of a porn film because he couldn't quite catch his breath.

"I lasted two weeks as a Cub Scout before I got sick of some man who wasn't my father telling me what to do. Why are we discussing this now?"

Stunt laughed, but Alex's hand around his cock tightened, and the sound turned into a strangled cry as he struggled. However, the rope held him to the wall—immobile, helpless, bound. Alex eased up, and Stunt managed to catch his breath. Even then, it took some time for him to find enough of his scattered brain cells to answer. "On my honor, I will do my best to do my duty to God and my country and always have a knife handy and slick prepared for any unexpected opportunity."

"I think you're getting that a little confused, possibly with an interesting porn video." Alex smiled and leaned in close enough to place an almost chaste kiss on Stunt's lips. The kiss contrasted sharply against Alex's hot hand, which pressed almost painfully hard against Stunt's balls while Alex's fingertips stroked his perineum. So many sensations rushed at Stunt in such a bewildering flurry, his brain couldn't quite figure out if he should pay attention to the gentle kiss or the rough handling of his genitals or the solid rope holding him to the wall. "I certainly am prepared for some things," Alex whispered into his ear. Shifting to the side, he pressed his hard cock up against Stunt's hip. "Do you feel that?"

Stunt nodded. Opening and closing his fingers, he strained against the rope.

Nipping at his neck, Alex moved his hand back up to Stunt's cock. He started with a slow rubbing motion along the length, but when Stunt started groaning, he turned to quick, short strokes. Slick fingers wrapped tightly around the shaft, and Stunt whined deep in his throat, desperate to come. His whole body felt coiled and overheated, and the ropes dug into his flesh because he couldn't support his own weight on his shaking legs.

Alex sucked lightly at Stunt's shoulder and tightened his grip. With a cry, Stunt came, his balls tight up against his body as he shot come across Alex's hand and hip.

Alex kept milking Stunt's cock with one hand, but with the other, he reached around Stunt's neck and pulled his head closer. Stunt rested his forehead against Alex's shoulder and let the shivering needs of his body overwhelm every thought. He breathed in hungry little gasps, and Alex petted his shoulder. But through it all, Alex's talented fingers worked at Stunt's cock, forcing him to stay hard. They stood like that in the twilight with motes of dust dancing in the air.

"You're killing me," Stunt finally said. Lifting his head, he looked at Alex, but his idiot husband didn't look too concerned. Actually, his idiot husband looked a lot like the cat that ate the canary.

"Oh, I haven't even gotten started," Alex said in a rather ominous voice. Then he wiggled his eyebrows and let his fingers trail over Stunt's stomach as he slowly sank to his knees. "I am so very curious. I mean, after I come, I'm so sensitive that I couldn't handle a blow job."

Stunt sucked in a breath. Oh God.

"I would find it torturous, but then I guess you have a different definition of torture." Alex's hot breath skittered across his cock.

Stunt did hurt. He hurt in that delicious way when pain and pleasure pressed against each other. He hurt in the way it hurt to sit in an overly heated hot tub. Twin sensations teetered ever so close to each other until the only thing that mattered was Stunt felt something.

The top of Alex's dark head leaned closer, and then a tongue ran over the head of Stunt's cock.

"Please. Oh Lord. Please." Stunt gasped out each word, his heart pounding loudly enough to drown out the sound of the rest of the world. Nope, his own heart and Alex's mouth on his cock... that was it. The rest of the world could be burning, and Stunt wasn't entirely sure he'd notice.

"I like the sound of that," Alex said, sounding mighty pleased with himself. "Of course, I like it more when you don't have the ability to talk at all." With that, he took Stunt's whole cock in his mouth. He slid down on the shaft until he was nose-to-groin.

Stunt screamed. It was a manly scream, but he couldn't rightly not scream, not when his whole body had become one over-sensitized nerve ready to catch on fire. Hell, it was ready to catch on conflagration.

Alex bobbed up and down, his clever fingers working at the skin behind Stunt's balls, and the pressure—the sheer need to come—built up until Stunt thought he might split like an overripe tomato. He shuffled his feet apart and twitched his hips forward in time with Alex's movements, but mostly he just stood there helpless while Alex did what he wanted.

Pulling back, Alex took a little time to blow little puffs of cooling air across Stunt's damp cock, making Stunt flail and kick out one leg until Alex captured his calf.

"This is how I like you," Alex said with a touch of smugness. Stunt rested his head against the wood behind him and tried to not spontaneously combust.

Stunt heard rustling as Alex stood, but at some point, Stunt's eyes had drifted shut, and he couldn't rightly convince them to open again.

"You are a stunningly beautiful man, Stunt Folger." Alex wrapped his hands around Stunt's thighs and lifted them.

Stunt would have accused the man of being a show-off, but he didn't rightly have the brain cells required to organize the syllables into coherent words.

Stunt's eyes popped open when Alex pushed his legs up and up. Hanging totally from the ropes, he watched as Alex brought Stunt's legs around his own waist. "Hang on," he said, and Stunt pulled him close.

Alex gave him a smile—a genuine, warm smile that reached something in Stunt. This wasn't just sex. Stunt weren't real experienced with taking relationships past sex, but he knew he was way past sex and into far more dangerous territory. Given that Stunt did like a little edge to his sex life, he'd gone out of his way to avoid emotionally dangerous territory, but now he realized he was in the middle of the emotional swamp with no escape in sight, not that he wanted one. It turned out he liked risking his heart about as much as he liked risking his body. That was a bit of a revelation.

When Alex got his hands around Stunt's hips, he lifted his own hips some. "I am going to enjoy this," Alex said before slipping a couple of fingers up inside Stunt.

"Ain't never had wall sex," Stunt managed, but with his cock hard and Alex pressed close with his fingers taking up rather personal territory, focusing was a bit difficult.

"You're talking again." Alex made an exaggerated expression of disappointment as he twisted his fingers and spread them.

Stunt threw his head back and near brained himself on the side of the stall as he gave a strangled cry. That was his prostate. Clearly, his prostate was very fond of Alex's fingers, because their introduction had gone rather well.

"Better," Alex said in an approving voice that mocked him. And yet, Stunt didn't mind being mocked. "Ready?" Alex asked, but it must have been one of them rhetorical questions, because Stunt felt Alex's cock pressing against his hole.

Easing forward, Alex pushed in, pinning Stunt even more firmly against the wall. All Stunt could do was hold on tight with his legs as the man started to deliberately rock in and out. The angle left Stunt bent in the middle and trapped his cock awkwardly between their hot, sweating bodies, but still… he was in heaven. Holding on to the only thing he could reach, the slats of the stall wall, Stunt rode the pleasure as Alex's thrusts grew harder and faster and more furious.

Stunt's legs ached with all the holding on and the rope burned across his chest, but all that faded as Alex became the center of his universe. Alex's whole face scrunched up, the intensity enough to leak out of every pore as his fingers pressed into Stunt's hips. Stunt waited until Alex thrust into him again, and just as he started his forward movement, Stunt tightened his legs. The force pulled Alex into him so hard their bodies slapped together.

"Fuck," Alex moaned, his face turning red, but that didn't seem like a complaint, so after he pulled back and began a new thrust, Stunt repeated his move. Alex's breath came like a freight train, and Stunt was starting to feel a little light-headed himself. But watching Alex come, watching that moment when his rhythm failed and he started lunging forward, tilting his hips and letting his mouth fall open, that was worth all the lack of oxygen.

Stunt's own cock was practically on fire with a need to come, the flesh hot and swollen, but the feeling of fullness balanced out all that pain. When Alex grunted heavily and came, Stunt was left hanging. Literally. He hung from the wall, his legs around Alex's waist and a dick up his ass. He waited for Alex to get control of his own breathing, he waited for Alex's fingers to ease off his hips. He waited, and he found watching his lover's exhausted body tremble was about the sexiest thing in the world.

Leaning forward on Stunt's helpless form, Alex let his cock slip free, and his fingers turned to slowly petting the bruises he'd made on Stunt's hips. Still, the barn was silent, and Stunt waited. When Alex shifted, Stunt loosened his legs and got his feet under him, even though his knees were still a bit wobbly. And still Alex leaned into him without speaking, their bodies sharing the heat they poured out into the world. Stunt was fever-hot.

"You are going to kill me," Alex finally whispered, the words tickling the little hairs in Stunt's ear.

"Only if'n you don't kill me first. Words like 'immolation' are coming to mind."

"Remind me to look that up later," Alex said, his voice slow with exhaustion. Putting his hands on the board on either side of Stunt's face, he leaned in until Stunt could smell coffee and musk. After long, heavy seconds, he finally pushed back. A honeyed smile spread across his face before he leaned in to place a chaste kiss on Stunt's lips, but then a frown quirked at his eyebrows as he reached down to stroke Stunt's cock. "You're still hard."

"I wouldn't mind coming again, but mostly I'm going to stay hard as long as you're doing something interesting to me."

"I hope that qualified as interesting."

"Oh yeah," Stunt hurried to assure him.

"Well then, let's see about getting you to come again, and then we can take a little rest before going for round two." Alex wrapped his fingers around Stunt's cock and started to sink down to his knees, but the ropes had loosened enough from all the struggling that Stunt could thrust his hips forward into the tight tunnel made by Alex's hand, and that's all it took.

Stunt hollered loud enough to wake the dead as he came hard enough his legs completely failed and he found himself dangling from the ropes.

Alex petted him, stroking the hair off his forehead as he murmured reassurances, but Stunt couldn't do much but just hang there helplessly and let his husband handle things. His body was officially on strike.

CHAPTER
17

"YOU know, now that we're ready to do this, it ain't sounding all that bright," Stunt observed as he crouched behind a tree and scratched his arm. He'd put his dirty, old uniform on, and the stink of it made his nose run. Alex gave him a cheeky grin. "I'm not joking," Stunt muttered, but seeing as how this was his dumbass plan, it seemed a little hypocritical to back out now.

Alex balanced a laptop on his knee and typed faster than a bootlegger avoiding a county regulator. "I'm almost there. People put way too much faith in wireless networks, and I can't even imagine why they think adding a number into their password is going to make one ounce of difference." He gave a dismissive snort.

"Seeing as how I mostly consider my computer a window into porn, I'm just going to sit here and nod my head like I understand any of that," Stunt said. He had married a nerd. It was downright disconcerting to see how nerdy Alex turned with a computer in his hands.

"Noob," Alex muttered, and Stunt pretty much ignored it, as he didn't understand what that meant. "Got it," Alex said, his voice low but full of joy. "Okay, I'm going to freeze each security feed for five seconds. That means we have five seconds to get to our next mark. Stop when you hit that white dead-looking tree that's losing its bark."

"You mean the birch?" Stunt offered dryly.

Alex rolled his eyes before giving a curt, "Now."

Stunt took off running and didn't stop until he skidded into the birch. Alex followed, his hand resting on Stunt's back for one second before he pointed to a rock. "There, now." Alex gave him a push, and Stunt scrambled for the mark. They continued this strange game of hopscotch until they stood panting in the shade of an outbuilding. It was new—gleaming white metal siding sitting on a brick foundation.

"We're clear." Alex grabbed at his laptop as it almost fell to the ground. Even though they hadn't run far, he panted heavily, and Stunt could feel his heart thump. "Okay, I've hacked the sheriff's computer system, and you people seriously need to invest in some IT security guys," he commented as he balanced his laptop on one hand and worked the keyboard with the other.

"I doubt anyone's given it much thought," Stunt said. Truth was, most people avoided the sheriff. There weren't many who spent time trying to get into the man's office or his computers. "Actually, does this have anything to do with all those doodads you put on the telephone wires?"

"Maybe." Alex sounded cagey.

"Then I know that no one's given it any thought. Who goes around hijacking wires unless they're giving themselves free cable? Has Elijah called in yet?" Stunt changed the subject as he realized he'd married the one idiot in the state who actually had gone hanging from telephone poles. And here Stunt thought he was the odd one.

"I don't see any calls," Alex said as he clicked away.

Leaning back against the cool metal side of the shed, Stunt considered Alex. "I'm near overcome with a need to buy you glasses and a pocket protector," he commented.

Alex looked up at him, frowning for a half second before his expression turned lustier. Holding his laptop out to the side, he moved in on Stunt, crowding into his personal space, but Stunt didn't back away. When Alex curled his hand around the back of Stunt's neck,

Stunt leaned in closer. "Be good or I'll spank you," Alex warned in a low, rough voice. "Or I'll refuse to spank you, and that might be even worse."

A shiver took Stunt. It had less to do with the words than the hungry expression on Alex's face. The danger also probably had something to do with the hard knot of excitement in his gut. Stunt's relationship with adrenaline was downright unhealthy at times.

Alex leaned in for a quick kiss before turning back to his laptop, but he continued to stand with a hip pressed up against Stunt. "There it is," he said in an excited whisper. "A report of someone seeing one missing Stewart Folger on the old Schmidt place." Alex looked at him. "This is the old Schmidt place, right?"

"Yep," Stunt said. "Are they coming?"

"Hell, it looks like your sheriff is calling in every deputy he has. Nothing like putting all your eggs in one basket." Alex clearly didn't approve of Sheriff Kennedy's approach. Maybe they did things different in the cities.

"Hey, if Elijah said it, the sheriff's going to believe it."

"I thought Elijah hated the sheriff. Doesn't that imply that the hate should go both ways?"

Stunt shrugged. "Hating someone ain't the same as lyin' to them, especially when a man's life might be in danger. The sheriff knows that Elijah won't lie about this, and he ain't exactly one to panic and go seeing ghosts. The sheriff has every reason to believe him."

"The logic here is oddly unlogic-like," Alex complained softly. Standing on the private property of a drug dealer waiting for the police to follow up on a fallacious report, Stunt couldn't exactly disagree. "But I guess I should just be happy this harebrained idea is working. Are you ready?"

Stunt's stomach took a flip and his mouth went dry as a desert, but he nodded. "Ready."

Alex wrapped his hand around Stunt's wrist. "I won't leave you. You're safe."

"Right. I'll keep right on a'telling myself that," Stunt said with a grim smile. When he'd come up with this plan, it'd sounded so easy. At least his part had sounded real easy. But now that he was here, letting someone tie him up in Garrido's shed seemed mighty unintelligent. However, when Alex moved, Stunt followed.

The building was fancier than most people's houses, with a little fake colored-glass window set next to a door and two bright blue planters making it look all cozy. But as soon as Alex pulled the door open, Stunt could see a plain old storage shed. He ducked into the dim light. After squeezing between two riding lawn mowers, he stood next to a rack of lawn tools.

"This'll work," Alex said. He shoved his laptop in his backpack and then pulled out a length of rope.

"I sure do hope so." Stunt thought he'd whispered that to himself, but Alex paused and gave him a worried look. "Let's do this before the sheriff comes and we've got even more explaining to do," he said in a firmer voice. If this didn't work, he wasn't real sure what criminal charges he might face for faking his own kidnapping. Well, not that he'd faked it, but he was definitely faking who the perpetrator was.

"You sure?" Alex asked as he came close, rope in hand.

"I've got to live up to my name, don't I?" Stunt said with his best smile.

"You are a bit of an adrenaline junkie. I get the feeling my husband is going to scare the life out of me one of these days." Alex ran his thumb along Stunt's lower lip. Another shiver traveled up Stunt's spine.

"Stop that before you go getting me hard, because you know how long it takes for me to calm down. It'd be beyond humiliating if the sheriff caught me with a big old hard-on."

"It's an amusing thought," Alex pointed out.

Stunt punched him in the stomach.

Laughing, Alex caught Stunt's wrist and started winding the rope around it.

"You're not doing this for entertainment, so get on with it," Stunt complained. Alex plus rope plus going slow was doing all sorts of things that could prove humiliating. Luckily, Alex obliged with quicker movements that felt more businesslike, even if Stunt's cock was still feeling a little confused.

Alex forced Stunt's hands toward the small of his back and then tied them at the wrists before winding the rope around his chest in a crisscross rope harness that didn't give Stunt any room to move at all.

"You don't have to be quite so thorough."

"Trust me. If Garrido's men caught you, you'd either be dead or tied up like a Thanksgiving turkey."

"Generally we shoot turkeys. We don't go tying them up."

Alex paused before he went back to work. "That really is a little disturbing."

"Why?"

"Because you're supposed to get your turkeys frozen at the grocery store, not go out and shoot a real bird."

Stunt rolled his eyes. City folk.

"Okay, where do you want to be sitting?"

"Sitting?"

Alex sighed. "If your feet are free, you should have found a way to run. So yes, you're going to sit down and I'm going to tie your feet." Alex rested his hand on Stunt's chest. "And then I'm going to stand guard over this shed and make sure you're safe the whole time."

Swallowing, Stunt nodded and silently reminded himself Alex was following Stunt's own dumbass plan. It didn't make him feel any better. He moved to the corner under the window. It seemed most of the bugs had avoided that space in favor of darker corners, so he started to go to one knee.

Alex's hands caught his arms and helped lower him so Stunt sat with his butt on the hard brick floor and his back against the sun-warmed metal. "This is going to be real comfortable," Stunt said sarcastically; however, Alex got to work tying his feet together.

"Now, you know the story?"

"I was walking on the trail and someone grabbed me, which feels oddly accurate for a lie." Stunt squirmed to find a more comfortable position. "I woke up in here. Some guy comes at night and gives me food and water and takes me out to take care of my business, but mostly I've just been sitting here, waiting to figure out why someone would want to grab a forestry technician, and seeing as how the guy who comes out in the pitch black of night doesn't really talk, I can't say I understand any of it."

Alex finished the knot, and Stunt realized he couldn't move at all. This would be a nice fantasy if it weren't for the potential for death at the hands of criminals.

"You okay?" Alex patted Stunt's knee.

"I'm hoping Sheriff Kennedy gets here real soon," Stunt admitted. He wasn't sure if he was more afraid of Garrido or of this whole plan backfiring, leaving Sheriff Kennedy to go after the real kidnapper—Alex. Either way, he was feeling a modicum of fear.

"I'll be outside covering you until I see the uniforms," Alex promised, patting the gun at his hip.

Stunt nodded, his mouth suddenly dry.

"Hey." Alex caught Stunt's face in his hands, cradling it as he leaned close. "We're going to be fine. It's a brilliant plan, and by the way, you aren't allowed to ever plan anything ever again. I mean it. You aren't even allowed to plan a garden party, got it?"

Stunt laughed. "Got it."

Alex gave him a quick kiss—a brush of lips against lips—and then he stood and headed for the door. Stunt wiggled around a little on the brick floor. "I really shouldn't make plans," he told the empty air after Alex had closed the door. At least now Stunt found it a little easier to relax into the role. With Alex in the room, he'd had to bite back all the fear before he'd done something stupid, like ask Alex to take him back to Elijah's place. One word, and Alex would have done exactly that, even if it screwed up their plans. Stunt wasn't used to having a lover who did that, who stopped and asked what he wanted.

One of the reasons why Stunt had such a liking for the clubs, other than a clearly out-of-control adrenaline addiction, was he never knew what he wanted. Before getting involved in the scene, he would have thought being gagged was a horror, but the moment the first Dom had slipped the gag in his mouth, Stunt had discovered the freedom that came with not having to figure out the next word out of his mouth—or not having to bite his tongue when he was on the verge of saying something stupid. And best of all, he didn't have to tell people what he wanted when he couldn't go figuring it out for himself.

But as much as those Doms had made Stunt feel good, they'd always been using his body for their pleasure. And Stunt had liked that. He liked that Doms got the pleasure they wanted out of him. He never wanted his Doms to go treating sex like some chore they had to do right. He never wanted his pleasure to be in the center of the room. He was always real careful to keep his list of hard limits as short as possible. No lasting marks, no visible marks, no scat or breathplay or blood. He'd tried to be considerate about doing what a Dom wanted.

However, when Alex looked in his eyes, Stunt could hardly breathe as he saw how much Alex wanted him to be happy. His pleasure was all about making Stunt happy, and that was a dynamic Stunt weren't real familiar with. Hell, Alex had gone along with this whole crazy scheme, and now they were in the middle of it, Stunt was very happy to admit it was a dumbass plan. He was all tangled up about what that said about their relationship.

Cocking his head, Stunt realized he was hearing voices. Loud voices.

Straining his neck up, he tried to see out the bottom of the narrow window, but it was too high for him to reach. The voices went on, rising steadily and sounding more like an argument than a police raid. Stunt dug his heels into the brick floor and tried to slide up the wall to get a better view. His head bumped one of the tools hanging from the wall and it fell with a loud clatter of metal against brick after hitting Stunt's back. "Gosh darnit," he muttered as he kept straining up. Something tickled his fingers, and he felt the slick of blood slip over his knuckles.

Great. He glared at the hedge cutters lying on the floor, and he could see the streak of red along one dull edge of the closed tool. Clearly the edge weren't all that dull because Stunt could feel the throb of the injury now. "Lord, if'n it's not too much to ask, maybe you could help me out a bit," Stunt said as he finally used the wall to push himself up a couple of feet. He knocked over a rake, but at least it didn't hit him.

Finally, Stunt could see out the bottom of the window, the plastic making everything look all weebly-wobbly.

Alex. Alex stood facing off against some man Stunt didn't know. Alex had his gun up and pointed right at the other fellow. The second man had his hand on his weapon, but it seemed he hadn't had a chance to pull it before Alex got the drop on him. Panic. Stunt was feeling panic as he realized something had gone wrong. The voices were still muffled, although now words were filtering through. Prison. Brother. Drugs.

Stunt put his cheek up against the narrow window and pushed as hard as he could. The damn thing was plastic. It should break.

Unfortunately, rich folks evidently bought a different kind of plastic from normal folks, because it held even as Stunt pushed harder and harder. His cheek was mushed up against the hard surface, but he could hear little creaking sounds now.

"You fucking bastard. Don't you even say that because I will blow your fucking face off!" Alex's anger came through loud and clear and he raised his gun a little more. The other man let his own hand fall off the butt of his weapon as he showed his palms. The anger startled Stunt, and he shoved harder on the plastic window. The bottom shattered, little colored pieces crumbling to the ground, but the two men outside didn't seem to notice.

Stunt could see them now. Alex's weapon shook slightly as he pointed it at a man in a dark suit with groomed hair graying at the temples. He looked like an actor.

The minute the guy opened his mouth, all that illusion of gentlemanly polish vanished. "Your brother was a coward. He talked to the cops. He deserved what he got," the man said coldly. Clearly, he was an idiot, because a smart person didn't go saying something like that to someone who had a gun on them.

"He was a kid." Alex snarled the words, his gun bobbing up and down as he shook with emotion. He was going to pull the trigger without meaning to at this rate.

"He was a dealer. Dealers that talk… they don't live long. That's the way it works." The man threw his hands out to the sides in an exaggerated shrug. "That's our world. That's your brother's world. He chose it. He had to live with the rules of the world he chose."

Alex shook his head. "I warned Garrido. I warned him to stay away from my brother."

The man laughed. "Your brother thought you were a loser. You were behind bars and still you were trying to tell him what to do." He laughed again, and the sound had an oily nastiness to it. "He made his choices, and he died for them. He would rather that than listen to his brother the rest of his life."

For a time, Alex stared at the man, and Stunt started getting reacquainted with prayer. They needed the sheriff real bad now. Finally Alex seemed to find his words. "Garrido murdered him," he whispered.

Stunt ached with a need to go out and offer some comfort.

The man in the suit took a step forward, and Alex took three steps back. "He was never important enough for Garrido to notice. He was a street player. I ordered Acosta to kill the punk."

Time stopped.

Stunt watched as the two men stared at each other, unmoving, unblinking even. None of this was making a lick of sense. A sane man didn't go saying stuff like that at the end of a gun. Not even Stunt was that stupid. Alex's chest rose and fell unnaturally fast, but the gun in his hands steadied. One shot would bring the other men a'running, and Stunt held his breath as he waited for it. One shot and Stunt's life would depend on whether the sheriff could show up before a whole hoard of thugs could overpower Alex. Being tied up during a Hollywood-style shoot out exceeded even his acceptable danger levels.

The man in the suit took another step forward, his arms settling in at his sides. "I ordered it because he talked. And you aren't going to pull the trigger because you aren't a killer." This guy seemed to be putting a whole lot of faith in that particular belief. Maybe as a drug dealer he had some sort of special skill at knowing who was most likely to pull a trigger. He took a step closer.

"But Alex, you have to remember one thing. I am. My friends are. Garrido definitely is. The only way you're going to survive this is if you run and keep running. I am going to go up to that house, and I am going to report this to Garrido, and then you will spend the rest of your life running from the bounty Garrido will put on your head. But if you run now and don't stop, maybe you can outrun death for a few days or a few years. You don't want to follow your brother to the next world this soon." A chill went up Stunt's spine. This fellow was serious as a bout of coughing in a horse.

Alex took a long time to answer. "You're going to pay," he whispered with his gun still aimed at the man's middle.

The other guy shrugged. "You're going to be lucky to get off this property without dying. If you pull the trigger, the sound will bring every soldier we have running, and you'll die. You didn't come here to die. I'm not worried about you. Run home, little boy. Run before you end up in a shallow grave." The man very deliberately turned his back. He turned his back on a man with a gun and he started walking toward the big house.

That was one cold bastard. Stunt had the feeling if that man had managed to pull his weapon before Alex got the drop on him, he would have put a bullet through Alex's head and gone for dinner after.

Stunt held his breath as the man walked away. He could almost taste Alex's need to pull the trigger. Here was the man who had ordered his brother's death, his back turned to present a clear shot. Stunt didn't doubt Alex could pull the trigger. He'd seen killing anger before, and it lived in Alex's gut like a parasite. Of course, Stunt weren't real sure what a dead body would do to the plan, but at least Stunt wouldn't have to figure it out. He planned to stick to the story that he knew nothing and he'd seen nothing. And he truly hoped he wasn't about to see the man he loved get killed.

Alex glanced over toward the shed, and he met Stunt's gaze for one second before going back to watching the other man stroll away. As bluffs went, this was about the best Stunt had seen. Either that or this guy knew something about Alex that Stunt didn't. On the other hand, what else could he do with Alex's gun pointed at his middle? If he tried pulling his own weapon, it would give Alex the perfect excuse to pull the trigger. Alex stood stiff, his fingers locked around his gun, and Stunt expected the loud bark and the spray of blood as the bullets tore through the man's back. He waited. And he kept waiting.

Alex watched the man go through the gate into the pool area before he lowered his weapon. Then he started right back for the door to the shed.

"We got to get out of here fast," Alex said as he reached for the door. Stunt was about to agree, but before he could, shouts came from the house. An artificially amplified voice yelled, "Sheriff's department," and the pops of guns sounded in the distance.

Surprise about took Stunt's breath. As much as this had been the plan, Stunt found himself surprised it was working. The cavalry was on the way. "Go, go!" Stunt shouted through the cracked window. Alex paused, his gaze going from the house to Stunt and back.

"This is the plan. Get out of here," Stunt yelled. With one last glance toward him, Alex turned and bolted for the woods. They were near enough to the edge of the property that Alex should be able to meet up with Elijah and get clear of any cops in the woods. Hopefully. Seemed Alex wasn't thinking all that clearly. Truth be told, Stunt didn't entirely understand why he hadn't pulled the trigger.

Since he couldn't do anything about that now, Stunt slumped back down to the ground and waited for his "rescue."

CHAPTER
18

STUNT'S discovery had meant every deputy in the county seemed to hover around him. Actually, every deputy from several counties. The ambulance folk had to shoo the police away so they could check his wounds. The cut on his hand looked pretty bad, but they were even more worried about the lump on his head. Stunt hadn't washed his hair at Elijah's because he could feel the scab and the knot from that first day when Alex had grabbed him, and he didn't want to make it break open. So that meant his hair had a trail of blood matted in it.

"How many fingers?" the paramedic kept asking, and every time Stunt answered, he got a little more annoyed with all the fuss. He tried to walk up to the main house, but the paramedic insisted on bringing a stretcher down.

"I didn't hurt my legs none," Stunt complained, but hands half helped and half shoved him onto the white stretcher. He spotted a familiar face and grabbed Guy Thompson's arm. "What's going on?"

Guy glanced over toward the paramedic for a second, but the man seemed obsessed with hooking Stunt up to more machinery than NASA had used to send a rocket to the moon. "The sheriff got Judge

Montgomery to sign an emergency warrant, and they're finding all sorts of things." He nodded toward the main house.

"Really? Like what?" Stunt tried to put on his best innocent face, but it wasn't an expression he was rightly familiar with.

"Like drugs," the paramedic said briskly as he finished taping things to Stunt's chest and then set a big old electronic thing on the stretcher between his legs. "The guy who bought this place is into drugs. Now we have to get you to the hospital."

Stunt rolled his eyes. "You don't have to go acting like I'm dying. I got tied up a bit."

The paramedic gave Stunt a dirty look, and Guy rested his hand on Stunt's shoulder. "City folk," he said softly. "Just let Jason take you up to the hospital and get you checked out."

"Fine," Stunt agreed unhappily. He couldn't exactly explain that he would rather go find Alex and make sure he was safe.

Guy and Jason started dragging Stunt up the rolling hill toward the house, and Stunt felt like a fool for lying still while they huffed and panted. A third ambulance man walked next to him and kept poking all the electronic equipment. "We're about there," Guy offered.

"I coulda walked up faster," Stunt said quietly, but no one paid him any mind.

The stretcher rolled easier when they reached the concrete, and now Stunt could see the doors all flung open and police walking through the lavish house. Rather than take him through the middle of the house, Guy led them around the side where a white-and-orange ambulance waited for them. The federal agents and their dark SUVs swarmed the front where Stunt could see a dozen or more men all handcuffed and sitting on the front lawn. His heart skipped along as he thought about having to give a statement to the FBI. Unfortunately, that made his heart-rate monitor beep along merrily.

"It's okay. They can't hurt you now," Guy promised. "I know you can pull some might big stunts, but I bet you never thought you'd get into something like this, huh?"

Stunt nodded. Thank the lord for his reputation, because folks were believing his story even quicker than Stunt had anticipated.

"Thompson, focus on the patient," the other paramedic ordered Guy.

"I am."

"On his vital signs," the paramedic corrected himself.

Guy rolled his eyes and mouthed the words "city folk" to Stunt again, but he did fall quiet, which was fine with Stunt. No one had much to say. The ambulance ran all the sirens as they drove the winding roads down the mountain. When they neared the hospital, Stunt could hear a commotion, and he tried to go up on an elbow to look out the window, but Guy pushed him back down onto the stretcher.

"Now, Stunt, don't you worry none. The hospital isn't going to let the press in. I swear. I don't know why those big-city reporters even care. They sure didn't show up when near half the county got burned in that damn fire a few years back."

"I think they care more about the kidnapper than me," Stunt said.

"Really? Why?" Guy looked at him, and Stunt's brain went running in a circle like a gerbil on a wheel as he realized what he'd said. Alex was the one who'd told him all about Garrido, and Stunt was supposed to be pretending that he didn't know him.

"Didn't you say he was into drugs and such? And with a house that size, I'm guessing we're not talking about mixing it up in a soda bottle," Stunt said with a shrug. His heart-rate monitor did another jig. Shit.

"Hey, don't you worry about him," Guy said, patting Stunt's shoulder. "By the time Sheriff Kennedy gets done with him, he's going to be a grease spot on the ground. And can you believe the feds showed up? And Drew has been torturing just about everyone, demanding that we find his best forestry technician. The man's been a pain ever since your truck showed up minus you."

Stunt realized Guy was trying to be comforting, but the guilt was starting to gnaw at him a bit.

"Here we go," Guy said as the ambulance stopped and started backing up. "We'll get you fixed right up."

Stunt endured another round of pats and whispered reassurances and good wishes as the paramedics rolled him into the county emergency room. Surprisingly, they took him right past all the curtained bays and straight into an elevator. They whisked him right up to the third floor where Doc Nesbitt stood waiting.

"You look like something the cat dragged in and the dog wouldn't eat," Doc Nesbitt greeted him. He was an older man with very little hair and very long, sharp fingers. Most of the people in town had reason to complain about how those cold fingers poked them every time they went to the hospital complaining of a stomachache. Generally, Doc Nesbitt terrorized them about blood sugar levels and kidney damage and then released them with a prescription and a strict order to stay away from Mountain Dew. The man had to have some sort of complex considering how often his orders were ignored. Maybe that's why he tended to poke folks so hard.

However, he didn't poke Stunt at all. He ran his fingers down Stunt's neck, feeling along the vertebrae as he looked into Stunt's eyes.

"Where does it hurt?"

Stunt blinked. "Um...." he stopped, not sure what to say. Doc Nesbitt didn't seem too surprised.

"Just take a few breaths and let your body start telling you things again. Does your head ache? Any sharp pains?" He leaned in to look at the bloody knot.

Now that Stunt thought about it, it did ache. "Some throbbing," he admitted.

"I'd be more surprised if there weren't any throbbing. Any sharp pains?" Doc Nesbitt carefully parted Stunt's hair.

"No."

"In your wrists maybe?"

Stunt looked down to see the bruised mess around each wrist. Now that he thought about it, he'd fought the ropes hard when Alex had faced off against that man. He hadn't noticed at the time, but now he could see the red, puffy results. Added to the bruises he'd gotten on his wedding night, he did look a right mess.

"They're more sore to the touch."

"Okay, can you move the wrists without pain?"

Stunt rotated his wrists around. "They're sore."

"No sharp pains anywhere?"

Stunt shook his head. "Only where it's cut."

Doc Nesbitt took Stunt's hand in his and looked at the wound. "It's fresh."

Stunt nodded. "I heard some noise, and I tried to stand up so I could knock against the window and get someone's attention, only I knocked a tool off the wall and it hit me."

A new voice offered, "Well now, that does sound like Stunt Folger."

Stunt looked up to see Sheriff Kennedy leaning against the edge of the door. The man always had a rough look to him, but right now he had bags under his eyes and he looked as edgy as a bear new-woke out of hibernation.

"Sheriff," Doc Nesbitt greeted him. "You need to ask any questions fast, because I'm having Stunt go in for a CT scan and we need blood work."

"A CT scan?"

"Possible concussion."

Sheriff Kennedy frowned and gave a quick nod. "Okay, Stunt, what can you tell me?"

Stunt blew out a breath and tried to collect his thoughts. Unfortunately, the damn heart-rate meter started speeding up anyway. Doc Nesbitt's hand landed on his shoulder and stayed right there.

"Someone grabbed me off the trail, pulled me backwards down the slope, and then my hands were being pulled back behind me, but I don't remember much except waking up in the shed."

"We found where you were grabbed. It looked like you gave 'em some trouble. Did you see anyone? Any faces?"

Stunt shook his head. "Someone would come in and give me water, but it was always after dark and I never got a look at a face."

He fidgeted in the hospital bed. The way Sheriff Kennedy kept giving him that real deep look was discomforting. They stayed like that, staring at each other, for some time before Stunt looked down and started studying the texture of his blanket. "So, nothing to add to your statement?" Sheriff Kennedy asked the words carefully, like he thought they might explode on him or something.

"No," Stunt said. He was tempted to repeat his rehearsed statement, but he figured he was stretching Sheriff Kennedy's credulity as it was.

"Stunt has extensive bruising to his wrists, most likely a concussion, a cut on his hand that needs stitches, and a host of other scrapes, dings, and general damage. Now isn't the time to go pressing him."

Sheriff Kennedy rubbed a hand over his face. "I'm not trying to push. I just want to make sure that all the Ts are crossed on this one. This man took one of ours, doc."

Doc Nesbitt nodded. "I know, Paul. I understand, but his probable concussion has me worried. Those can be unpredictable. A shaky memory isn't a good sign, but it isn't unusual either."

"So he's not going to remember?"

Doc Nesbitt shrugged. "There's no way to tell. That looks like a bad hit, and head injuries are notoriously difficult to predict. I'll keep him here for at least twenty-four hours to be careful, and some memory might return. It might not." Doc Nesbitt turned to Stunt. "Have you had any balance or coordination problems? Any vomiting or vision problems?"

Stunt squirmed. "Not that I noticed."

Sheriff Kennedy moved to the other side of the bed, and Stunt was starting to feel a little trapped. "Stunt, I know you've been hurt, and I understand that some people don't want to get too involved with the police, but did Elijah Pierpont have anything to do with this?" For one second, the room went deathly silent.

Stunt blinked, his brain not fully engaging with his mouth for a few critical seconds. "What? Elijah would never hurt... well, okay, he would if I went and tripped over his still, but I never did that and Elijah has never been one to look for trouble." He scrambled to get the words out. Elijah had done nothing but help them.

"I would agree, only I also would have said that Elijah would never come to me for help, not even if his house were on fire. Now he comes to me because he thinks he saw you, only that's real hard to believe when you've been locked in a shed for days. You can see where I'm a mite bit confused." Sheriff Kennedy gave Stunt a really hard look.

"He's family, sorta," Stunt said. "My grandfather and him were distant cousins, and you know Elijah ain't going to let strangers hurt family. I don't know how he knew I was there, but that's why he'd go to you if he couldn't get the job done himself."

"Family." Sheriff Kennedy raised an eyebrow. "Really? That's the best you can do?"

"Paul, don't go upsetting my patients," Doc Nesbitt said firmly. "In fact, why don't you go wait anywhere other than this room? Whatever happened and whatever reason Elijah had for getting involved, it doesn't change the basic facts. Stunt is injured and there is substantial evidence of a serious assault." He reached down and raised up Stunt's hand. The bruises around his wrist were purple bleeding into green. "You can't ignore evidence."

"I'm not looking to ignore evidence, and a deputy will be in here to take pictures, but I am looking to understand all the evidence. The feds are about two steps behind us, and they'll be here just as soon as they figure out all the parts we didn't bother telling them."

"Well, since memory troubles are one of the major symptoms of a concussion, I think you're going to need to look elsewhere. At this point, Stunt isn't a reliable witness for anything after his head took that hit." Dr. Nesbitt crossed his arms and faced off against the sheriff. Sheriff Kennedy was a good six inches taller with a Burt Reynolds mustache, but Doc Nesbitt had a mean glare and a sharp finger he didn't mind poking into people's chests.

"One question," Sheriff Kennedy said. "Stunt, right now, did Elijah do anything I want to know about?"

Stunt looked at the sheriff and swallowed. Chances were the sheriff would want to know about a whole mess of things, but that didn't mean it would do any good in the world to put him in the position of knowing any of it. "I trust Elijah with my life. I know he'd never do anything wrong," he said firmly.

Sheriff Kennedy looked at him for several long seconds before he gave a nod. "That's good enough for me. I'll let the feds know that Stunt's memory is a little scrambled and they're going to have to rely on forensics for this one."

"Is there enough forensics?" Stunt blurted out, suddenly worried. He didn't want to lie under oath but he needed Garrido out of his community.

"If I had this much physical evidence, I could convict the President of the United States. You don't worry none about that," Sheriff Kennedy promised. "The kidnapping is a given, and with the injuries you've suffered, we'll probably get him for assault on a federal officer—maybe even attempted murder, because I can't imagine what else they planned to do with you. The feds are even suggesting that they might go down for attempting to kill a witness, because that's about the only reason for them attacking you—because you saw something. Your work records say you were on the trail just north of the Garrido property when you vanished, and that's where we found evidence of a struggle and kidnapping."

"I heard two men...." Stunt frowned as he honestly tried to remember what the men on the path were saying when they'd passed the spot where he and Alex were hiding. Of course, Alex's gun pressed to the base of his head had been a bit of a distraction at the time. "I was just off the path, and someone said something about the boss not liking the idea of a federal employee so close to his property."

"You're sure about that?" Sheriff Kennedy took out a notebook.

"Nope," Stunt said. "That was right about the same time I hit my head, so I'm a little fuzzy on the details." Like Alex lying with his body pressing Stunt into the mud. He planned to stay fuzzy on that last bit.

"Well, even if we don't get him for interfering with a witness, he'll go down for enough other charges that he's going to have a long time to consider how unfriendly Tennessee folk can be when we're riled."

"If that's all you need," Dr. Nesbitt took out his pointy-poking finger and got the sheriff right in the chest, "then you need to get out and let my patient rest. And don't even think about coming back until tomorrow." Each order came with another poke until Sheriff Kennedy was in full retreat. Dr. Nesbitt kept poking at the sheriff until he was out of the room and the doctor stood at the door.

"Call if you need anything," Dr. Nesbitt said with a smile. "The nurse will be in here to take you to have that head scanned and get your hand stitched up." With that, he left the room, pulling the door closed behind him.

Leaning back against the rough hospital sheets, Stunt blew out a huge breath. It worked. His dumb plan worked. A smile curled the edges of his lips until his cheeks ached, but he just couldn't stop smiling.

CHAPTER
19

STUNT opened the door and froze. Alex stood there, with a bad haircut, in a denim jacket that looked like it came straight out of Bass Pro Shops. With his truck parked on the curb, he could almost pass as local. "Alex," Stunt said softly.

"Hey." He looked uncomfortable and unsure—two words Stunt never thought he'd associate with Alex. Now himself... Stunt was all kinds of unsure, especially after three weeks of not seeing hide nor hair of the man who'd promised to love, honor, and cherish him. Stunt had been starting to think it had been a concussion-induced hallucination, only now Alex stood on his doorstep, shifting nervously from foot to foot.

"Come on in," Stunt offered, pushing the door open as far as he could.

"Thanks." Alex's whole body seemed to uncoil at the offer. As he strode into the living room, he magically transformed back into the Alex Stunt knew and had completely tangled and borderline inappropriate feelings for. "I didn't know if you were going to invite me in or call the police."

"Calling the police on my husband, that ain't exactly a good way to get along."

"Husband." Alex sounded real thoughtful as he pronounced the word with exaggerated enunciation. "I won't hold you to that agreement. You did what you had to when I put you in a bad position." Alex was back to looking nervous and guilty, studying everything in the room—everything except Stunt.

With a sigh, Stunt closed his front door and leaned against it. "I warned you up front—people round these parts take marriage vows seriously. I ain't exactly looking for ways to get out of it."

Alex finally looked at him. "I don't want you to feel trapped into this."

Stunt felt something close to relief wash over him. Alex was still trying to take care of him, and this time it didn't have anything to do with Garrido or Elijah or anyone else. "I've been missing you," Stunt said. He wanted to say more, but he wasn't sure how. Instead, he changed the subject. "So, I hear Elijah has some California cousin a'visiting, some guy named AJ. I don't suppose you know anything about that?"

Alex shrugged. "Alejandro Jesus Soto, but the second Elijah tells people I'm his kin, the grandson of his brother who decided to walk away from the mountain after the war, they seem to assume I'm AJ Pierpont."

Stunt blinked as that fact sunk into his brain. "Alejandro Jesus Soto? You don't exactly look Mexican." He wandered closer, wanting to touch but not sure how to find that place where they could be comfortable touching.

Alex raised one eyebrow in a look that bordered on disgust. "Well, thank you for that bit of stereotyping. First, I'm not from Mexico. My parents were from Venezuela. Second, there are plenty of blond-haired, blue-eyed people south of the border. Not everyone who speaks Spanish has Indian blood… and actually, I don't even speak Spanish."

Stunt laughed. "Well, I guess we just found a subject that annoys you as much as insults about my accent offend me. So, no discussion of accents or names. Got it." He dropped down onto his couch and pulled one knee up under him. He found he couldn't stop staring at Alex. His hair looked messier with the haircut, but he'd shaved. Stunt itched to run his fingers over the smooth cheeks.

Raising an eyebrow, Alex studied him. "The way you said that, it sounds like we're negotiating hard limits."

"Does it?" Stunt smiled as a frisson of excitement ran up his spine. He hoped it sounded like negotiation. As much as he'd tried to deny his growing discomfort, the fact was he'd missed Alex. He'd missed the way Alex talked rough and then ran hands gently over his body. He missed the strength and the tightly controlled emotions that seemed to flow just under the surface. He had himself a real good crush on this man who felt so strong about doing the right thing, even if it meant putting his life on the line. Now, Stunt was not going so far as to say Alex had been in the right—Stunt didn't hold with taking hostages. However, he could admire the passion.

Alex took a step closer. "So, I hear Garrido is blaming some stranger."

Stunt gave a dark laugh. "Yeah. One of his lieutenants claims some guy from California came all the way out here, kidnapped me, ran me through the security unobserved while I was unconscious, tied me up in the shed, and then kept running through one of the best security systems on the planet to give me food and water. All without ever getting caught, and when there's no evidence that this random Alex guy is even in the state."

"That sounds a little crazy."

"Yeah, that's what the FBI thinks. They aren't buying it."

"So, the prosecution is going forward?"

Stunt nodded. "There's a lot of evidence, even if the star witness is having memory problems. The sheriff is getting a little weird about my assault case, but when they searched the house, the FBI techs found all sorts of evidence on their computers. Apparently, someone didn't have time to erase the files, and that seems to have surprised everyone. In the past Garrido always seemed to know when the feds were coming.

Unfortunately for Garrido, Sheriff Kennedy doesn't issue invitations before crashing through your front door."

"Sometimes the mountain way of doing it works better," Alex—AJ agreed. Stunt stared at Alex and tried to get himself to see an AJ in there. The denim and bad haircut were very AJ-ish, but the dark blue eyes with their intense stare were all Alex.

"Why didn't you shoot him?" The question popped right out even though he'd told himself over and over he shouldn't go prying into that particular business.

Alex's eyebrows went up. "Who?"

"The guy in the suit. You had a gun on him. You could have shot him, and he turned his back on you."

Alex sighed and ran a hand through his short hair. "If he had pulled his gun first, he would have killed both of us. Or worse, he would have captured and tortured us. I know that, but when he came out, when I got the drop on him…." Alex hesitated.

"He said he ordered your brother's murder."

"You heard that, huh?" Alex turned his back, and Stunt felt oddly excluded from Alex's thoughts. He wanted to see Alex's face and judge his emotions. "I guess I decided that I could be Alex Soto, vigilante, or I could be your husband and put worrying about you ahead of my brother. I can't carry both of you—you and my brother."

"So you became AJ Pierpont?"

Alex turned back to face him before giving a little shrug. "I didn't know that was an option at the time, but I knew that I needed to take care of my husband." Alex let his gaze slide down to the floor as his body seemed to grow quiet. Eventually, he looked back up, those blue eyes searching Stunt's face. "What are you thinking?" Alex asked, and Stunt realized he'd been staring too long.

"I guess I'm just trying to get used to seein' you as AJ Pierpont."

"I suppose it is strange for you, marrying a Pierpont," Alex said.

"I always did like AJ Pierpont," Stunt said. "Mind you, I probably wouldn't have married him, seeing as how I'm not on real good terms with preachers, but when Elijah found out I was sleeping with his grandnephew, marrying him suddenly seemed a far better option than annoying Elijah."

"Annoying Elijah is dangerous," Alex agreed dryly.

Stunt raised an eyebrow.

"Don't ask," Alex said, holding a hand up. "Because I am not going to tell that story. Let's just say that I was ready to run to your side faster than probably would have been safe, and we had a little discussion about what a man had to do to protect his family, even if that meant staying away from them."

"He threatened you?" Stunt guessed.

"It went beyond a threat." Alex shrugged. "He informed me that if I wanted to act like a spoiled little boy who couldn't control himself instead of a married man with responsibilities, he could arrange to treat me that way."

Stunt cringed as he considered what that might mean. As much as he didn't like the thought of Elijah going after Alex, he couldn't avoid the warmth at the idea of Alex trying to rush to his side. As the weeks had gone on, Stunt had started to feel abandoned and downright terrified the marriage hadn't actually meant anything to Alex.

"Exactly." Alex made a face. "But he's right that as a married man, I had to take care of my husband. That's what it means to love and cherish someone, and I needed to not put you in a difficult position by showing up and making everyone ask awkward questions." Alex paused, and Stunt tried to figure out how to say something about the use of the "L" word in the middle of that sentence. Before he could figure anything out, Alex continued. "Is anyone asking you awkward questions?"

"Um… surprisingly, no. Mostly, I'm not saying anything at all, and everyone is letting the evidence do the talking. The evidence is kind of damning." Stunt rubbed his wrists. The bruises were gone, but there was still a long red line where the hedge trimmers had cut him. His mouth was working, but his brain was still churning on that last bit.

"I hear you had a concussion."

Stunt laughed. "Yeah, I guess I did. Who knew?"

Alex moved in and sat on the couch next to Stunt and ran his fingers through Stunt's hair. "I should have known. I'm sorry."

Letting his eyes fall closed, Stunt leaned into that touch. "I didn't even tell you I'd hit my head."

"I was too focused on Garrido."

Stunt leaned back away from Alex, and Alex allowed it. He leaned back himself, putting more distance between them. "So, is this revenge enough? Is it enough to have them in jail?" Stunt asked. After a life of one-night stands and sharing Doms, he found he didn't want to share Alex with anyone or anything, not even this all-consuming need he had for revenge.

Alex's eyes got comically large. "You think—" He stopped and shook his head. "Do you think I am still looking for revenge? Do you think I care about Garrido at this point?"

Stunt swallowed as the dark emotions seemed to swirl around them. Without waiting for any sort of permission, Alex leaned forward, crowding into Stunt's space.

Alex kissed him. Hard. There was nothing tentative or unsure, just the solid press of Alex's lips against his. Stunt's cock hardened as Alex's fingers dug into his upper arms, pinning him against the arm of the couch. When Stunt parted his lips, Alex slid his tongue in and shifted so his weight pinned Stunt down. He tried to raise an arm, but Alex caught him by the wrist and pressed it down next to Stunt's head. By the time Alex gentled his hold, Stunt was all but boneless. He thought he'd seen Alex's dominant side before, but clearly that had been a watered-down version.

"I love you, idiot." Alex fisted Stunt's shirt for a moment before ripping it open.

Stunt grinned. "It's probably proof that I am an idiot, but I love you too. I was also unreasonably fond of that shirt."

Alex stood and pulled him to his feet, where he swayed dangerously before Alex caught his arms. "Tough shit." Alex pushed the shirt over Stunt's shoulders so the fabric fell to the floor.

"Ain't you the stereotype?" Stunt twitched his body, and he had a flash of panic as Alex studied him. Maybe this wasn't the sort of husband Alex wanted, and when the hell had Stunt started caring if his lovers wanted him to change?

Alex stepped closer, forcing Stunt into a full retreat until he had his back up against the living room wall. Then Alex put his hands against the wall on either side of Stunt's head and leaned close. "Yes. I am a stereotype. Now, get on your knees and show me if you can hold up your end of this stereotype." Alex whispered the words, and Stunt felt a hard shiver go through his body.

Stunt dropped. The wood floor stung his knees when he fell, but he focused on unzipping Alex's jeans. Alex's cock pressed out, and Stunt took a second to run his hands up and down Alex's legs before he finished pulling the jeans and underwear down.

"Fuck, yes," Alex gasped out.

Smiling, Stunt leaned close and kissed the rounded head, cupping Alex's balls. Before Stunt could decide what to do with his prize, Alex grabbed Stunt's head.

"Ready?"

"Yeah." Stunt didn't even ask what exactly he was agreeing to, but when Alex put the tip of his cock against Stunt's lips, he opened his mouth. Alex slid in deeper than Stunt had expected. Given some time to prepare, he could deep-throat with the best of them. But the fact Alex wasn't giving him time was a whole new level of hot. Stunt moaned around the cock as Alex pistoned in and out of his mouth. When Alex pulled out, Stunt twirled his tongue around the tip of the cock, and when Alex thrust in again, he sucked hard.

He felt a gut-deep trust, which erased any shadow of doubt. He'd been in about the worst position ever, and Alex had been there with him. Knowing that, knowing Alex would do anything to protect him and that Alex was taking all the control was enough to make Stunt come in his pants like a teenager.

Giving up any attempt at predicting what Alex might do, Stunt leaned back into the wall and let Alex set the pace, his thrusts slowing.

Stunt reached out and rested his hands against Alex's legs. He could feel the muscles tremble under his touch. Alex slid deep into his mouth, the head of his cock nudging the back of Stunt's throat. Stunt swallowed instinctively, and Alex made a strangled sound. Under Stunt's hands, Alex's legs began to tremble and his whole body froze in place.

Without warning or even the smallest sound, Alex shot his load. Swallowing quickly, Stunt looked up at his husband. He could feel the soft gray invading his world. Yes, his cock still ached with a need to come, but more than that, Stunt just wanted Alex to tell him what to do. He didn't want to have to think. Funny, normally it took a whole lot more than getting ordered to his knees for his brain to white out this far.

Alex ran his thumb over Stunt's cheek, his cock still in Stunt's mouth. "You are so beautifully gone, aren't you?"

Stunt grunted. He didn't want to think about the answer to that. He was happily in a place where he didn't feel the need to think at all.

Alex stepped back and took his cock away. Stunt licked his lips, the salt of Alex's come still sharp against his tongue.

"Strip," Alex ordered.

Stunt didn't hesitate. He couldn't. He stood and his body worked on autopilot, kicking off his pants and underwear so his cock bobbed out, obscenely hard.

Alex watched, his arms crossed as he let his gaze travel over Stunt. "Where's your bedroom?" he asked once Stunt was naked and shifting uncomfortably. Normally, leather or ropes held Stunt down, but as much as he felt pinned by Alex's presence, he couldn't quite figure out what to do with his hands.

"That a'way." Stunt jerked his head toward one of the doors.

Alex nodded and took Stunt by the arm, reminding him of his sheer physical strength as he guided Stunt toward the room. He pushed the door open and seemed to take inventory for a moment, looking around the room. Stunt's quilt lay on the ground at the foot of the bed, tangled in his sheets. His headboard had a couple of robe ties draped over it, waiting for Stunt to play a few self-bondage games, and dirty clothes spilled out of a white plastic laundry bin.

Alex pushed him to the middle of the room and slowly circled. Stunt let his head fall forward as he waited. The man had come, so who knew how long he would play with Stunt, keep him hard and waiting, and there was a hot, clawing need in Stunt's gut that made him want to grab his cock and start jerking off. But he couldn't. Alex was there. So he would wait.

Alex ran a hand over Stunt's shoulder and back, and an embarrassing whimper slipped out before Stunt could stop it. He needed more. But Alex limited himself to running a single finger across Stunt's chest as he circled around the front.

He stopped and let his torturous finger glide over Stunt's chest and down to where dark tiny hairs started. Stunt's cock twitched as Alex stopped there, his finger hovering just north of where his real curlies started.

Panting, Stunt fisted his hands and tried to control himself as Alex finally continued to walk around, his arm slipping around Stunt's waist. "You are so fucking beautiful. I think I'm keeping you."

Stunt closed his eyes, yielding when Alex pulled him close, his arm locked around Stunt as immovably as iron.

"So," Alex said, "let's finish that talk about hard limits. Where are yours?"

Stunt blinked, his brain cells scattered on the wind like dry leaves. It was real hard to gather them all back up and have any sort of coherent thought. Stunt leaned, letting his head fall back onto Alex's shoulder. "I'm not into puppy play, and I'd rather not have marks that other folk are going to see. I get enough grief without bringing it down on myself."

Alex chuckled, and his fingers traced small shapes onto Stunt's skin. "That you do. So, roleplay? Bloodplay?"

"Roleplay's fun. I'm hoping you're not into bloodplay." And that was not the same as saying no to bloodplay. Stunt assumed Alex had been around the community long enough to hear that difference.

For a second, Alex paused in his finger tracing. Then he returned to his exploration and he mouthed Stunt's curved neck and sucked until Stunt could feel the heat rise to the skin. While Stunt was distracted, Alex pulled at one of Stunt's nipples, and the heat shot through Stunt. "I never want to see you hurt again. Now tied up, writhing in need and suffering, that sounds good."

Between the heat in his abused nipple and the words, Stunt nearly lost control. Grabbing at Alex's arm, Stunt arched his back. He could hear his every ragged breath as he tried to get enough oxygen to feed his racing heart. "Please," he begged softly, and Alex's hand drifted over Stunt's stomach and reached down and cupped his balls. Stunt widened his legs and thrust forward, but Alex's hand simply followed, denying him the friction he needed to come.

"You need something?" Alex sounded amused.

"Bastard."

"Be nice—I might not do this," Alex warned as he fisted Stunt's cock, squeezing once before he stroked gently up and down.

Stunt couldn't resist—he thrust wildly into that touch. No rhythm, no finesse, simply a desperate need driving him into wild action.

"Stop," Alex ordered.

Stunt moaned and dug his fingers into the arm around his stomach, but he forced his body into a brittle stillness. He couldn't stop himself from coming, though. His come spilled out over Alex's fingers, and Stunt shook as he forced himself to stand still. The lessening of the need, the small relief of orgasm never came. Alex's warm breath against his skin kept his cock as hard as ever.

"You are beautiful," Alex said. "And I am going to have so much fun playing with this." He used his fingers to explore Stunt's hot skin and hard cock.

Stunt writhed in his hold. When Alex tugged at a curled pubic hair, Stunt's hard cock twitched, and he fought that strong arm around his waist for a half minute, but then Alex's hand returned to gentle stroking. Stunt found his own body matching pace with Alex, his struggles gentling under Alex's petting.

The pleasure and the lack of control sent him drifting away from reality. Alex's hot skin pressed up against him; hot breath danced over his skin. He was so hungry for this. For weeks Stunt hadn't gone to the clubs because he didn't want a Dom, he wanted his husband. He let himself drift on the helpless pleasure of submitting to Alex.

"You're going to scream," Alex promised in a whisper, and Stunt's whole body shivered with need. He wanted that. Every breath took effort. His brain conjured images of Alex holding him down, tying him down, forcing the screams out as he twisted in pleasure. Alex's hands, Alex's body: those were all that existed in Stunt's world. Well, that and Stunt's very hard cock. As long as Alex's hands held him, revenge and feds and Doms all faded to nothing.

Alex threaded fingers through Stunt's hair before fisting it, forcing him to turn his head. Then Alex kissed him. Stunt's lips burned from the rough pressure of Alex's mouth, but still Alex held him captive, the grip on his hair denying him the ability to move even an inch. When Alex finally released him, Stunt gulped down air, his head swimming from a lack of oxygen, and still his cock ached.

Alex herded him toward the bed, and Stunt willingly followed. He ended up standing at the foot of the bed, and with one push, Alex put him stomachdown on the white sheets. When Alex's shirt hit the ground, Stunt wanted to be able to reach out and run his hands over Alex's strong chest. He would have, only his limbs felt too heavy to lift and there was a strange hum in his head that made it hard to think.

Alex crawled onto the bed and pushed Stunt's legs apart to kneel between them, urging Stunt closer to the headboard by lifting his hips. Stunt struggled to cooperate despite his leaden limbs. When Alex had him where he wanted, he captured Stunt's arm and raised it up to the headboard. Then he slowly tied one end of the robe tie around his wrist. The terrycloth was soft against Stunt's skin, but the feeling of being tied made his heart pound faster anyway.

Stunt squirmed as the pressure on his cock grew, but Alex ignored that tacit request for some relief as he caught Stunt's other wrist. Using the other terrycloth tie, he secured Stunt. Sitting back on his heels, he seemed to study Stunt's helpless form. Watching over one shoulder, Stunt could only wait as dark hunger shone from Alex's face. A smile made him look devious, but before Stunt could worry much, a hand came down on Stunt's unprotected butt.

Stunt yelped in surprise, and the heat rushed into his ass.

"That's a good color on you," Alex said, his voice fond. He brought his hand down again, and the sound of the slap rang in Stunt's ears a half second before the sharp sting registered. Sucking in a breath,

Stunt arched his back and pulled against the ties. However, Stunt was helpless as Alex brought his hand down three more times, each time a little harder. Stunt's ass burned, and his cock was about to fall off by the time Alex leaned close and placed a kiss on each of his burning cheeks. The brush of lips across the hot skin made a full-body shiver run through him.

Shifting to the end of the bed, Alex ran his hands down Stunt's calf as though trying to memorize every inch of him. A strangled giggle slipped out of Stunt when Alex let his fingers dance over the bottom of Stunt's feet. "I'm going to remember that," Alex promised. Stunt groaned as he thought of what Alex could do with that little piece of information. "Now lie still or I'll tie your legs so tight that you can't move at all." Alex paused with his hands resting against Stunt's ankles. "Of course, eventually I'm going to do that anyway, but right now, I don't want to take the time to try and find all the toys, so you can just lay there and let me play."

He ran another finger over the bottom of Stunt's foot, and Stunt gasped and jerked. Alex caught his ankle with one hand and slapped Stunt's red ass with the other. Stunt yelled, which brought another slap, and Stunt's whole body tingled with life. Alex lowered himself down onto Stunt's back, his whole body covering Stunt's. "You like that?" he whispered in his ear.

"Yeah," Stunt admitted.

"Thought so." With a chuckle of his own, Alex pushed himself up again. Fingers brushed against the inside of Stunt's thighs as Alex returned to his meticulous torture.

Stunt gasped and clung to his headboard as Alex ran his fingers down the inside of Stunt's legs right back to his feet. This time when Alex tickled the bottoms, Stunt was prepared, but he still couldn't resist the need to try to escape. Three more slaps landed on his ass, and Stunt groaned as his cock seemed to soak up all the heat from the spanking. Alex rested his weight against Stunt's back again, the pressure keeping every bit of Stunt utterly trapped.

Stunt could feel his whole body sink into the stillness. Even his heart seemed to slow as Alex lay on him, his fingers tracing lazy circles against Stunt's shoulder.

Eventually, Alex slid backward and returned to his explorations. He ran his hands over Stunt's hot ass and cupped each cheek for a second before letting his splayed fingers move on to the small of Stunt's back. He lingered over Stunt's flanks, but Stunt was too lost to react.

Then Alex moved on to Stunt's arms, stroking up and down before teasing Stunt's underarms. Stunt twitched as his body recognized he should be ticklish, but he didn't have the energy to respond. He could only lie still and wait for Alex. Nothing else existed.

Alex ran fingernails over Stunt's hot ass, bringing four trails of fire to life, and Stunt cried out and nearly came, his body twitching, but then Alex lay next to him and muttered soothing words. Alex's fingers mapped out some strange language as they created little circles against his skin. When Alex's fingers slipped between Stunt's ass cheeks, he keened low in his throat and fisted his hands.

"Lube?" Alex asked.

"Bedside table." Stunt gasped the words out. Words had become fish darting between Stunt's outstretched fingers, and he couldn't think straight. When Alex's newly slicked fingers slipped between his cheeks and into his ass, Stunt cried out. His ass burned, his cock ached, his whole body overwhelmed him with a thousand different whispers, and Alex's hand ghosting over his flank, Alex's fingers pressing up into his body… it was all too much. Stunt squirmed and cried out again.

Alex rubbed his slick thumb over Stunt's perineum as he pressed his finger in farther. Arching his back, Stunt tried to give Alex more room to work. It was as close as Stunt could come to begging because words had slipped away. Alex teased with a slow in-and-out motion that made Stunt whine with need. A second finger joined the first, and Stunt surrendered to the burn of muscle stretching the heat of his ass.

Then Alex was gone, the connection broken, and Stunt struggled to look over his shoulder. Alex was there, looking down with his own hard cock in hand. With one of his wicked smiles, he pressed his cock inside Stunt's barely stretched hole. He began to thrust hard and fast, and Stunt could feel another orgasm pressing close. Sweat rolled down his neck, leaving cool trails in its wake. When Alex paused to lift his hips, Stunt struggled to get his legs to fold under him, and then Alex was back inside, his thrusts wild and uncontrolled. Each one shoved Stunt closer to the headboard, and he pushed back into that hard fucking. This was what he'd needed. He needed to know Alex wanted him so much he couldn't control himself.

Alex gave a guttural cry and rammed into Stunt, their bodies slapping together. The fog that had clouded Stunt's brain solidified into hot white lights flaring so brightly in his mind that the world became a pale ghost in comparison. Only Alex's cock and Alex's fingers pressing deep into his flesh really mattered.

Stunt came hard, his orgasm slamming into him so fast all his muscles tensed. Behind him, Alex gave another cry of his own, but Stunt was gasping for air. He could only writhe under Alex's weight as waves of pleasure blurred the world.

For a long time, he lay under Alex's weight. His ass was too hot, and his cursed cock was still hard, but none of those things meant as much as the tidal wave of endorphins carrying him above the pain. Alex stroked his forehead, brushing a few stray hairs back. Normally, Stunt kept his hair shorter, but he hadn't gotten it cut since before meeting Alex.

"You okay?" Alex asked softly as he played with one of Stunt's sweat-damp curls.

Stunt could only hum his pleasure. He didn't want to poke the happy bubble where he lived right now. Alex kissed his forehead and then shifted around to lie next to him, one leg draped over the back of Stunt's knees.

"Yeah, I think we're both okay," Alex whispered.

Stunt hummed again and let his eyes fall closed. They really were.

CHAPTER
20

STUNT groaned and stretched. Oh yeah. His ass definitely hurt in all the very best ways. He was overstretched and overly sensitive in a way that could only mean he'd got rode hard and put up wet.

"Is that a happy groan or a 'holy crap we went too far' groan?"

"If you think that's too far, then you don't know me well," Stunt taunted. Opening his eyes, he turned his head to find Alex propped up on one elbow. The morning sun slipped in around the edges of the curtain, and Stunt was a little surprised to find he'd slept through the night.

"Now that sounds like a challenge."

"Are you planning on sticking around to find out?" Stunt held his breath.

"Seeing as how my husband is crazy in love with this damn mountain, and my adopted uncle has loaned me his truck with very clear rules about what I can and can't do with it, it does seem easiest to try and find a job in town." Alex laughed. "God, a job. I haven't held an honest job since I was seventeen and hadn't yet figured out how to crack security codes on the really nice homes." He shook his head but was smiling like the thought amused him, so Stunt took that as a good sign. "So now, I reckon I'se a real local," Alex announced in the worst mountain accent Stunt had ever heard.

"Oh Lord. No. No, do not ever talk like that." He sat up in bed.

"What? Ain't you a'likin' my accent?" This time it was more of a perverted hybrid between gangster and mountain. It was truly hideous.

"Seriously, someone is liable to shoot you if you talk like that."

"What? If I go up yonder, ain't folk gonna to appreciate my talkin'?"

"I may shoot you," Stunt warned.

Alex laughed and caught Stunt by the back of the neck before pulling him in fast for a kiss. Stunt yielded, wrapping his arms around Alex's waist. "Now," Alex said, his mocking accent gone, "I do believe I'm going to take my husband out for breakfast with the last of my ill-gotten gains."

"You want breakfast? After a kiss like that?" Stunt put on his best pout.

"I plan to wear you out in all sorts of ways, so you need your strength." Alex frowned. "Unless you have to go to work…."

"Nope. I got a one-month leave to recover from the emotional scars, only I seem to be short any emotional scarring."

That earned him a nice big Alex grin. "Good, then go get some clothes on so I can feed you." He rolled off his side of the bed. "Aw crap. I left my suitcase in the truck."

"Your suitcase?"

Alex turned to face Stunt. "I was hoping…."

"Get your suitcase. I'll clear out some drawers in the dresser," Stunt hurried to say.

Moving clothes and getting Alex settled took the better part of an hour, so the morning was turning into midmorning before they hit Sadie's Café for breakfast. Stunt nodded to several of the regulars.

"Stunt. AJ," Angie greeted them.

Stunt looked over at Alex and raised an eyebrow.

"She goes to the same church," Alex whispered.

Stunt's world tipped a bit onto its side. "You go to church?"

Alex shrugged. "Uncle Elijah," he said with a sheepish grin.

Most of the tables were empty, but Stunt headed for the very back anyway. He was having another of those moments where the world seemed to be changing a little fast, and a nice quiet corner was sounding good. Alex followed without comment.

"What'll you boys have?" Angie yelled across the room.

"Ham and eggs," Stunt yelled back as he slid into the old green booth with its torn Naugahyde. The corner Stunt had chosen was on the back wall opposite the door to the kitchens, so it was quiet. Then he chose the seat with the back to the door so Alex could see the café.

Alex slipped into the other side of the booth and scanned the room. He might be a nerd when he had a computer in his hands, but he still looked every inch the predator as he watched the room.

"How about you, AJ?"

"Pancakes," Alex called back. "Other people do get table-side service, right?" Alex asked in a low voice that didn't carry far.

Stunt shrugged and watched as Angie headed for the kitchen. "Locals don't. Angie's on her feet enough without catering to people who can just as well shout across a room."

"So I'se is a local." Alex smirked as Stunt couldn't control the shudder of horror.

Angie came over with a basket of tiny muffins just in time to hear. She gave Alex a cross look and tsked at him before putting the basket of muffins right in front of Stunt. With a roll of her eyes, she headed back toward the kitchen.

Stunt leaned closer. "Death is still an option, you know. I'm a forestry technician. I know all the poisonous plants and all the best places to hide a body." He didn't register Alex's sudden alarm until a voice spoke out behind him.

"Now, Stunt. I know you ain't threatening people." Stunt twisted around in his seat to find Sheriff Kennedy standing behind him. Stunt looked back at Alex with his eyes wide.

"So, you'd be AJ Pierpont." The sheriff tilted his head toward Alex.

"Yes, sir. Nice to meet you," Alex offered in his most polite tone. His back was still stiff.

The sheriff took his hat off. "Move over and make room for an old man." Without waiting for Alex, the sheriff shoved right into the narrow booth. Stunt could see the shock and mild horror on Alex's face. "So, Stunt Folger has taken up with one of the Pierponts. That couldn't have anything to do with Elijah calling in the cavalry for you, could it?"

Stunt traded a look with Alex before clearing his throat. "I can't say I remember much."

The sheriff snorted before reaching to steal one of Stunt's little muffins. "You can't say, huh?"

"Sheriff, is there something you needed?" Alex's voice sounded brittle.

"Nope. I'm avoiding my office," the sheriff said in a confidential voice. "It seems the feds think we're downright incompetent. The clothes Stunt here was wearing, I reckon we burned them because they were so soiled. Days being locked up and he would have made a right mess out of them. And if'n we don't have any recordings of the call sending us up to that place, well, that's just our old computer system. I do keep telling folks that accidents happen when the taxpayers don't upgrade old systems." Sheriff Kennedy put on an overly concerned mask. "We should have someone upgrade those old things."

"Sheriff." Stunt stopped, fear tangling up in his guts. From the look of sheer panic on Alex's face, the man might have made a run for it if he weren't trapped in a booth by an armed officer of the law.

The sheriff looked back and forth between them. "Preacher over at Saw Creek says that you and AJ here took your vows a while back."

"Whatever you're trying to say, just say it," Alex growled out.

"I'm not trying to say anything, son. I'm just pointing out that perhaps you two idjits shouldn't be trying out for *Mission: Impossible* any time in the near future. So, do you plan on telling me what happened when you got into it with Garrido's henchman? I mean, I am assuming you're the Alex they're trying to lay all the blame on. Of course, it's hard to blame you for several years' worth of drug receipts or a plan for how to turn my county into a distribution hub using the local bootleggers as drivers."

"What?" Stunt's voice cracked.

"It seems like he had a real fine plan all set and ready to go."

"Land o'Goshen," Stunt muttered in shock. His friends. His people. They were going to ferry that poison for a drug lord. Some days Stunt figured he didn't know people at all.

"I reckoned you didn't know, Stunt. You never have been one to stand by while people did wrong. I am, however, wondering where you fit in." Sheriff Kennedy gave Alex a mild look. "One of Garrido's goons says you got the drop on him when he came out to investigate a strange sound. Is that about right?"

"I don't know what you're talking about." Alex sat stiffly, holding the edge of the table.

"Really? I suppose you're the sort to know that by physically trapping you here and then pointedly not reading you your rights, I can't use anything you say in a court of law." Sheriff Kennedy stole another of Stunt's muffins. "I also know that as far as old Elijah's concerned, you're kin. That means I'm about as likely to go to war with you as with a bad-tempered bear. Oh, I'll do it if there's need, but mostly I prefer to just leave sleeping bears to sleep. So, convince me that you're not more trouble than Garrido, and I might go back to my office and lose some more evidence all accidental-like."

"He's not," Stunt said, rising up to Alex's defense.

Sheriff Kennedy gave him an amused look.

Alex spoke carefully, his voice strained. "I wanted to stop Garrido. That's it."

"And pulling a weapon on that goon?"

Alex's fingers tightened on the edge of the table until his knuckles turned white. "He came out when I wasn't expecting him. He would have killed us, both of us, if I hadn't pulled my weapon first."

"So you let him walk back in the house and get reinforcements, and you were going to do what exactly?" Sheriff Kennedy thunked one elbow down on the table and gave Alex a real sharp glare.

Narrowing his eyes, Alex leaned closer. "I knew you were coming. I just needed to either protect Stunt or hide him long enough for you to show up. Running had come to mind, and if you'd been any slower, we would have done exactly that."

"How—" Sheriff Kennedy stopped. "You know, Garrido's lawyers tracked down the older brother of this Soto kid killed back in California. Alex Soto is a thief who did time for assault. From what I hear, he might have the computer skills to hack my sad, old system. Did I mention that my system got hacked? This all turned out to be very interesting."

Alex stared at him. Time drew out, the world slowing around them as he and Sheriff Kennedy eyed each other.

Sheriff Kennedy bowed out of the contest first, reaching over to take another of Stunt's little muffins. "But then AJ Pierpont, he doesn't have any good cause to care about Garrido, at least not beyond the fact that his sworn husband might have been in danger." Sheriff Kennedy looked from one of them to the other. "While I don't have any idea what you two actually did, if you ever do it again, I will find an excuse to throw you both in a jail cell. Separate jail cells. Understood?"

"Yes, sir," Stunt hurried to agree.

Sheriff Kennedy gave Alex the hairy eyeball. "Yes, sir," Alex finally offered.

With a smile, Sheriff Kennedy pushed himself up from the table. "Well, now that I have that settled, I guess I'm going to bite the bullet and go back to talk to those feds. It's a good thing they found so much evidence of the drug dealing, otherwise they would be absolutely inconsolable, seeing as how the kidnapping charges are turning out to be a little dicey. I would worry about them blaming me for all this mysteriously disappearing evidence, but those folk do seem quick to believe we're all a little stupid around here. Of course, the locals know better. Right?" Sheriff Kennedy included Alex in the meaningful glare.

"Mountain logic has a lot more logic than people might think," Alex said.

"That it does, son. Stunt. AJ." With a tip of his hat, Sheriff Kennedy turned on his heel and headed out of the café.

Stunt could feel his heart pounding as his brain sifted through about a million new facts and tried to put them all in their proper places. He'd had to do entirely too much mental adjusting lately. The kidnapping might not have left emotional scars, but this stress might. A sudden thought hit him.

"Wait. Are you wanted anywhere? Did you jump parole or leave parole or whatever you call it when you don't do what you're supposed to be doing?" he asked, panic rising up to press at the base of his throat.

Alex gave him a fond look. "Nope. Apparently, I had a bad attitude, so I got denied parole and served my whole time. I'm free to go wherever I want, and the state of California doesn't have a say in it."

Stunt sagged back into the seat as his fear evaporated.

Alex scooted back to the middle of his seat. "Well, I guess your plan didn't work as well as you thought," he said in a voice that sounded almost amused. But this was not amusing. This was not even a little amusing.

"Don't go there," Stunt warned.

"What? You don't want me to—"

Stunt poked his fork in Alex's direction. "Oh no. If you finish saying that, you are going to be missing a limb, and I will make sure it's one that you're particular fond of."

Stunt glared as Alex looked entirely too amused.

"For the first time in my life, I think I like a lawman," Alex said, and he sounded rather shocked by his own admission.

"You say that to Elijah, and you're like to get disowned."

"Well, then I'll have to be careful to not say it around him." Alex reached out and caught Stunt's hand. He held it right there in public.

"Well, really." Stunt looked up to see Mrs. Spinell staring down at them disapprovingly. "And in public." With a sniff, she turned and stalked off.

Stunt groaned. Not only was Mrs. Spinell one of the more vocal gay-haters, but she was the biggest gossip in town. "If you were a real local, you would have known to avoid doing anything juicy in front of Mrs. Spinell, because by the end of the day, every single person in this town is going to hear all about us holding hands in public." Stunt sighed. He loved his town, but sometimes he didn't like it all that much.

Alex's fingers tightened. "Do you want to stop, to hide this?" He leaned forward with this concerned expression that made Stunt's heart tighten just a little.

With about anyone else in the world, Stunt would have said yes. He would have said upsetting folk wasn't worth it. "Fuck 'em," Stunt whispered, the word feeling odd in his mouth, like a too-large marble rolling around and clicking against his teeth.

Alex laughed. He gave one of those big Alex grins and started laughing. "Deal," he said.

"Now are you boys making trouble?" Angie asked as she set two plates in front of them.

"Yep, always," Stunt agreed as he gave Alex a smile.

"What fun would life be without a little trouble?" Alex added, and he tightened his hold of Stunt's hand. "We do seem to excel at it."

Stunt smiled at his husband. They might have more than their fair share of bad luck, but Stunt always had liked a little trouble. He closed his hand around Alex's, twining their fingers together.

LYN GALA started writing in the back of her science notebook in third grade and hasn't stopped since. Westerns starring men with shady pasts gave way to science fiction with questionable protagonists, which eventually became any story with a morally ambiguous character. Even the purest heroes have pain and loss and darkness in their hearts, and that's where she likes to find her stories. Her characters seek to better themselves and find the happy (or happier) ending.

When she isn't writing, Lyn Gala teaches history in a small town in New Mexico. Her favorite spot to write is a flat rock under a wide tree on the edge of the open desert where her dog can terrorize local wildlife. Writing in a wide range of genres, she often gravitates back to adventure and BDSM, stories about men in search of true love and a way to bring some criminal to justice... unless they happen to be the criminal.

Also from LYN GALA

Contemporary Romance from LYN GALA

http://www.dreamspinnerpress.com

www.ingramcontent.com/pod-product-compliance
Lightning Source LLC
Chambersburg PA
CBHW070122260626

47160CB00004B/1582